$\mathcal{S}oul$ of **COURAGE**

Jeanette L. Ross

Soul of Courage is a work of fiction. However, John Lothropp and his family were very real, as well as King Charles I, Bishop Laud, Bishop Juxon, and the officer Tomlinson. All other characters or any resemblance to actual persons either living or dead is entirely coincidental.

Many believe John was imprisoned at Newgate. However, there is a chance he may have been in the Clink prison (this issue is addressed at the end of the book). The author placed him at Newgate. A few other happenings in this book were inspired from historical information as well. However, most events in this book, including events during his incarceration, are entirely fictional and come from the author's imagination.

Fortunately, a few letters and journals written in John's hand were preserved. The author used these as inspiration for some of John's narrative. References to records from the Star Chamber were also used. Any other narrative, unless otherwise stated, is entirely fictional.

Scripture taken from the King James Version of the Holy Bible

Poetry of Rick Oyler comprising *Courageous Souls* and the sonnet *For Jane* used by permission of the author.

Cover photograph and author photograph by Kathryn Jensen

Cover design © 2017 Jeanette L. Ross

Printed in the United States of America.

ISBN# 978-0-9989796-0-1

This book is dedicated to my four beautiful children.
We are creating our own story together.

Dear Reader,

Years ago, I grew fascinated with the life of an ancestor of mine named John Lothropp. Several spellings of the name exist including Lathrop, Lothrop, Lothrope, Lowthroppe, and so on. However, I chose to use Lothropp, as that is how he signed his name and is true to the time period.

I found several books on his life, which mostly consisted of genealogy books, reference books, and one biographical sketch. Over a period of about five years I read each of them, some more than once. As I read, I became further enthralled with the man and the great story that unfolded before me. It niggled at my mind until one day I sat down at my computer and started writing. The book you have before you is the product of those thoughts.

This is primarily a work of fiction inspired by events in his life. I did not attempt to write a biographical novel, which has been done previously by Helene Holt with her work entitled *Exiled*. I wrote this story with the hope of bringing his life and his struggles to light in a different way.

John was first and foremost a family man, with fourteen children from two consecutive wives. After receiving his Bachelor of Arts degree from Queens College at Cambridge in 1606, he was ordained a deacon in the Church of England. He later received his Master of Arts degree and was admitted as Perpetual Curate for the parish at Edgerton in the county of Kent. He had a great love of God and a faith so strong he endured overwhelming hardships in his search for a place to worship in a way he felt to be true and correct.

He was born in 1584 in Etton, East Riding of Yorkshire, during which time Queen Elizabeth sat upon the throne and William Shakespeare was about to begin his acting and writing career. Through John's life, he witnessed the subsequent reigns of King James I and King Charles I, which was a time of great transition in British government.

It was during the reign of Charles I that there was a sharp disagreement between the Church and Parliament. Charles was partial to a church full of pomp and ceremony, with bishops dressed in lavish robes and cathedrals extravagantly built and decorated. He believed in the divine right of kings and felt he could govern according to his own desires.

Hundreds of ministers renounced their positions and left the Church, including John Lothropp. This spawned several new religions consisting of the Independents (later called the Congregationalists), the Separatists, the Puritans, the Baptists, and so on.

William Laud was at that time the Bishop of London. He was merciless in his search for anyone who refused to take an oath of allegiance to the Church. His most ruthless law officer was Tomlinson who, with his band of agents, combed the streets searching for anyone who would attend a religious service not sanctioned by the Church of England. Stiff punishments were meted out which included large fines, long-term imprisonment in disgusting prisons, public humiliation in the stocks, nose splitting, and branding, among other horrific mutilations I desire not to name.

I can no better describe the man than did Amos Otis who conducted exhaustive research on John Lothropp and his descendants in the 1800s. He wrote numerous articles originally published in the *Barnstable Patriot* and later reprinted in *Genealogical Notes of Barnstable Families*.

Amos Otis wrote, "John Lothrop and his followers were held by the people to be martyrs in the cause of Independency [sic]. No persecutions—no severity that their enemies could inflict, caused him, or a solitary one of his followers to waiver—they submitted without a murmur to loss of property, to imprisonment in loathsome jails, and to be separated for two long years from their families and friends, rather than to subscribe to the forms of worship that Charles and his bigoted prelates vainly endeavored to force on their consciences, and compel them to adopt. No power could thus compel, they considered it far more glorious to suffer for the cause of Christ and his visible church than to submit to arbitrary power, though with submission came worldly wealth and temporal distinction."

In another article Otis stated, ". . . all must admit that he [John] was a good and true man, an independent thinker, and a man who held opinions in advance of his times. Even in Massachusetts a half century has not elapsed since his opinions on religious toleration have been adopted by the legislature, accepted by the people, and incorporated into the organic law of the state."

I am proud to call John Lothropp my ninth great-grandfather. His life has inspired me to grow stronger in my own convictions. Writing this work of fiction has brought him to life in my mind, and I hope that you, dear reader, will feel the same. I have taken artistic and literary license in telling his story. I pray that I have done justice to the man, his family, and his followers.

Faithfully,

Jeanette L. Ross

England

1632-1634

Amidst the great challenge of uncertain choice,
Many are doubtful and ponder their lot.
Yet some will rise forth and lift up their voice,
Courageous souls by which freedom is wrought.

LAMBETH

Gnawing pain jabbed at the reverend's bare, calloused toe. He lay atop a bed of moldy straw clumped on the stone floor, a threadbare cloak pulled over his thin body as he shivered against the dank air of London.

He'd been sleeping in the devil's pit for so long now it felt as though time had ceased its forward journey. Raising his head up from the ground, he spied a filthy bit of vermin chewing the dead skin of his big toe.

He lifted his foot and kicked it away. "Get thee hence, rat! I will not be your supper this night."

The rat scurried across the floor and over the bodies of John's cellmates, bringing a cry from William, a young lad who huddled in the corner of the room.

Young William never spoke. How had the boy come to be in this place, and what had triggered his silence?

The vermin, filthy and scrawny, scuttled through a hole between the stones and was gone.

John plumped up a bit of the foul-smelling straw and laid his head down. It eased his pain from the cold, hard floor.

Mold rooted onto any obtainable surface, including walls, floors, and wounds. An odious stench permeated the walls of Newgate prison. John pulled the cloak over his mouth and nose to filter the inescapable odor.

As sunlight slowly faded, he quivered from the chill of approaching night. Thick London fog slipped through an iron grate in the wall above John and crept over the men's bodies crowded together in the cell.

Cold slithered through the room, snaking around his legs and over his body like a serpent in search of its prey. Ruthless, it sapped his strength and further chilled his bones.

John pulled the rough-worn cloak tighter around his body. His family had sacrificed a few shillings for the privilege of no irons about his wrists and ankles, plus the cloak and bit of straw.

Tattered garments clung to his filthy skin, causing a rash which spread across his back and down his body. He scratched at lice living in his long, tangled mass of hair and beard.

Being with lost souls, doomed to spend time in Newgate prison, brought despair to his soul. Its walls were filled with robbers, murderers, and multifarious prisoners. The never-ending onslaught of their anguished cries assaulted his ears and plagued his mind.

John maintained hope that one day he'd be set free to hold his beloved once again. He closed his eyes and visualized his wife's lovely face. He missed the soft curve of her lips as she smiled at him, the sweep of thick lashes as they closed over gentle brown eyes. His heart ached with loneliness and the desire to have her soft body next to his. A tortured whisper came forth. "Oh, Hannah, how I long to be by your side."

His thoughts were disrupted when a raspy voice assaulted his mind. "What'd ye say, Reverend? Longin' fer somethin', are ye?"

John opened his eyes only to see the man Raif crouched on his knees, bending over him. Spittle from his mouth landed on the reverend's cheek. John's shoulder popped as he brought his hand up to swipe at the dribble with his sleeve. Raif's greasy insect-filled hair mingled with his lice infested beard and rubbed across John's arm.

"I said nothing. Now, get your odiferous self away from me." John pulled the cloak over his head.

"Sure as day, ye spoke. I heard ye saying how pitiful ye are, poor ol' reverend, so lonely an' all."

"Leave me be. There is nothing for you to worry over."

"Aye, there be, Reverend. I need be worryin' over that fine cloak ye have. It be high time ye pass it on over to me." His hand grasped the cloak and pulled.

A low growl rumbled out of John. It grew louder as he pulled the cloak from his head and rolled up onto his knees. Rising, he bent forward and loomed over Raif.

"Do you think to take what is not yours?" John's voice roared with the strength of an enraged lion. He pointed at Raif. "Thou shalt not steal!"

Raif cowered and held his gnarled hands up alongside his head. He peeked up at John like a frightened mouse. "Ye misunderstan' a poor wretch, Reverend. It be yers." Lowering his hands, he turned and scrambled on all fours over a few bodies. He hid in the darkness of his corner.

John scrunched his body into a sitting position and leaned back against the wall. Cold's frigid fingers grasped at him as he pulled the cloak up to his chest.

Twenty men were caged within the tiny cell, it being about eight feet wide and ten feet long. Men either slept side by side on the floor or while leaning onto one another for support.

John imagined the walls drawing closer every day. The ceiling hung low, which prevented him from ever rising to his full height. He'd reconciled himself to be either sitting or lying most of the time.

His children's faces tormented his mind. Thoughts of them living in poverty—their hungry bellies crying out for food—haunted his every waking hour.

He thanked God each day for his precious Hannah, who supported his cause. He longed to worship God with the conviction of his soul. Hope of release lay in pledging his oath to the Church of England. He could not, in good conscience, deny his beliefs and make such a pledge. Therefore, he remained in prison, but he felt deficient in his duties to his family and to his congregation.

Deep within John's core, a shudder began. It spread like a fiend throughout his body. He groaned in agony as his bony shoulder blades knocked against the wall. To ease the pain, he leaned forward and stretched his back.

A groan stole from his lips.

The touch of a hand on his shoulder startled him. His young friend Tibbot's thin arm reached up from a makeshift bed.

"What is wrong, m' lord? Are you ill?"

"Nay, the cold has gotten the best of me."

"'Tis a chilly night. I pray we're alive, come morning."

John rubbed Tibbot's arm. "Let's not think that way. How do you fare, Tibbot? Are you still feeling poorly?"

"Aye, my body aches. I fear the worst is yet to come."

"I will continue to pray for your health. Keep the faith, my young friend."

From the moment John had arrived in perdition, a chill dwelled within him. It spread through him like the call of a siren threatening to take his life. John lowered his head and bore a silent prayer.

My Most Glorious God—hast Thou forsaken me? Why dost Thou ask so much of me? I am but a humble man who desires to do Thy will. My soul falters, and I know not what to do. I ask for added strength to survive this trial and return to my family once again. In Thy Holy Name, amen.

He lay down and rolled onto his side, resting his head on an arm. Sleep was an elusive maiden in the dark abyss.

After a time, he dangled between waking and sleeping. A sound pushed at him. It prodded his mind and urged him awake.

The Keeper.

Thud, clomp. Thud, clomp.

John's head snapped up at the thud of wood on stone. The pounding of the keeper's crutch echoed down the hall. He recognized the rattle of keys against the old wooden door.

John whispered to his cellmates. "Stand up men. The Keeper is at the door. Hurry! Arise before he enters." As John got to his feet, he leaned down and rubbed Tibbot's shoulder.

"Tibbot, you must get up." Tibbot shifted his weight until he was in a sitting position. John reached down to help the boy stand.

The door scraped outward on its hinges until it came fully open. Light from the Keeper's oil lamp gradually illuminated the corridor until John could see the ugly face of Jervis.

The Keeper's bulky body tilted to one side as he grasped the wooden crutch tucked under his arm, his right leg ending in a stub at the knee. Palsy affected the left side of his face, causing his mouth to droop. Slobber ran a constant course down his chin.

Jervis stepped through the door, bringing his lantern with him. A yellow glow spread across the men within the cell. John raised his hands to block the glare and awaited the Keeper's word.

Light played across one side of a stranger's face who stood beside Jervis. Long, dark, straggly hair draped down the other side. Ragged clothes covered most of a thin body, with dirty arms folded against the cold night air. His feet were bare and coated with grime. John wondered what had befallen the man and why he'd been brought to Newgate.

Jervis said, "Make room fer yer new mate. This here man 'as come to live with ye."

With a shove, Jervis sent the newcomer stumbling into the room. John instinctively reached out and caught the man in his arms. They toppled backward. John's head cracked against the wall as both men fell with a thud onto the unbreakable floor.

A loud cackle came from the Keeper. "Oh, Lothropp, did ye have a lit'le fall?" Jervis's laughter filled the cell.

The newcomer grumbled in John's ear and lifted himself from the floor. He stepped to the opposite wall and leaned against it with an air of indifference.

John rolled up onto his knees. His friend Colin reached down and offered a hand, which John willingly accepted. He arose once again, rubbing where his skull had hit the wall. Leaning toward his friend, he whispered, "Thank you, Colin."

Jervis said, "Hrrump . . . ye bunch o' jackanapes make me sick." He turned on his crutch and clomped through the opening. He sniggered and said, "I 'ope there be room fer yer new bloke."

The gaoler's loud cackle filled the air. Hinges, rusty with age, creaked and groaned as Jervis closed the thick oak door, taking the light with him.

John shuffled back to his spot under the window grate and leaned against the wall.

Scraping, tussling, mumbling. Men maneuvered for position. Then silence filled the room.

Darkness enshrouded the cell like someone had drawn a cloak over the whole of it. John lay down on his straw bed and closed his eyes, turning his thoughts to better times. Days when he'd been home, surrounded by his beautiful Hannah and their six lovely children. Days when he'd served in the church, bringing the spirit of God to his congregation, and to his life.

His body relaxed upon the straw. The enticement of sleep had begun to pull at the corners of his mind when a low gravelly voice broke its way into the quiet of the night.

"And just where do I sleep?"

Several of the men mumbled.

Colin spoke, "I do not give a care where you sleep. Just keep your mouth shut."

The new man's voice drifted over John in the darkness. "It's too dark in here. I cannot see where to go."

John worried for the new soul enslaved within his cell. He said, "You're the new man, you must find your way. Mayhap someone will move and make some room."

A few men groaned. John heard some shuffling. The room fell silent once again.

For a second time, sleep called to John. Thoughts of home and family usually brought him peace. Tonight, he was unable to conjure their faces. He lay awake all through the night.

*****

As dawn approached, sunlight streamed through the grate in the outer cell wall and washed over John. It must certainly have been over a year since he'd lived in this box with these men.

He sat up and took in the scene before him. His eyes came to rest on the person Jervis had brought in the previous night.

The new man sat against the wall, his head lying to one side. Long, stringy brown hair fell across his face. His beard hadn't grown too long, which meant he'd not been imprisoned for longer than a few months. As he watched, the man slowly lifted his head, brushed the hair from his filth-covered face, and locked eyes with John.

There was something about the man's dark green eyes that brought unrest to the reverend's soul. John pushed himself up into a sitting position and watched the new man. Try as he might, he couldn't figure why the stranger would elicit such a response from him.

John broke the silence and asked, "What are you called?"

Dark eyes watched John, but no words came forth.

"How long have you been incarcerated?"

An intense stare tore into John. *Why does he watch me so?*

"Do you hail from London?"

The stranger rubbed a palm across his brow and drew it over his face and beard. Using his fingers, he combed his hair back, pulled it into a mass, and tied it into a knot at the base of his neck.

"Well, John Lothropp. I'm surprised you do not know who I am."

7

The use of John's name and the sound of that voice sent fire down the length of his spine.

Who was this man?

John said, "Pray tell, who might you be?"

The newcomer shifted his weight until he sat fully erect. His gaze deepened as he stared at John.

"I am Gryffyn Cane."

Shock and anger reared in John like a riled stallion. He pulled back on the reins in an effort to control the beast. Jumping to his feet, he hit his head against the low ceiling. The steed pawed at the ground. John did all he could to control the creature as he watched the man who had betrayed him. He lifted his hand and pointed at the man.

"You! How can it be my misfortune to have you in this cell? You have ruined my life!"

The angry stallion within gave John new strength. He moved across the cell and grabbed Gryffyn Cane by the front of his shirt, pulling him to his feet.

"I should beat you where you stand for what you have done to me and my family."

John pushed him against the wall, pressing his forearm into his neck. He clenched his other hand into a fist, preparing to strike.

The jangle of wrist shackles jarred John from his thoughts as someone grabbed his arm. Shackle chains thumped onto his back and side.

"Nay, Reverend, do not do it." Colin spoke into John's ear. "Remember your wife, your children, your congregation. If you set off a fight, you will suffer great punishment, perhaps even death. It does not matter who he is, or what he's done to you. Remember your family."

Anger still coursed through John's body. His muscles were taut against Gryffyn Cane's neck. This person had betrayed him and left him at the mercy of wicked men.

How many others were incarcerated because of Gryffyn Cane?

How could John ever forgive him?

Colin said, "I beg of you, think of Hannah. Think of your young ones."

John gradually gained control of the stallion, and the acidity of his ire began to subside. Colin was right. He must remember Hannah. He must remember his children. He must remember his congregation. He leaned back and pulled his arm away from Gryffyn Cane's neck.

A low snarl rumbled in John's chest. "You'd best stay away from me."

John returned to his spot under the grate. Colin joined him, and both men pressed their backs against the wall and slid down, coming to rest on the floor.

Colin asked, "Reverend, what has the man done to cause you such anger?"

"He is responsible for my incarceration, as well as many others from my congregation." John raised his arm and pointed at Gryffyn Cane. "He is the one who took me from my family!" John met the steely gaze of his former friend. Anger boiled to the surface once again.

How can it be that this man comes to be in this place, at this time?

Gryffyn Cane sat down, leaned against the wall, and crossed his legs. An arm rested on each knee. He watched John with the intensity of an eagle to a field mouse.

John said, "Look at him! He shows no remorse and watches me with a challenge in his eyes."

Colin leaned into John and whispered, "Nay, do not show your anger to such a man. It only speaks of weakness. Control is strength. Be strong, my friend."

John saw the truth of Colin's words and lowered his gaze. Gryffyn Cane had already taken his freedom—John would not let him take his soul as well. He pressed his back against the wall and stared over at his nemesis. The man turned his head away.

Colin whispered, "Tell me what happened."

Speaking in low tones, John began. "I was the Perpetual Curate of the Egerton Church. Yet, I left my ministry."

"Why did you part from it?"

"I found many problems with the doctrine of the Church. I felt the King and the Archbishop had filled it with corruption. So I left and joined with the Independents and taught them as their minister. I was arrested, and several others from my congregation, as well."

John watched Gryffyn Cane for any sort of reaction to what he was saying. The man kept his head rolled to the side.

"A group of us were in Blackfriars at the home of a congregant the night they found us. I didn't know it at the time, but someone who I considered a friend," John inclined his head toward Gryffyn, "had betrayed me to Bishop Laud.

"In May we were brought up before the Court of the High Commission, where we were questioned by Laud and five other bishops for hours. They insisted we sign an oath of allegiance to the Church. We could not sacrifice our souls to do such a thing because we believed the Church had deviated away from many true Bible doctrines, and we refused to sign. Therefore, Laud sent us to rot in prison."

Colin said, "So you sit among thieves and murderers because you love the Lord? Because you trusted a friend?"

"Aye, in the words of the Psalms, 'Yea, *mine own familiar friend, in whom I trusted, which did eat of my bread, hath lifted up his heel against me.'*
i

He scrutinized the man who had once been a close confidant. "Why did you do it, Gryffyn? Why did you turn on your friends?"

Gryffyn Cane slowly rotated his head and leveled a steely glare at John. "Bishop Laud was willing to offer a price for your capture—I was willing to take it. Others from the congregation were inconsequential victims."

"Inconsequential victims? How can you say such a heartless thing about your friends?"

"Friends? True friends would not have led me astray from the real church of God. When I belonged to the Church of England, my life was good. However, I believed your talk of incorrect doctrine and an unjust King, and I joined with the Independents."

Gryffyn Cane shifted his weight and leaned back, keeping his legs tucked under him. "After I began to meet with your group, my mother became ill. No doctor could find what ailed her. I felt her only hope lay in God. I implored Him to save her. When the months went by and she didn't improve, I begged him to take me instead. She is gone now and, as you can see—I remain."

He let out a sigh and leaned back against the wall. "I asked myself this question. If God was truly in the church I followed, why didn't He give me what I asked for? I was willing to make the ultimate sacrifice, yet He didn't do as I bade Him. Instead, God took my mother, who was a humble, loving, and innocent soul. I soon came to realize I was in the wrong church, praying to the wrong God—and you were the one who lead me there."

Sadness overcame John. "Why did you hide this from me? Together we could have worked through your troubles." If he had known the truth of Gryffyn's pain, perhaps he could have helped him, long before anger transformed Gryffyn into the vindictive man who sat before him today.

Realizing the deep pain Gryffyn must have felt over his mother's death, John tried to put away his anger. "I am deeply sorry for the loss of your mother."

Hatred spewed from the lips of Gryffyn Cane as he leaned forward again and watched John. "You do not have the right to feel sorry for me. I left the Church of England and followed you. To punish me, God took my mother. You were the leader of the congregation and are foremost responsible for my pain and loss."

John ran a hand over his face while he struggled to put his thoughts into words. "Gryffyn, God does not punish us for where or how we worship. All He asks is that we follow Him. In truth, He shows great mercy in all things—even as we walk this world imperfectly. We know according to God's mercy, we will be born again through the resurrection of Jesus Christ."

He continued, "I am sad you believe God took your mother because you joined with the Independents." John felt genuine sorrow for

11

Gryffyn's pain and turmoil. However, betrayal burned strong within his soul.

"Nevertheless, it does not give you the right to turn on your friends. You have caused egregious harm to many people. I pray I might forgive you some day. But, that day isn't today."

John turned away from Gryffyn Came. Resentment still coursed through him. He moved to his place under the grate and made ready to lie down upon his bed of straw.

A low growl came from the corner of his cell. He squinted into the darkness. There seemed to be the silhouette of a dog sitting in the corner. He turned to Colin.

"Colin, did you hear a strange sound?"

"What sound?"

"It sounded like the growl of a dog." John pointed toward the corner. "Do you see the shadow of a dog over there by William?"

"Pray, forgive me, but I do not."

Was it real? Was the black dog of Newgate more than the wild imaginings of deranged men?

John peered into the darkness, yet now, all he saw was William sleeping against the wall.

"It must have been a trick of the light. I see nothing now."

Colin said, "Aye, this place can do strange things to one's mind."

John lay upon the straw once again. He pulled the wool cloak over his head, and turned to face the wall.

How did he have the dreadful misfortune of Gryffyn Cane being placed in his cell? Did Jervis know who the man was?

Reaching out, he let his fingers play across the stones until he found the row of previous hash marks. He continued to rub across the lines until the end of the top row. Holding one finger to the mark, he reached his other hand into his pocket and pulled out a small, jagged rock. He brought it to the wall and began to scratch against the stone.

One more day in hell.

LAMBETH

A rank odor filled the air. Thomas held a hand over his nose and mouth as he picked his way over food, trash, and sewage tossed from doors or poured out of windows.

Newgate was on the other side of the Thames; otherwise he would have avoided the London Bridge altogether. The cost of a ferry ride across the river was too great a sacrifice. He must save every bit of the money he earned as a waterman. He needed it to pay the gaolers for passage through the prison gates and into his father's cell.

Rowing his wherry boat across the river would require him to leave it moored at a dock while he continued on toward Newgate. He could not take the risk of someone stealing the boat while it was left unguarded. Ergo, the bridge was his only option.

His neck throbbed at the weight of the muslin bag of goods he wore thrown over his shoulder. A large strap angled across his chest and kept it secure. Thankfully, Frederick was a great friend to his father, and he'd scrounged up some food and supplies for Thomas to take with him to Newgate.

He remembered the dreadful night when he'd heard his father had been arrested. Every day, he felt his father's loss. He was aware of it when he walked through the house, when he noticed his father's Bible sitting on the sideboard, when he spent time with his ailing mother, or when he soothed a younger sibling during a dark and lonely night.

People jostled against him and brought his mind back to his present situation. He bent his head down and pressed on through the crowd. One foot in front of another, with fervent intent, he moved toward Newgate prison and his father.

Foul street smells filled his nose. Somehow, through it all, the smell of freshly baked bread broke in, and he lifted his head to breathe in the delectable aroma. Gazing down the bridge, he spied a weathered bakery sign with a loaf of bread carved into the wood. The bakery sign called to him and brought a rush of saliva to his mouth.

He steeled himself against the scent. He must continue forward and allow no distractions. Even still, he wasn't prepared for the sight of pastries, tarts, cakes, and custard which filled the window shelves of the bakery. Marzipan in the shapes of animals, birds, fruits, and baskets tugged at his heart.

Oh, how delicious! Maybe I could spare a few pennies towards a sweet? Nay! I must stay the course. My goal is to see Father.

He adjusted the bag over his shoulder and pressed into the throng of people once again. The Chapel of St. Thomas sat at the bridge's center and would afford him a quiet place to pray. It was his immediate objective, and he must remain focused.

Horrid odors pressed in on him and overpowered the sweet bakery smells. Several shops were passed before he arrived at the entrance to St. Thomas.

An arched entry held large Gothic eight-panel doors which seemed to say, *Come inside.* He pushed the doors open and stepped through.

Such a pleasing fragrance greeted him. He inhaled deeply, filling his head with the scent of the church. Incense smoke imbued the air with the strong aroma of sandalwood, which helped mask the horrific smells right outside. He released the doors, letting them close softly behind him.

Pews filled the church and were lined down each side of the main aisle, like children awaiting their turn for communion. Peace sat in every corner of the sanctuary. He saw no one, so he set off down the aisle toward the front of the nave.

Beautiful vaulted ceilings rose above the altar. Thomas was amazed at the gracefully carved stone, which resembled huge fans coming together at the middle. In the center of the arch was a glorious stained-glass window depicting Christ holding a small child. Other children surrounded Christ, holding onto His robes or sitting at His feet. A golden halo encircled His head, which seemed to glow as sunlight passed through the glass, and a riot of color blazed across the room.

Thomas moved to the altar and slid his hand along smooth and shiny mahogany. He brushed his fingers over the surface of a delicately carved fruit and ribbon swag which swept across the face of the altar.

Taking a pew a few row backs and kneeling down, he clasped his hands together to pray.

My most beloved God, I come to Thee with a prayer from my heart. I thank Thee for my wherry business so I was able to earn the money in my pocket. I pray it is enough to pay the fees required before I am allowed to see my father. I beg of Thee, help him that he may be safe and come home soon. Please bless my mother so she will gain her strength and might get well again. I pray for Thy spirit to abide with me as I continue on my journey this day.

In the name of Thy Holy Son, amen.

Thomas remained kneeling for a time as he thought about his life and his family. His heart broke with the pain of his father's imprisonment. His shoulders bent low with the burden which had been placed upon his young back. His soul faltered at the discouragement of his mother's illness.

A gentle voice broke through his reflection. "May I be of service to you, my son?"

The kindly face of a vicar smiled down at him. Thomas slowly arose from his kneeling position. "Thank thee, Your Grace, but I am well."

"Oh, my dear boy, it does not seem so to me."

"Pardon, Your Grace, I should have said I *will* be well. I was making my way across the bridge and thought to enter and pray. I will be on my way now."

The burden of his father's imprisonment was something he didn't intend to share. His responsibility was to take care of the family in his father's stead. He squared his shoulders and feigned a smile.

"Thank thee kindly, Your Grace. The sun continues its path across the sky, and I must hurry before I lose the day."

The vicar smiled and said. "I understand, young man. My prayers go with thee."

Thomas nodded his head and turned for the door, the smile quickly fading from his face. He picked up the muslin bag and made his way back down the aisle. The heavy, wooden doors creaked on their hinges as he pulled them inward.

At a small break in the crowd, he pressed in and resumed the journey. He jostled his way through the people and weaved between the carriages. A sense of relief filled his mind when the bridge finally emptied onto Thames Street, where he turned left and headed toward the corner of Newgate Street and Old Bailey Road.

He thought back to the days before his father's incarceration. Those were good days. The family came together each night for a dinner made delicious by his mother's wonderful cooking. They sat around the dinner table, his father at the head, the family engaged in lively conversation.

Thomas trudged along watching the ground, head down, shoulders hunched forward. For a moment, he forgot about the criminals and pickpockets who inhabited Thames Street. People banged and bumped him from every turn, yet onward he pressed.

Something caught his right foot, and he gripped the bag tightly as the street rose up to meet his face. Cobblestones scraped across his palms and he hit the ground, his head and shoulder thumping onto the cold, hard stones.

Gritty street grime filled his beard and spread across his lips. He spat it upon the cobbles and pushed himself up onto his knees. A sound blow caught him between the shoulder blades. He once again fell to the street, scraping his palms across the stones.

Turning to view the dingy faces of two young ruffians, he noted malicious smiles displaying rotting teeth.

The taller of the two said, "Ge' up, man. Wha' you doin' on th' street?" His mouth twisted in a sneer as he kicked Thomas in the side and grappled for the bag.

Thomas jumped to his feet and pulled the bag out of the boy's reach. He could not allow this boy to take the supplies meant for his father.

"Dinna yer ma teach ye 'ow t' walk?" said the short one. He swept his leg across Thomas's ankles in an attempt to trip him up again.

Thomas kept his balance and looked from one boy to the next.

Tension grew in his stomach. He pulled the bag into his chest and stood tall, staring down at the two hooligans. The boys backed slightly away. Thomas noted no stubble shadowed their chins. Their bodies were thin and emaciated. He could see they were merely boys, pretending to be men.

With a deep voice, he said, "You boys had best be on your way before I get truly angry."

The taller boy reached for the bag. Thomas stretched to his full height and deepened his stare. He placed a hand on the taller boy's chest and gave him a shove backward.

His gaze fixed on the shorter boy, Thomas could see hesitation in his eyes. He pointed his finger down the street. "Get going, both of you!"

Both boys jumped at the gruff sound of his voice. They took off down the street, disappearing into the crowd.

Thomas rolled his shoulders and rubbed the back of his neck, bringing a jolt of pain from his injured palm. Abrasions and dirt spread over his palms, evidence of his run-in with the cobbles. He rubbed them across his pant legs.

Would he ever arrive at Newgate?

The attack had caught him unawares. If he lost the money, his visit to Father would fail. Slipping a few fingers into his purse, he checked for the coins. One, two, three . . . he continued counting until all coins had been accounted for.

He pulled the drawstring on his purse and tucked it back into the waistband of his breeches. Most people seemed to be about their daily tasks and were not a threat, nor did they care what was going on around them.

Head high, shoulders back, bag pulled into his chest, Thomas moved into the horde of people and continued down Thames Street. Skies above shone bright and clear, in direct contrast to his mood. He growled at the sun.

Why do you shine brightly when my mood is so dark?

He persisted in his trek toward Newgate as he made his way onto Fleet Street. Day began to cool and crowds began to thin. Turning onto to Newgate Street, he glanced up to see the imposing stone towers of the prison jutting into the sky. They stood like a dark and sickening giant, ready to swallow all who dared enter its realm.

Repulsion slithered through his body, slipping across his abdomen and around his back. Taking several breaths, he pushed the sickness down and trudged forward.

At long last, the old Roman gate stood directly in front of him. It had been enlarged into a prison many years ago. Its tower rose tall and majestic, with chiseled stones stacked in perfect order. A tall arch spanned the entrance, a large keystone at its center with a gate of strong iron cross-thatched bars to fill its opening.

Two gallows stood to each side of the tower. Four men hung from the beams jutting out into the street. Their bodies rotted while they dangled from ropes cinched around their necks. An oppressive, putrid stench filled the air.

Thomas pulled a kerchief from his pocket and pressed it over his nose and mouth, his other hand grasped the muslin bag. He stepped up to the gate and peered through the iron bars. Darkness beyond the gate was thick and eerie. Nothing within could be seen.

Holding the cloth away from his face, he called out, "Ho, the gate! Is anyone there?"

Uneven footfalls echoed from the darkness. It was a strange sound. *Thud, clomp. Thud, clomp.*

A grotesque shape emerged from the darkness and took the form of a man as it slipped into the sunlight. Thomas felt his stomach lurch as he viewed the most dreadful face he'd ever seen.

Deep wrinkles cut down the creature's face. One eye watched Thomas while the other pointed to one side. His face drooped down on one side and seemed to be sliding off his head. Slobber dribbled through a deep crevice at the corner of his mouth. Drool gathered into a drip at the bottom of his chin, and the man wiped it away with his sleeve.

Thomas's gaze was fixed upon the eye that stared off into nothing. The gaoler emitted a heavy sigh, and a terrible stink filled Thomas's nostrils. He recoiled at the scent and stumbled back, pressing the kerchief over his nose and mouth.

"What be it ye want? Ye came callin' at m' door. Now talk, lad."

Thomas swallowed hard. He stepped up to the gate again. "Umm . . . umm . . ."

"Speak up, boy, or I be leavin'."

"Umm . . . I . . . umm . . . I have come to see my father . . . sir."

"Sir!" Spit flew in Thomas's face as the man erupted in laughter. "I 'ave n'er been called sir afore. Wha' ye can call me is Jervis. I be th' Keeper 'ere."

Thomas used the kerchief to wipe the spit from his face, a shiver of revulsion passing through him. "Might I see my father?

"'Ave ye brought the fee?"

"Aye."

"I need one shillin' t' open th' gate." The man stretched his arm through the gate with his palm facing upward.

Thomas retrieved a shilling from his purse and quickly placed it in the man's hand. He watched in shock as the gaoler turned and disappeared into the darkness.

19

Pulling the kerchief from his mouth, he said, "You, sir! Come back! I paid my money, now let me in."

Sounds of grinding metal filled the air. The gate slowly began to rise. Thomas stepped back from the bars as the gate rose higher and higher, coming to a stop about two feet above his head.

The Keeper stepped from the darkness and waved him in. He turned and disappeared into the blackness once again.

Smells of urine and body odor grew thicker as Thomas passed beneath the gate and into the holding area. Folding the kerchief so the man's spittle was on the inside, he held it over his nose again and scanned the room.

Darkness clung selfishly to each corner of the chamber. His eyes adjusted to the dark. A bit of sunlight shone through the archway and fell upon a large wooden door, which had a heavy black knocker marking its center.

"Jus' who is it yer lookin' t' see?"

Thomas jumped at the sound of a voice piercing the darkness.

Jervis stepped into the sunlight, which cast a revealing light across his face. Deep shadows played in every line and crevice, giving him a manifestation of the walking dead.

Thomas sucked in his breath. His voice shook as he said, "I am here to see my father—John Lothropp."

"Tha' mammering hell-hated ratsbane! Tha' will cost ye another shillin', just fer sayin' 'is name." The gaoler thrust his palm forward.

Anger rose from deep within Thomas, but with care he pushed it back down. He must keep his head, or he might pay all his money to the Keeper and still not be able to visit his father. Pressing fingers into his purse, he retrieved another shilling, placing it on the out-thrusted hand.

The gaoler snapped his hand around the coin. "Tha' will do fer now. Ye must pay more once yer inside, so there'd best be others." He grabbed a lantern and lit the wick.

"Follow me." Drool hung in a long string from his chin and lay upon his shoulder.

A shudder passed across Thomas's back. The thought of his father in this sickening place brought a chill to his heart.

With the bag of supplies held close to his chest, Thomas trailed the Keeper to the large oak door, where another gaoler stood against the wall. The man reached out and grasped the large black door handle, stepping back to pull the door open.

Jervis turned back to the other gaoler and said, "Be sure an' close th' gate directly."

"Aye, tha' I will," the man replied.

Jervis passed through the doorway and headed down a long dark corridor. Thomas followed close behind. He slipped over slimy stones as he struggled to keep his balance. How did the Keeper walk over such slippery ground while missing one leg and relying on a crutch? The Keeper's lantern bobbed back and forth as he clomped from crutch to foot.

Thud, clomp. Thud, clomp.

Clammy air closed in around Thomas. They moved ever deeper into the guts of Newgate. The Keeper stopped at an intersection of corridors, turned right, and continued down another long hallway. Thomas trailed the Keeper into the inner recesses of what seemed to be the underworld.

Onward they plodded, until at long last Jervis stopped at a door and held his lantern high. The door was made of thick oak planks with a small metal grate inset about chest high, which was cross-latched with flat, iron bars.

Jervis pulled a large key ring from his belt clip and fumbled through different keys. He stuck one key into the door and turned. There was a loud scrape and a grunting sound as he pulled on the door. Rusty hinges screeched and groaned in objection. Thomas stepped back to make way for the door to open out into the corridor. Once the door had fully opened, the Keeper turned to Thomas and held out his hand.

"Tha' be four shillin' fer th' time with yer pa. I be waitin', so ye'd best get on wi' it."

Thomas reached into his purse and felt out four shillings. He placed them in the Keeper's palm. Tears stung his eyes, but he dared not wipe them away and bring attention to his emotions.

How can Father be in this loathsome place? Oh, my most beloved God, please help me. I must be strong!

Jervis held his lantern forward and stepped through the door. He hollered into the cell. "All ye men stand again' th' wall."

Anxious to see his father, Thomas bent down and moved into the cell. He tried to straighten up, but his head thumped against the ceiling. Light from the lantern revealed several men hunched against the walls, some rising from the floor. The room seemed too small to house even four men, yet he counted twenty within the cell.

Jervis called out, "Reverend—step forward."

A man shuffled into the light. Hair and beard were tangled into one large mass. Torn clothes covered most of a body thin beyond compare.

The gaoler clomped over and poked a finger into the inmate's face. The man flinched and turned away.

Jervis held the lantern up to the reveal the pitiful face. He turned to Thomas and said, "Ye see this man? He be who ye came to see." A sinister chuckle escaped his lips.

As light from the lantern illuminated the man's face, Thomas studied him. He wondered if it could possibly be his father, the Reverend John Lothropp. His mind couldn't reconcile what stood before him with the image of his beloved father.

The bedraggled man turned his face toward Thomas. Bright blue eyes flickered in the lantern's light. Those were the eyes of his father! A deep sob tore at his soul and threatened to escape. Thomas covered his mouth to stifle the cry.

The inmate's eyes lit up, and he stepped forward. "Praise God! Thom, my boy, can it be you?"

Jervis called out, "Ge' back! Ye know th' rules. Ye must stand again' th' wall." He shoved John back against the wall. "Now, Lothropp, ye stay where ye be."

Thomas moved forward, but thought better of it and stood his ground. His father and the gaoler glared for a moment.

Jervis leaned back on his crutch and wiped at his chin. "Lothropp . . . it fills me with vexation to come here this day, yet this boy 'as come fer ye. He only be paying for a bit o' time, so I'll not be leavin'." Jervis turned back to the doorway and set the lamp down on the ground. Lantern light cast a grotesque shadow upward onto the Keeper, making him look sinister as a demon.

"Yer time began when this 'ere boy hollered at th' gate." He surprised Thomas with a forceful push forward. "Ye asked fer your pa, well, thar he be."

Thomas stumbled to catch his balance. Anger and frustration from his terrible day rose to the surface. He had taken enough. He raised his hand toward Jervis.

"Thomas! No," John called out.

Thomas flinched at the sound of his father's voice. Events of the day had worn on him, but he'd best not raise a hand to this man. He eased his arm down to his side, though his eyes remained fixed on the repulsive little creature.

A slow smile spread across the Keeper's mouth. He shook a fist at the boy. "Ye'd best beware yer actions, lest yer father pay th' price."

Conflicting emotions churned in Thomas's stomach. If he allowed his anger to spill over, his father would suffer the consequences. Thomas turned from Jervis and moved toward John.

"Oh, Father. How I have missed you." He reached his arms out, and father and son came together in a warm embrace.

"Words cannot express how much I have missed you, my son." John clung to Thomas.

"Hrrump . . . sickening," said Jervis. "Makes me wanna puke. Yer shillin's only buys ye so much time."

Thomas pulled back from his father to straighten up, but his head once again banged on the ceiling. He turned and glowered at the Keeper. "I will not make you wait for long. Please leave us in peace and let us have the time I've paid for."

23

Jervis shrugged his shoulders. "Hrrump."

Thomas turned back to his father.

John said, "Please forgive me, my son. I wish we could meet under better circumstances."

Thomas studied his father's eyes. Months of deprivation and pain surged into his thoughts. Though he was glad to visit his father, frustration over today's events flowed into his mind. "This is where you have chosen to be. What can I say about it?"

"Oh, Thom, please understand my plight. I must be faithful to the Lord, to the congregation, and to—"

"What of us, Father? Are you faithful to us?"

John rested a hand on Thomas's shoulder. "Of course. Every waking moment I think of my family. I worry you—"

"It may be, yet still we suffer." Hard work, hunger, and loneliness stabbed at his heart. He lowered his head and slid his foot across the stone floor. Tears stung at the back of his eyes. Squeezing them tightly, he pushed the tears away and lifted the muslin bag to show John. "Here, let me show you what I brought—"

"Shh . . . nay, Son, keep it closed." John guardedly took the bag from Thomas. He whispered to him, "Keep your voice quiet."

John slid the bag down next to his legs and kicked some type of fabric over the top of it, pushing it behind him. He whispered in Thomas's ear, "Where did you find excess? You didn't take food from the mouths of the family, did you?"

Thomas whispered back, "Nay, Father, 'tis from Frederick. He brought us food and clothing and even some toys for the children. He says these items are for you."

"Frederick has been released from prison? Thank the Lord! How long has it been?"

"It has been barely a fortnight. He is gaining his strength back and looks better each time I see him."

"It fills my soul with joy to hear such good news. He is a true friend. Thank him for these things and tell him I am forever in his debt."

"I will, Father." Anger and frustration drained from him as he took in the deprivation he saw standing before him. "You are so thin. Do you get any food at all?"

"We have water soup once daily. It has a bit of bread in it. At times, we are allowed some meat. Though, without some pence for the fire, 'tis given to us raw. I cannot bear the raw meat, but I drink the soup."

Tears threatened Thomas, and he struggled to keep them under control. He failed the task as one slid down his cheek. "I have a few coins I can leave you for the fire, Father."

"Nay, son, you keep them. You must save them to pay your way back out of this prison. I cannot bear the thought of you being held here for lack of funds."

John pulled Thomas into his arms. "Please, Son, do not shed a tear for me. I am here doing the Lord's work." He moved back to look into Thomas's eyes. "I long to know how your mother and the children fare."

"The children are fine. However, I am sorry to say Mother is sick. Jane is always by her side and takes good care of her."

"Pray tell, how did this come to be? She is a strong woman, able to run our household, as well as care for many parishioners."

"The doctor says that is what caused her sickness. Many of the parishioners fell ill, and Mother tended to some of the families. It seemed to hit the children the hardest, and you know how much Mother loves the little ones. She couldn't let them suffer, and was gone day and night caring for them.

"Though, in reality, Jane believes 'tis a broken heart. Mother misses you so much. I grieve to tell you this, Father, but she is now weak and bedridden. I hear her crying at night when she thinks no one is about."

John rubbed a hand over his face, pulling at his beard. "Oh, my beloved Hannah. I wish I were there to care for her. Tell her I miss her and love her dearly. Pass my love onto the children, as well, especially to my sweet Jane for her devotion to your mother. Every day, I picture each of you so I won't forget your faces. I cannot imagine how much the children have changed."

"Not as much as you would think, Father. They send their love."

"You have changed, Thom. Your beard is filled in and trimmed into a nice shape. You have grown so tall—you seem to be a man."

"Father—I am now eighteen." Thomas stood as tall as he could in the cramped quarters.

"Aye, you are a man. Forgive me for not seeing that."

"I have had to become a man, Father."

John put one hand around the back of Thomas's neck and the other on his shoulder. "You are a good son, and I thank the Lord for you every day. However, I worry the burden you carry is too great."

Thomas noted the concern etched across his father's face. "Worry not for me, Father. I am fine."

"I have no doubt you stand tall in my place while I am away."

"I do my best, yet I miss you so. My faith wavers, and I wonder if peace will ever be in our lives again."

"I miss you as well, my son. I pray daily for the courage to stay strong. I pray God will guide us to a place where we can live and worship in peace."

"Father, all my life I have heard you speak of a special place God has in store for us. I need to have faith, yet I struggle to find it."

"Be assured, Son, your faith will come. Put your trust in the Lord, and He will guide you." John's reassuring hands clutched Thomas's arms. "I will be home soon, Thom. I feel it in my soul. Embrace your mother and the children as well, tell them I—"

"Tha' be all ye paid fer. Out wi' ye, lad," Jervis said.

"Oh, Father . . ."

John stretched up and took his son's head in his hands. Thomas leaned into him, and John kissed him on each cheek.

"I will be home again. Do not despair."

His father's reassuring words calmed his troubled heart. Jervis grabbed Thomas by the collar and yanked him away.

"Tha' be it. Out—now."

Thomas stumbled back as Jervis pulled him out into the hallway. The Keeper leaned down and picked up the lantern. He lifted it high and stepped through the door.

Thomas peered into the darkness of the cell. "I love you, Father. I will come again."

Jervis mocked Thomas and said with a cackle in his voice, "I love you, *Father.*" He leaned back and let out a loud guffaw.

From the gloom, Thomas heard his father's voice calling out. "Thomas?"

"I am here, Father."

"Be well, my son."

"I will, Father, I will."

A hand grasped his shirtsleeve and pulled him away from the cell door. Turning toward the gaoler, Thomas stared him in the eye. "Keep your hands off me, you slithering, grimy stump of a man."

The Keeper matched the boy stare for stare. Thomas waited until Jervis cleared his throat and turned back to push the cell door closed, scraping the key into the lock.

Jervis was clearly a cruel man. Thomas prayed his loss of control would not cause his father any undo harm. Knowing his father was trapped inside of that insidious cell, at the mercy of this horrible creature, filled Thomas's soul with anguish.

The gaoler edged around him and thumped down the hallway. The echo of Jervis' crutch bounced across the walls. Gloom began to swallow up the lantern's light as the Keeper clomped his way down the hall and back toward the gate.

Thud, clomp. Thud, clomp.

Lantern glow shrank smaller and smaller. A knot tightened in Thomas's stomach. He'd best hurry or perhaps be left in this horrific place for good. Slipping and sliding over slimy stones, he caught up to Jervis and followed the lantern down the hallway. He worked his way out of the darkest place he'd ever seen. Upon reaching the outer door, the Keeper turned and held his hand out once again.

"Now ye must pay a fee to leave this 'ere place. Since ye be th' son o' tha' gnashgab reverend, and since ye felt th' need to snipe at me, ye must pay one shillin' fer me to open th' door and two more to open th' gate."

Thomas matched the man's glare as he reached into his purse and prayed he had three more shillings. As the coins gathered into his fingers, he counted. One . . . two . . . three . . . four shillings remained in his purse.

Relief filled his mind. He grasped three of them and placed them into the palm of the outstretched hand. How many more shillings would be required? He prayed it wasn't more than one.

The Keeper's hand snapped closed around the money. He turned and pushed the door open, allowing sunlight to stream into the hallway. Thomas squinted and brought his hands up to block the glare.

Jervis clomped his way across the holding area. With the grind of metal on metal, the gate began to rise. Thomas strode toward the gate.

A gruff voice echoed across the enclosure. "Step back! Ye don' leave 'til ye pay th' final fee."

Sweat broke out on Thomas's forehead. How much would it be? The gate was now open. He could always make a run for it, but surely his father would pay the price.

Jervis clomped his way over to where Thomas stood. He held his hand out one last time. "One last shillin' before ye pass under th' gate."

"I already paid my shillings to pass under the gate."

"Tha' were fer me to open th' gate. One more to pass under th' gate."

Thomas reached for the last coin in his purse, but he came up empty. Where was his last shilling?

His fingers swept every part of the leather pouch. He grasped the bottom of his purse and pulled it up through the drawstring opening. The coin fell to the ground and rolled across the floor, coming to a stop against Jervis's crutch.

Thomas stepped forward and leaned down to recover his coin. Jervis lifted his crutch, positioning it over the top of the shilling.

Thomas snatched his fingers away and arose to watch the gaoler. "Let me retrieve my money."

"I see no money 'bout this place."

"Very well." Thomas glared down at the Keeper. "I have paid the fare. I am going to pass under the gate and be on my way."

He stepped under the gate and out into the bustle of London. His mind urged him to run, but his spirit warned him to walk.

Don't look back! Stand straight and tall. Walk slowly.

He headed down the street, but took the opportunity to check whether or not the Keeper watched him. No vile, repugnant figure stood at the gate. His stance relaxed while he made his way toward the bridge.

Anguish over his father charged in and overwhelmed his emotions. A heavy sob threatened and he pushed forward, not noticing the people around him until he was nearly knocked off his feet by someone in the crowd.

London Bridge was near. Pandemonium surrounded him, and the clop of horse's hooves battered his ears. He shoved his way past several carriages and through hordes of people as he continued to press into the throng.

Newgate's stench endured, so the smell of the bridge barely assailed his senses.

Emotions battered his soul. It had been wonderful to visit his father, yet the conditions he suffered were almost intolerable for Thomas to contemplate. His soul cried out for solitude, even in the midst of so many.

One glance down the bridge brought notice of the ramps, which had been drawn up to allow small ships to pass through. Nineteen arches spanned the twenty-six-foot-wide bridge. Water rushed around the pilings and between the arches, gushing out the other side on its way to the ocean.

Elbowing through the crowds, Thomas made his way to the last building before the raised ramps at the center of the bridge.

Sounds of rushing water beckoned him. He edged around the building and headed to the waist-high wall. Water swirled around the bridge pilings but slowed as it met the wide expanse of the Thames.

A wherry boat whooshed out from the arch beneath him. Passengers held tightly to the boat, a look of terror on their faces. He knew too well the fear and exhilaration of shooting the bridge, as he'd done so many times himself.

His mind reeled from the experience at Newgate. Rumors of the horrors of prison ran rampant, but until today, he had not understood.

Oh, Father, how will you ever survive that hellish place? My heart breaks with sorrow for you.

A sob threatened to shatter Thomas's willpower. He rubbed it away with the palms of his hands.

What will I tell Mother? She will ask me questions and will want to know everything. I don't know if I can bear telling her. She is so ill, what if the news of Father makes her worse?

Thomas drew in deep, ragged breaths as he slowly gained control of tears hovering on the edge of his resolve. He lowered his hands and placed them atop the wall.

A small sailing vessel emerged from between the ramps of the drawbridge as it made its way downriver. The pull of the sea taunted him. Oh, how he longed to step aboard and sail away from his troubles.

Unexplored worlds lay beyond the shores of England, waiting to be discovered. Perhaps he could hire onto one of the large ships heading to the New World. He imagined himself at the bow of a ship, wind whipping through his hair, salt water stinging his skin. Would Emma be at his side?

Though he'd only met Emma a few months previous, he was falling more in love with her every day. He recalled the touch of her soft skin against his fingers, her bright blue eyes staring intently into his own, her lips pressed against his mouth. A shiver ran up his spine.

Perhaps he could persuade Emma to join him on his travels. Did she have a sense of adventure to match his?

He longed to bring her home and introduce her to his family. He knew his mother would fall in love with her, as he had done. Jane and Emma would certainly become close friends. If only he could pull Emma into his circle and acknowledge their relationship. Emma's father had given his permission for the courting; however, Thomas didn't want to bring her into the mess of his life quite yet.

Once his father returned home and when his mother overcame the illness plaguing her, his life would return to the happy place it had once occupied. After which, he would allow Emma into his home life, but for now, he would continue to keep her a secret.

Something rubbed against his legs and brought him from his thoughts. What was it now? He heard a quiet sound and realized a mewling cat wound between his ankles. A soft chuckle broke free of his lips. It was time he gained control of his fears. It was time to step up and be a man. Thoughts of Emma and sailing ships quickly fled.

Standing straight and tall, Thomas pushed his shoulders back, lifted his head high, and headed home. Back to his family. Back to his mother.

Back to his life.

LAMBETH

Crisp, springtime air caressed the surface of the River Thames as it wound its way through the maze of boats and alongside cobblestone roads. Jane shivered as the wind curled up through her hair, sending long strands swirling around her head. Using both hands, she gathered her hair to one side, bringing it down over her shoulder.

She took Edmund's proffered arm and gazed into the face of the man she dearly loved. "Oh, the air is so cold this evening, Edmund." His strong jawline, wavy brown hair, and eyes the color of the sea painted a picture in her mind.

Jane loved the full-skirted Carnation pink dress she wore. It brought out the blush in her cheeks. She'd also chosen her favorite broad-brimmed hat, with a wide pink ribbon she tied in a bow under her right ear. Her mother had made ribbon flowers and attached them to the hat, along with some feather plumes, which flowed jauntily over Jane's shoulder.

She had taken great care in dressing this morning. She'd pulled her long ringlets into a bunch at the side, letting them flow down her shoulder. However, the breeze whipped up again and her hair flew around her head, making it hard to see what was right in front of her.

Removing her hand from the crook of Edmund's arm, she gathered her messy curls into a bun at the base of her neck. She loosened the bow and tucked the wayward hair up into the hat, retying the bow tighter than before.

Another gust of air whisked around her ankles, threatening to lift her skirts. She quickly pushed them down in an effort to keep things where modesty required. She pulled the thick wool cloak tighter around her shoulders.

"Are you all right, my love?" Edmund asked.

"As long as the breeze leaves me alone, I'll be fine." She smiled up into his fascinating eyes. Jane tucked her hand into his arm once again as they continued their walk down Willow Street.

She felt loved and protected when on the arm of her strong, handsome man. Though her brother Thomas was tall, Edmund stood a good two inches taller. She was secure on his arm each evening when they took their walk along the river. She loved him dearly, and each night she prayed for her father's release from prison, after which he might allow Edmund to formally court her.

London loomed large and foreboding on the opposite side of the river. The tall, daunting Tower of London was striking across the landscape. St. Paul's Cathedral, which had lost its spire in the lightning strike of 1561 when it fell through the nave roof, was a wonder to Jane. It saddened her to see the flat roof where the spire should have been. Why they never rebuilt the spire, she would never understand.

The style and architecture of ancient buildings were of great interest to her. Though London held many wonderful structures, Jane preferred the peace and quiet on the bank side of the river. She loved living in the beautiful countryside of Lambeth.

"Thank you, Edmund, for carrying my basket of vegetables."

"It is my pleasure to aide you, my sweet." He pulled her arm into his side.

Jane smiled up at him. "I am so grateful to the Allen family for allowing us to spend time picking vegetables in their garden. And thank you so much for helping me." She rubbed her hand across

Edmund's shoulders as she considered his deep blue eyes. Lost in his gaze, she was caught off guard when someone from behind thrust her into him.

"Oh, dear! I beg of you forgiveness, Edmund."

He pulled her even closer. "Worry not, sweet Jane. I welcome your advance."

The rising heat of a blush climbed up Jane's cheeks. She lowered her head as a slow smile spread across her lips. How would she ever survive until her father returned home?

"Come, Jane. Let's find a place away from the throng which surrounds us."

She allowed him to take her arm and guide her through the crowd. They passed several street vendors and worked their way to the side of a small brick building, which sat by the river's edge.

Even though many people surrounded them, Jane found herself alone with her dearest. Edmund put the basket on the ground and pulled Jane into his arms.

"Nay, Edmund, you know we cannot." She put her hands up and gently pushed against his chest.

He took her hands in his while his eyes implored her for more.

"Do not play me the fool, Jane. I love you, and you love me in return. I want to be with you always."

"I do love you, Edmund. However, you know my father is in prison. Hence, he cannot give his permission for you to officially court me."

Edmund stroked the backs of his fingers gently against her cheek. "I do know that . . . ," he lowered his hand and Jane caught the glimpse of a pout in his eyes. "Yet I often wonder if he will ever be released, for it does not seem so to me." He hesitated. "My patience runs thin these days. I want to call you mine now."

Jane stretched up her hand to touch his cheek. "Surely, you know the desire of my heart is to be with you always. We must have faith that my father will soon be home, then he will—"

"Jane! What are you thinking?" Behind her, a deep voice interrupted her thoughts.

Cold waves of shock flashed up Jane's spine and across her shoulders. She pulled from Edmund's embrace only to turn and look into the angry eyes of her brother Thomas. Her hands flew to cover her mouth, and she spun to squarely face him.

Thomas stood with arms akimbo. Anger seethed across his face. Jane felt his intense blue eyes cutting into her heart. Though she knew Thomas was angry, she was anxious about his visit to Father in prison. Pushing her concerns about her brother aside, she pulled her hand from her mouth and asked, "Oh, Thom! Pray tell, how is our father?"

"Dare not ask about our father when you have, just now, been in the arms of Edmund." Thomas glowered at her. "Father has not given his permission."

"I am sorry, Thom. I should not have allowed so much closeness with Edmund. But I am eighteen and a woman now—I should be able to decide my own fate and not be required to wait for permission."

Thomas's icy stare began to melt. "I understand your feelings, but Father must decide your fate. Nevertheless, let us put it aside for now."

He inspected Edmund. "I do understand your love for my sister. However, I must insist on distance from one another until permission is given."

Edmund stared down at Thomas for a moment longer than Jane thought necessary. He said, "All is well, Thomas. In future days, I will keep my distance."

"You must surely understand my situation. I stand in the place of my father while he is away."

"I comprehend your predicament," Edmund replied.

Thomas reached up and put one hand on each of their shoulders. "My sympathy is with you, but I beg of you, patience."

Jane nodded. "We will be patient." She took Thom's hands in hers. "Pray tell, how is our father?"

Thomas looked toward the ground. "He is thin and barely even looks like himself. The prison was horrific. I feared the worst. Yet, the worst was far greater than I could have imagined."

Jane brought her hand up to cover her mouth again. Her stomach wrenched to and fro. Edmund reached over and put his arm around her shoulders. Thomas glanced up and fixed his eyes upon the arm. Edmund lowered his hand, and Jane shivered as the breeze slipped between them. She pulled her cloak tighter around her neck and clutched it to her chest.

"Oh," she cried. "Our poor father, will he ever survive?"

Thomas shook his head. "I do not know . . . though he says we must keep the faith."

Dismay seemed to burn a hole in the pit of her stomach. "How will we do such a thing?"

"Father remains hopeful, so we must stay strong for him. Let's go home and talk about the visit. Though I do not want the younger children present. I worry about them, and about Mother. I'm fearful of how the news will affect her."

"Be that as it may, she will want to know everything."

"It's my greatest concern. I will go in to her. But first, I need to rest. I am exhausted."

"Perhaps rest for a bit, but not for too long. I'm sure she will realize when you get home and will call for you."

"Aye, you are probably right." Thomas turned to Edmund. "I ask you to pardon us. Jane and I need to head home."

"Very well, Thomas. Pray, forgive my insensitive behavior."

Thomas rubbed a hand across his bearded jaw. His sigh was deep as he put a hand on Edmund's shoulder. "Thank you, Edmund. Worry not, the incident is over, but please watch your closeness with my sister in the future."

Edmund turned toward Jane. "My heart will always be with you. Until next time, my sweet." He tipped his hat and continued on down Willow Street. Her heart fell as he disappeared into the crowd and was gone.

Thomas picked up the basket and extended his arm to her. She tucked her arm into his and leaned her head onto his shoulder.

"Jane, I must say that I have some misgivings about your beau, Edmund. He appears to be a gentleman and aboveboard, but there is something in his demeanor that brings me caution."

"Oh, Thom, Edmund is a good and kind man. There is nothing for you to worry over."

"I pray that is true, my dear sister, just be cautious. For now, let us return home quickly. I am exhausted."

It had been wonderful to be with Edmund today, yet the sorrow of her father's imprisonment and her mother's illness tore into her soul.

"Thank you for all you do for us, Thom. I cannot imagine what you experienced today at Newgate. Your strength and courage inspire me."

Thomas pulled her arm into his side. "You are sweet, Jane. Your words are appreciated."

She patted Thom's arm and smiled up at him as they continued down Willow Street, heading toward home.

*****

Jane and Thomas turned down the lane near their home. The latticed windows of their cottage sparkled with the setting sun. She had always loved the brick foundation topped with the timber frame filled in with wattle and daub. All was covered with vines of ivy rising up to the second story of the house. Thick thatched roofing had grown even thicker over the years, as they'd added more thatch to prevent leaks.

Her mother's lavender plants along the fence line wafted a beautiful scent across the breeze. Thomas held open the gate for her to pass through and they both walked up the cobblestone path, which was surrounded by holly, linden, daffodils, roses, and saffron crocus.

She spied the younger children playing among the willows. "The children are playing in the trees. Let's walk quietly so they won't realize we're home."

Taking Thomas's arm and passing between the two small oaks framing the gate, Jane followed the path up to the arched oak entry door of their home. Thomas lifted the latch and quietly pushed the door inward, allowing her to step through before him.

Jane tip-toed across the wooden floor and made her way toward the hearth. Floor boards creaked and groaned. Thomas followed close behind. She pulled the cloak from her shoulders and hung it on a big wooden peg next to the hearth. The warmth of the fire beckoned her.

A soft voice called from the other room. "Janey, have you returned home?"

Thomas brought his forefinger to his lips, imploring Jane to be quiet.

"Janey, is that you?"

Glancing toward Thomas, she shrugged her shoulders and mouthed the words, *Forgive me.*

"Aye, Mother, it is me."

The expression on Thom's face irritated Jane. When he shook his finger at her, she reached up and grabbed it in her hand. She inclined her head toward the bedchamber and fixed her gaze on him. "Thom, don't–"

"Please, come here, Janey." The soft voice called out.

Jane whispered to Thom, "Pray, tell her you are home. She will want to hear of your visit with Father."

Thomas shook his head. Softly he said, "Nay, I need to gather my wits before I can face her."

"I understand, Thom, though she will be awaiting your arrival." Jane turned and headed to her mother's bedchamber. She motioned for her brother to sit by the fire. Thomas sat upon the large chair near the hearth.

Upon entering the room, Jane went to her mother, whose forehead glistened with sweat. Jane placed the back of her hand against Hannah's cheek. It was hot to the touch. Sickness beat at the pit of Jane's stomach.

Nay, Mother, you must not grow worse. I cannot bear to lose you.

"You are so hot, Mother. Let me fetch a cloth and some cool water for your forehead." She desperately wanted to leave the room before she gave in to tears.

"I would be grateful for a cool cloth, though bring it later. For now, I desire your presence."

Her mother patted the bed. Jane smoothed the blankets and sat down. Reaching up, she swept Hannah's hair from off her forehead.

Hannah said, "Have you heard word of Thom?"

Did she have to ask of Thomas so quickly?

Jane dropped her head against her chest. She didn't want to mislead her mother, yet she felt a certain loyalty to her brother.

"Janey? What is it?"

She gave her mother a sideways glance and knew where her loyalties must lie.

With a slow sigh, she said, "Thom is in the hall resting by the hearth. He worries about telling you of his visit to Father."

Hannah placed a hand on Jane's arm.

"Please, dear, have him come to me. I need to know about my husband."

"I long to hear about Father too, yet I fear what he has to say."

"I understand, my child." Hannah patted Jane's arm. "Please, fetch him for me."

Jane rose from the bed and went into the hall. Thomas sat on the large, stuffed chair. His head sagged to his chest, his breathing slow and deep.

She watched him for a moment. She figured he must be exhausted from the long walk to Newgate and time spent in the prison. Not desiring to awaken him but realizing she must, she patted him on the shoulder.

"Thom . . . Thom . . . ," she whispered.

Thomas groaned and stretched his arms above his head. "Why did wake me? You know I longed for a rest."

Jane lifted a finger to her mouth, asking him to speak quietly. "Mother desires your presence in her bedchamber."

Thomas turned toward her, his eyes filled with accusation. "You promised not to tell her I was home and to give me some time to rest."

Months of caring for her mother and concern over her father being in prison, along with Thomas's frustrating reproach, combined to set off her emotions. She stared Thomas squarely in the eye. With a stern but soft voice, she said, "Have a care for me. You know I did not want to tell her. She asked if I'd heard anything from you. I couldn't lie."

Thomas jumped up and pulled her into his arms. "Oh, my poor sister, you are right. Please forgive a sorry fool."

"I suppose I can forgive you." Jane pulled back. "Let's go together and see Mother."

Jane grabbed Thom's hand and set off toward their mother's bedchamber, pulling him along with her. They entered the room, and Hannah motioned for them to sit on a bench along the wall.

Jane sat down, while Thomas went to his mother and tenderly took her into his arms. Hannah reached up and put her arms around his neck. "Thank you, my son." She pulled back from him and took his face into her hands. "Pray tell, how is your father?"

Thomas laid his mother's hands back onto her chest and turned to join Jane on the bench. He leaned forward and placed his elbows on his knees. Rubbing his hands over his face, he pulled a ragged sigh in and out, in and out.

"Well, first . . . he remains faithful to the Lord."

"Oh, Thomas, I doubt not that he remains faithful to the Lord. I desire to know how he is doing."

"I beg of you forgiveness, Mother. I fear the truth will cause you pain."

"Whether it be painful or not, I must know for myself. Tell me."

"Mother, I will tell you, but only if you will allow me to stop when you become fatigued."

"Very well, my son. Bear this in mind, I want to hear all about your father and all about the prison, for that is where your father currently resides."

"Even about Newgate? Surely, you dare not."

"Surely, I dare—begin."

Thomas straightened up, pushing his hair back from his face.

41

"First, he tells of his love for you. He misses you so." A heavy sigh escaped him as he continued. "Yet . . . he is weak and quite thin. I fear he fairly starves."

Hannah gasped and brought her hand to her mouth. Jane's eyes stung with tears, and she blinked them back. Mother needed Jane's strength and not weak emotions right now.

A tear slid down each side of her mother's worried face. Arising from the bench, Jane went to the bed and sat beside her mother.

"Surely he must not tell you. You need to rest, Mother."

"Nay, I must hear it now, in case I cannot bear to hear it later." With a catch in her voice, Hannah said, "I am fine now . . . continue."

Jane saw her mother's resolve strengthen as she prepared for what came next.

Thomas related the details of his trip to Newgate. Tears flowed down her mother's cheeks throughout the recap of Thomas's visit. Jane's heart broke as she saw the pain this news brought to Hannah. She longed to take the pain away, but could not.

Thomas told of the horrible keeper, whose smell was putrid, and how he mistreated John. He continued his tale as the sun slipped down onto the horizon and darkness invaded their home. Jane thought she could bear no more, yet there was still more to bear.

Thomas described Newgate to them: a large oak door with a giant metal knocker that led into dark and dreary passageways; cries never ceasing from poor wretches crowded within filthy cells; gallows where dead men still hung, though they reeked of death and decay.

Jane realized Hannah was quite pale and distraught. Her heart wrenched with sympathy for her mother. She eyed Thomas and bade him stop. He seemed to understand and brought his narrative to a close.

"I will visit him again, once I am able to earn more money to pay my way."

Hannah said, "Come here, my boy." She motioned for him to sit beside her. Jane stood and moved back over to the bench while Thomas sat on the bed next to his mother.

"You are a good son, and you fill your father's shoes well." Hannah cupped his cheek in her palm. "It must have been a horrible experience. Rest assured your father is grateful. *I* am grateful. I love you, Thom. Thank you for your bravery today."

Thomas leaned down and gave her a kiss on the cheek. "I know he will be home soon, for he told me so."

"Thank you, my son. You give me hope that I will see him again one day."

Hannah reached back and grasped her pillow. As she lifted her shoulders to tuck it under her head, she let out a loud groan, and her hand flew to her chest.

"Mother? Mother!"

NEWGATE PRISON

Sleep had come and gone throughout bitter, cold hours of darkness. Stiff muscles groaned in protest as John rolled onto his side. He lay for several moments until he felt the urge to open his eyes. He peeled back his lids, only to look into the sickening face of Raif.

"What do you want, Raif?"

Startled, Raif said, "I merely checked if ye be well."

"Pray tell, why is your filthy hand upon my bag?"

Raif stared at the ground. "It be not, Reverend," he lied.

John lifted his head and leveled his eyes at him. "Release the bag."

Raif spat at him. "Nay."

"Need I arise?" John leaned forward and stared intently into Raif's eyes.

Muttering, Raif released the bag. "Yer eyes flash like a steel blue sword tha' pierces me clean through."

Raif slowly eased the other hand behind his back. John grabbed his wrist and tugged it forward, forcing him to drop what was in his hand. Raif whimpered as an apple fell and rolled onto the floor. It came to rest in front of his knees.

He watched John like a frightened rat. "Ye are a reverend and ye must forgive."

"Go back to your corner and leave me be."

Raif turned but reached for the apple. John snatched it up.

"Back to your corner." John opened the bag and put the apple inside.

The insidious man crawled away, mumbling something John could not hear.

"Do you have more to say?"

"Nay . . . nay . . ." He disappeared into the gloom of his corner.

John turned toward Tibbot to determine how he'd fared through the night. Tibbot lay facing the wall, an eerie pallor covering his arms and legs. Alarmed, John arose to his knees and shook him.

"Tibbot—awaken." John grasped his shoulder and rolled him onto his back. His stomach churned when Tibbot's head lolled to one side.

"Tibbot! Tibbot!"

Tibbot lay silent and unmoving. John's heart thudded as he stared at the man, so young and frail. He had suffered grave illness after being thrown into this pit.

John had tried to protect him from the horrors of Newgate. His stomach roiled, and he felt sick as he stared at the limp body of Tibbot.

Collapsing against the wall in sorrow, he let his head fall forward into his hands. He mourned the loss of his young friend in silence, though a few tears wetted the stone floor.

"Nay . . . Tibbot. I cannot bear losing you." With his own family far from him, he had grown to love Tibbot like a son. What would he do without him?

He heard a faint voice in the dark. "I am here . . . though I am not well."

"You do live!" John pulled him up into his arms. "Thank the Lord." He held onto him, rocking him back and forth like a baby.

"I am grateful for the warmth, Reverend, but you can set me free now."

John chuckled and released Tibbot, gently rolling him back onto the ground. He rummaged through the bag Thomas had brought to him. Amidst a few articles of clothing and a blanket, he found potatoes, apples, and nuts. He pulled an apple from the bag.

John said, "For you, I have an apple." He lifted Tibbot's hand and placed the apple thereon.

The boy's hand felt warm, yet he trembled as though he were chilled. John worried he had contracted gaol fever. He watched Tibbot growing weaker every day. He had often complained of pain in his head. John hadn't seen evidence of the rash yet, but he feared it was coming. Tibbot was only fourteen, the same age as his son Johnny— would Tibbot survive the dreadful nature of this place?

"Eat this, my boy, it will give you some strength." John curled Tibbot's fingers around the apple.

Tibbot's eyes filled with tears. "Thank you, m' lord." He took a small bite of the fruit. "Mmm . . . something so sweet, I ne'er did taste."

John smiled and rubbed his arm. "Eat up, my young friend."

He rummaged through the bag, removed a blanket, and began to spread it over Tibbot.

"Nay, Reverend, it is for you." A cough rumbled in Tibbot's chest. John waited until it passed.

"I desire you to have the blanket." He finished pulling the blanket over Tibbot. The bag had included a nice pair of woolen socks. John found them and began to pull one onto Tibbot's foot.

"Nay . . ."

John pointed at him, wagging his finger back and forth. "You must not argue with a reverend." He finished pulling the sock onto Tibbot's foot.

Tibbot wiggled his toes in the sock. "It be warm. Thank you, m' lord."

John pulled the second sock over Tibbot's other foot. "You stay warm and get better."

He arose and turned toward Colin. Stretching his hand forward, he offered him an apple or a potato.

"I'll take a potato, thank you, Reverend," said Colin.

John moved onto the next man and offered an apple or potato. Working his way around the cell, he came to Raif and pulled up short. The man remained pressed into his corner, eyes averted. John considered him for a while. He dug in the bag and pulled out an apple.

"This is for you, Raif."

The little man cowered at John, and they regarded one another for a few moments. John thought he saw a crumb of humanity still left inside the callous man. Raif reached up and snatched the apple. He grunted and turned back into the darkness of his corner, mumbling to himself.

Perhaps he was wrong.

He soon arrived where Gryffyn lay. John hunkered down in front of his former friend. The man seemed to be in slumber, with an arm flopped over top of his head. John watched him for a few moments. How did he have the rotten misfortune of being detained in the same cell with this man? It was beyond his understanding.

Did God want him to forgive the man who had wreaked such havoc and sorrow on the lives of so many? Was this a test of his very soul?

Gryffyn's chest rose and fell with each breath. John pondered whether or not he could share what little substance he had with this particular man.

"Keep moving, John Lothropp. I'm not interested in anything you care to give me." Gryffyn Cane pulled his arm away from his face and fixed John with a hardened gaze. "Get away from me. I don't need your pity."

John considered the man who had betrayed him. Perhaps one day he might find a way to forgive his old friend. John felt a little quiver deep within his soul. Maybe someday.

He got to his feet but stayed stooped so as to not hit his head on the ceiling. He moved on to William, who sat with his back against the wall, staring into the cell.

"William—a potato or an apple? William?"

John squatted down in front of him. "My boy, do you sleep while you stare?" He realized William's eyes held a vacant look. Bitterness hit the bottom of his stomach. It was clear God had called William home.

John reached up to close the boy's eyes. He was stiff and cold. Had the icy night air frozen him to death?

John's heart broke for this boy who had been lost and forgotten by the world. Never had he been able to coax a word out of William during the months they'd shared this crowded cell.

He placed a hand over William's eyes, warming the skin until finally the lids softened and he could brush them closed. "Be at peace now, William."

This horrible place had stolen another life.

John shuffled back to his spot against the wall and slid down. Slumping forward, he felt the sorrow of William's death tugging at his soul. Would he share the same fate as the young boy?

Tibbot said, "What ails you?"

A great sigh escaped John's mouth. "William has gone to our Lord today."

"Mayhap William is the lucky one."

"Do not speak so, Tibbot. We must break free of this place and return home. We must have faith." John pulled himself up again and turned to rest his forehead against the stone wall. There was no place for privacy in this cramped and crowded room.

Sorrow beat at him like a wave crashing on the shore. The current pulled at him. Despair threatened to drag him out into a sea of misery. He wanted to let go and float away.

How much longer will this trial persist? When will God release me from this torment?

He struggled against the tide until he pulled himself onto the shore. He must have faith that even in this darkest of prisons, God was still by his side.

Did God not allow His Own Son to be tested until the end? Am I greater than He? Nay!

He lifted his head upward toward Heaven and began to pray.

"*Yea, though I walk through the valley of the shadow of death, I will fear no evil: For thou art with me.*" [ii]

Colin put his arm around John's shoulder, his shackle chains clinked on John's back. "I beg of you, do not allow this place to get the best of you."

John peered over his shoulder and smiled at the man who'd become his friend here in prison.

With a reassuring pat on the shoulder, Colin said. "The Lord is with you, Reverend. I see it in your face. All will be well for you."

"Thank you, Colin. Though we live in this horrible place for now, you have been a good friend, indeed."

"And you, as well, Reverend."

"I cannot abide William's body in here. It brings to mind the possible fate before each of us."

John trudged over to the door. He pounded on the wood and called out for the keeper.

"Jervis . . . Jervis . . ." When no one responded, he pounded against the door again and bellowed. "Jervis! A man is dead."

Silence filled the hall.

"Jervis! Come to this cell. There is a dead man within." John continued to pound on the door until Colin touched him on the shoulder. He jumped in surprise and stopped for a moment.

"Reverend, it is of no use."

"What else am I to do?" He shrugged Colin's hand away and continued to pound, yelling into the hall. "Pray help me, someone . . . a man has died."

John ceased banging on the door and cocked his ear toward the grate. A thud echoed down the passageway. Was it the sound of Jervis's crutch? With renewed energy, John pounded.

Colin said, "Reverend, he cares not a whit for you. Come and sit, we can tell him of William when he brings the soup."

"Nay, Colin, I cannot abide it any longer. William sits dead in the corner."

A piercing scream slashed through the air of the prison. Startled, both men jumped back from the door. Sounds of commotion drew closer. It was as though a fiend from hell traveled down the hall.

Another scuffle, and a few men shouted.

"Get 'im!" one said.

"Grab 'im now!" said another.

Screams of the damned pierced the air. The scuffle drew closer. John pushed his face into the grate and peered down the hall.

A gruff voice yelled, "Grab his legs, lest he get away."

The passageway grew brighter. A lantern bobbed along the corridor. John noticed the silhouette of a wooden crutch.

Thud, clomp. Thud, clomp.

The Keeper.

An unfortunate captive flailed his body about and clawed at two gaolers.

"Halt!" Jervis stopped the straggly band of men and turned to the prisoner. He jutted a finger into the man's face. "Th' powers tha' be 'ave condemned ye t' death. Do ye want a slow death, or do ye want a quick end? It be yer choice. So, stop yer infernal strugglin'. If ye comply, it be quick. If not—"

"Please," the man begged. "I am not at fault! I do not deserve to die."

"Well, tha' be of no concern to me." Jervis turned to the other men. "Take 'im to th' gallows."

"Please, no!" the man screamed. The gaolers resumed their struggle with the poor, condemned wretch as they passed John and continued their journey.

John called out to Jervis, who clomped closer to the cell door. "Jervis, I beseech you. A dead man lies within this cell."

The Keeper stuck his face up to the grate in the thick oak door, his stench assaulting John's senses. John wanted to pull away, but knew he must not.

Jervis said, "What worry be tha' o' mine?"

"You are the Keeper. You must do your duty and take the body away."

"Oh, ye reckon so? Who be it tha' died?"

"It is William."

Tapping his right forefinger into the palm of his left hand, Jervis said, "When 'is family place a few shillin' in my hand, I will take away th' body. Until then, he sleeps with ye." Jervis turned and clomped away.

Thud, clomp. Thud, clomp.

John called down the hallway. "No! Jervis, please, you must remove the body. I entreat you to return."

The men continued to struggle with the condemned prisoner as they made their way farther down the corridor. The lantern's glow was soon swallowed up by the thick darkness ever present in Newgate.

In resignation, John lowered his head and stepped away from the door. He maneuvered around his cellmates, shuffling toward the double grate in the impenetrable outer wall. Colin's leg shackles jangled across the floor as he followed the reverend.

If John peered through the grate and turned his head just so, he could see the thick wooden beams of the gallows.

Stories in the darkness of the prison told of the black dog of Newgate and how he escorted condemned prisoners to the gallows. The hound would sit vigil by their side until they were dead. A long-lasting howl would send their souls up to heaven—or down to hell.

John pressed his face up against the grate, cocking his head to the side and craning his neck. Jervis and the two gaolers led the condemned prisoner toward thick wooden timbers. The inmate had ceased his struggle. With head hung low, he trudged along the path to his impending death.

There looked to be one dark four-legged creature padding alongside the doomed man. John leaned back and adjusted his stance so he might stretch up higher to get a better glimpse of the canine.

No dog followed the man.

He was sure the dog had been there a moment before. Did he witness the Black Dog of Newgate?

"What do you see, Reverend?" Colin said.

John thought about Jervis and his cronies taking that poor man to the gallows.

"I see small men who get a little authority and think themselves big."

He drew from the grate and slid to the ground. Fluffing the straw, he lay down and pulled the cloak over his shoulders.

Oh my most beloved God, please save this wretched soul. I beg of Thee my freedom so I might be free to find a place for my family to live in peace—a place where we can all be free, where we can worship Thee without fear of the authorities. I pray to Thee, bless my wife that she may get well. I cannot bear to lose her. Please let Thy Holy Spirit watch over my family while I'm away. In the name of our Holy Savior, amen.

Night slipped into the cell as John finished his prayer. His beautiful Hannah came to mind. Thoughts of her struggling with illness plagued him—being without her tore at his soul.

Sleep eluded the reverend. Though his eyes were open, the cell was black and he saw nothing. Images of his wife and children tortured his mind. So close, yet so far away. Lids grew heavy with sleep. He prayed its sweet release might attend him.

In the distance, an ominous howl filled the air.

LAMBETH

Fog enshrouded the countryside, climbing over rooftops, curling around trees, seeping under doorways. Nothing escaped its tenacious journey as it made its way across the ground and into the Lothropp household.

Jane pulled a shawl over her shoulders and tied it in a knot at her chest. Warmth emanated from the hearth in the large gathering hall, though the bedchamber still held onto the night's chill.

Hannah had given them a scare with her episode a few weeks back. Jane was thankful Doctor Mead, a surgeon from her father's congregation, had offered his services to the family free of charge.

The doctor believed Hannah's chest pain was brought on by pneumonia, so a bloodletting had been necessary for her well-being. He'd also left some opium to help with the pain and to allow her some much-needed sleep.

He'd warned Jane about the need for her mother to repent of the sin which had brought on her illness. All the bloodletting would come to no use if she didn't repent. He made it clear that God would punish the sinning soul with illness until the time of true repentance. If

Hannah did not honestly repent, he explained, God would take her soul.

Jane didn't agree with his opinion. How could the doctor consider her mother some kind of sinner? Hannah was the strongest, kindest, most caring woman Jane knew.

If only Father were here! He would know what to do.

She sat on the bench across from Hannah's bed and watched her breathe. It seemed a struggle for her mother to pull in every shallow, uneven breath. Jane leaned forward and placed an elbow on each knee. She pressed fingers to her face and rubbed her swollen eyes.

Oh, Mother, you are the one who knows how to care for the sick. I need you to help me! Yet I am the one who must find a way to help you.

Sunlight fought its way through the mist, though the gloomy day still won the battle. The house remained cold and dreary, matching the emotions of the worried daughter within its walls.

Her mother's health failed more each day. Jane ached for the days when Hannah had been strong and had run this household with a firm but loving hand. How would Jane ever stand in her place? Hopelessness surrounded her. She felt as though it might fairly choke the breath from her.

There must be a way to overcome such feelings. How do I accomplish such a thing?

She had grown close to her mother through these days of trial. Jane valued the stronger bond forming between them. Her heart ached, not knowing if her mother would get better or be taken to Heaven.

She rose and stepped over to the bed. Her mother lay still, skin as pale as the white bedclothes. Jane pulled the covers up and gently tucked them in around Hannah's neck. The movement caused her mother to stir. Slowly, she opened her eyes.

"Good morning, my sweet daughter."

"Oh, dear, Mother. I didn't mean to awaken you."

"Worry not, I was already waking." Hannah began to push against the mattress. "Will you help me sit up?"

"You must rest, Mother."

"I can rest while I sit. I grow weary of lying here."

"As you wish. Let me help you."

Jane took hold of her mother's hands and carefully began to pull. Hannah tried to help, but a low moan escaped her lips.

"Oh, Mother!" Memories of the dreadful night Hannah had her episode came flooding back.

With a groan, Hannah said, "I will be fine, continue."

Hannah held onto Jane's arm while she pulled her into a sitting position.

Jane said, "Continue to hold my forearm for a moment while I fix your pillows."

With Hannah grasping her arm, Jane reached around and plumped the pillows, arranging them against the headboard.

"There we go, now you can lie back again."

With a ragged sigh, Hannah relaxed back against the pillows.

"Are you comfortable? I can arrange them again."

"Thank you, my dear, they are fine."

"Pray tell, Mother, do you want some leek pottage? You must be hungry."

"Yes, that would be lovely."

"Doctor Mead says your strength is returning, though he admonishes you to pray daily."

Hannah inhaled deeply and pulled the covers tighter around her neck. "I wonder at the doctor's words. Strength does not seem to be returning, no matter how much I rest and pray. Mayhap I need another bloodletting. There is such pressure in my chest."

"Mother, please do not allow it again. It sapped your strength rather than helping it. I don't trust the doctor's opinion." Not wanting to discuss it any longer, Jane patted her mother's arm. "I will go and get you some pottage now."

Before Jane could walk away, Hannah grasped her hand and pulled her back. "The doctor is not what worries me the most. I am more concerned your father won't be released from prison before the Lord takes me." A few tears gathered in her eyes and slid down her cheeks.

"I must do all I can to try and get better so I can be strong for him. If it means another bloodletting, I must endure."

Jane sat on the bed and brushed her mother's tears away.

"Oh, Mother. Do not speak so. You will surely get well and see your husband once again."

"I pray for that, my sweet girl." She wiped at her cheeks and smoothed the bedclothes over her chest. "I'm sorry I have shed so many tears lately."

"Worry not for the tears, Mother. It is frustration with your circumstance and your weakness. You have done so much for this family. It's high time we returned the kindness."

Hannah squeezed Jane's hand. "Thank you, my dear. I do appreciate your strength."

"My strength? I feel anything other than strong."

"You are stronger than you know. Search your soul. You will find there is strength and courage already within you."

Jane rested her head on her mother's arm. "You are the strong one. All my life I have watched you care for the parishioners, tending the sick, bringing them food, sharing of your talents and your loving heart. Never once have I heard you complain."

Hannah rubbed her hand across Jane's back. "It is always a pleasure to serve God's children. No matter how difficult your own life is, there is always someone having a worse time of it. When you reach out to help those in need and stop dwelling on your own trials, you will begin to see the gifts and blessings with which God has blessed you. You will begin to see yourself for who you truly are and will find the strength hiding within you."

"*You* are my strength, Mother."

"No, Janey, you are your *own* strength. Never forget that." Hannah reached up and cupped Jane's cheek in her hand. "Now, I have one more question for you." A smile spread across her face. "Is there bread that I might have with my pottage?"

Jane chuckled as she arose from her mother's bed. "Aye, there is. I will fetch it now. Oh . . . umm . . . do you have the energy to help me with my embroidery after you've eaten? I would love your help. I have truly made a mess of it."

"It would be my pleasure and a good distraction for me."

Jane left the bedchamber and headed to the hearth for Hannah's pottage. Only a few embers remained from the fire. She grasped the metal fire fork and poked at the embers until a small flame emerged. The wood box held only a few pieces of wood. She arranged them under the pot with the existing embers.

She used the pot puller and grasped the kettle which rested within the large inner hearth so she might stir the pottage remaining from last night's dinner. As she did so, there came a knock at the door.

Calling out to her mother, she said, "Mother, I fear it will be longer than I first thought. The pottage is only warm, but I have added more wood to the fire. Also, someone knocks at the door."

A gentle voice came from the bedchamber. "Very well, Jane. I will rest a while."

Jane rested the pot puller on the hearth and moved toward the door. The iron door handle stuck a bit, but she worked it free and pulled the door inward.

A swell of mist flooded the entry and swirled around Jane's ankles. Frederick stood before her, stamping his feet back and forth against the cold, cloak flapping behind him in the breeze. His arms lay folded across his large barrel chest, a hat firmly within his grip.

"Oh, Frederick, please enter quickly so the fog might stay outside where it belongs."

Jane stepped back and allowed him to enter. He wiped his feet across the doormat and moved across the threshold. She pushed the door shut against any additional fog invasion.

"Thank you, Jane. It's quite chilly out there."

"Brrr . . . you have braved an unpleasantly cold day. Come over to the hearth and get warm by the fire." She rubbed her hands up and down her arms in an effort to get warm.

"Oh, my dear, you seem to know my innermost thoughts."

Frederick made his way across the front hall and over to the fireplace. Two padded chairs sat at each side of the big, open hearth. He chose the larger of the two while Jane chose the smaller chair at the opposite side.

Frederick watched her. "How is your mother since her spell a few weeks past?"

Jane brought her index finger up to her lips to signal the need to speak quietly. "She is still quite weak. Bedrest wears thin and she longs to be up and about. The doctor tells us she must continue to pray for God to forgive her. Yet, I do not believe Mother could have committed any kind of sin to bring this illness upon her."

Keeping his voice low, Frederick said, "I know the doctor thinks he is correct, but do not believe his thoughts about sin and illness being connected. He speaks of an old tradition. She is ill for another reason."

"I thought so, yet the doctor—"

"The doctor is wrong about your mother being sick because she is a sinner. Do not listen to him in that regard."

Jane lowered her head. "Mother fears she will never see Father again."

"Ah, the reason for my visit today. Are the young children at home?"

"Nay, they are enjoying a day at the Allen home. Thomas is working. It is only Mother and me."

"Good, good." He continued speaking in quiet tones. "I came to your home today so I might converse regarding your mother and father. I am concerned about Hannah's health, which has greatly deteriorated. It is time we prepare for the worst."

Jane's hands flew to her chest. "Oh Frederick, I fear the same thing. I worry I have not taken proper care of her. I am so inept in the ways of medicine."

She leaned forward, pressing her head into her hands.

Frederick arose and crossed by the hearth to where Jane sat upon the other chair. He laid his hand on her shoulder. "It's not your fault she is deteriorating. You have been unfailing in your mother's care."

"Do you think so? I feel so guilty. I try to aid in getting her strength back, but she continues to grow weaker."

Frederick patted her shoulder. He leaned down to whisper closer to Jane's ear. "My dear, you have done a wonderful job. Do not fret." He arose again to his full height.

"Thank you for your words. They bring me comfort." She leaned forward and brushed her hair back from her face. "We have been saving our money so Thomas can visit our father again soon."

The floorboards creaked and groaned as Frederick stepped back toward the chair he'd vacated. He sat upon the chair again and leaned forward so Jane might hear his hushed voice. "That is all good. However, I have been investigating a temporary release for your father. I learned I might be able to petition the Bishop at Lambeth. He may have the power to allow a provisional liberty. I believe he will consent, considering your mother's illness."

Jane leaned closer to him. "Oh, Frederick, that would be wonderful. When can you begin proceedings?"

"It may take a while to get an audience with the Bishop. Therefore, I must submit the petition immediately. I came to speak with Thomas about it and get his permission to submit the petition."

Jane sat up abruptly. "Oh, yes," she said in a loud voice. She flinched and covered her mouth with her hands. She hushed her voice to a whisper. "You most definitely can move forward with this. I will inform Thomas when he gets home."

He arose, and in a soft voice, he said, "I must take my leave now."

Jane stood and followed him to the door, where she reached up and gave him a warm embrace.

"Good day to you, Frederick. You are a good friend to our father . . . to our whole family."

Frederick patted her shoulder. "I love your father as though he were my own brother."

He turned and pulled the door open. Mist swelled around him as he disappeared into the fog.

Jane shivered for a moment before she pushed the door closed. Thoughts of Father coming home brought emotions from within. Emotions she had previously hidden.

The house felt empty without him there. His strength and kindness had filled their home with peace. His absence, and Hannah's continuing illness, had drawn the serenity from their lives.

Their home must no longer be a sad and dreary place. The possibility of Father returning, if even for a short while, brought a little smile to her lips. She must find the strength to carry on.

Something grew within her soul. Whether it was strength or determination, she did not know. She would, however, use it to her own end. She must do whatever was necessary to bring some peace and quietude to her family.

They had lived in sadness for too long now. The situation was not going to change of its own accord; she must make it happen. How was she going to accomplish such a task?

She must find the strength. The strength her mother spoke of. The strength hiding within her soul.

NEWGATE PRISON

Every nerve in John's body screamed as he looked up into the face of the Keeper. He'd been wrested from his sleep by two large gaolers, who now pulled him to his feet.

John stood as tall as possible in the cramped quarters. "Take your filthy hands off me!" He faced his enemies with a growing concern. Why were they here, and what did they want with him? Was he headed to the gallows?

"Shut yer trap, Lothropp, an' ye will fare better," said Jervis. Spittle disgorged from his throat and landed in a glop on his chest.

The two gaolers dragged him toward the door. John lifted his legs and straddled his feet across the door opening, pressing a foot against each side. With a grunt, the larger man wrenched John away from the door jamb and began pushing him into the passageway.

Struggling against the men, John attempted to break free. He'd watched them haul more than one poor wretch to the gallows over the last several months. Now, it seemed he faced the same destiny. What had he done to warrant this punishment?

The gaoler succeeded in pushing into the corridor, and he pressed John's face against the opposite wall, smashing it into the stone. The

gunge from years of water seepage mashed across his cheek and pushed into his mouth. He thrust at the slime with his tongue and spat it upon the ground.

Jervis thumped up to John and stared him straight in the eye. "Why do ye make it so hard on yerself, Lothropp?"

"Why do I go to the gallows? Has the King placed a death sentence on religious dissenters?"

A loud cackle erupted from Jervis, and he began to speak. "Lothropp, ye—"

John heaved up and shoved the men back into Jervis. The men clamored to find footing on the slippery floor. The Keeper's crutch clanged to the ground. The sound bounced around the hall, echoing in John's mind.

"Ye will pay fer that," Jervis said.

Seizing the moment, John broke free and darted down the hallway, his hands dragging along the walls. He felt the muck collecting on his fingertips. It was dark, and he dared not run without the wall to guide him. His feet slipped over stones covered with slick, wet grime.

No light bounded through the corridor, nor did it bounce across the walls. He heard a scuffle coming from the passageway behind him. In desperation, he felt around for somewhere to hide.

Nothing.

He heard Jervis's voice. "Men, find him! Nary a man ha' escaped whilst I ha' been th' keeper."

John continued through the dark, feeling along walls, slipping over mossy stones. Sounds of feet tramping against stone followed him. Clawing through the dark, he made his way down the corridor, pressing farther into the guts of Newgate.

His body slammed into a flat stone wall at the end of a dark corridor, bringing a loud grunt from deep within. He fell to his knees in submission. Pain radiated down his arms and into his chest. Slime clawed at his soul.

Oh, my dear God, I need thee. Please guide my path. I am lost in Satan's grasp.

Sweat ran in rivulets down his face, stinging his eyes and burning the open sores on his face. He used his sleeve to mop at his brow. A sigh of frustration filled his lungs.

Words of the Psalms played through his mind. *Rest in the Lord, and wait patiently . . . Be still, and know that I am God.*

The pounding of wood on stone snapped him out of his thoughts. *Thud, clomp. Thud, clomp.*

Jervis and his two cohorts were closing in on him. John struggled to control the fear in his heart and to put his trust in the Lord. Standing, he bent forward and breathed deeply. Little by little, he took command of his fear. His vain attempt at escape must cease.

Sensations burned within his chest and spread throughout his body. The Lord spoke to his mind.

Fear not, I am watching over you.

His breathing slowed, and he leaned against the wall. If it were his time to die, it would be as it should. He stayed against the wall and awaited the arrival of the Keeper.

Lantern light bobbed down the passageway toward him. Shadows grew long and fearsome on the floor, bounding across the stone like a demon.

Raising the lantern above his head, Jervis shouted, "Thar 'e be! Get 'im!"

The two men ran forward, each grabbing one of John's arms. "You figured thar were no escape, did you?" the larger man said.

They turned and dragged John back down the hallway, where he came face to face with Jervis.

The Keeper stuck his repulsive face up to John and spit with each word. "So, ye thought to break free." John saw a flicker in the darkness as the blunt end of Jervis's crutch slammed into his stomach. A loud grunt exploded from him, and he fell to the ground. He wheezed and spat, trying to suck air back into his lungs. The hard floor gave him no relief. He lay there, not knowing what the gaolers would do next.

Jervis leaned forward with his crutch and pressed the bottom end into John's cheek. "Nary a man can ge' away from Jervis."

The two gaolers each grabbed an arm and yanked John to his feet. They dragged him along the passageway. He paid little heed to where they were taking him, stumbling between them, turning where they turned, stopping where they stopped. Light from Jervis's lantern bounced across the walls.

John matched the pace set by the two men. He glanced over his shoulder to see if the Black Dog of Newgate followed him. No dog padded along behind him. Was he to die alone? Or would the hound appear? He feared the gallows, where dead men were left hanging as a deterrent for crime.

Jervis approached a thick oak door. Pressing a key in the lock and turning, he pushed the door open. John's captors pushed him through the opening and released him into the holding area.

John rubbed his eyes, blinded by the glare coming through the bars of the gate. He rolled his shoulders back and tried to stand up straight, though his back screamed in protest.

He blinked his eyes and scanned the room, wondering what came next. He stared in disbelief when he noticed Frederick standing near the gate mechanism.

"Frederick? Is that really you?"

"Aye, John, it is me."

"Oh, my dear friend, you are too late. I fear I go to the gallows this day."

Frederick raised his eyebrows, a look of surprise on his face. "What say you?"

"I beg of you, Frederick, care for my family in my absence."

"Nay, John, you do not face death today. It is Hannah who is in trouble. You have been granted a temporary pardon. I came to take you home." He laid a hand on John's shoulder. "I am grieved to tell you Hannah is nigh unto death. She longs for you to come home so you may commend her soul unto God. She wants you and no other."

Anguish rushed at John like a dark demon charging forward to steal his soul. "Oh God, I beg of Thee, take me, not her!" He stared toward the sky. "Not my beloved Hannah."

"My friend . . . look at me."

John pulled his gaze from heavenward and regarded his friend.

Frederick said, "It is her time, and she needs you, John."

Cold, icy fingers squeezed John's heart. What would he do without Hannah by his side? She was his tower of strength. Thoughts of her had kept him sane over these many past months of incarceration.

"Come, John, let's leave this place."

Though frigid fingers still held his heart in their grasp, John stepped forward, toward the gate.

Jervis said, "Hold on. Jus' cause ye 'ave a pardon, tha' don' mean thar be no fee." He held his palm up in front of Frederick.

Reaching into his pocket, Frederick retrieved his purse. "Just what is the fee, Keeper?"

"Tha' be two shillin' t' raise th' gate and two shillin' t' step under it."

Frederick opened his purse and counted out four shillings, placing them in the Keeper's palm.

Sputtering, Jervis said, "Ye'd do well to remember tha' ye be liable for 'im. If he does not return, it be ye what takes 'is place."

"Have no concern. He will return."

"It best be so, or ye will pay th' price."

"I understand," Frederick said. "Come on, John, let's be on our way."

Frederick circled an arm around John's waist.

The large gaoler turned the mechanism that lifted the metal gate. It squealed and groaned as it rose up in front of John and Frederick.

Jervis banged his crutch onto the ground. He threw his head back, crowing into the air. "Ye'd best remember 'is return, or I will ha' ye for my guest." The miserable gaoler turned on his crutch and thumped his way back through the doorway and down the hall.

Thud, clomp. Thud, clomp.

John's body stiffened at the sound. Frederick pulled him in closer. "Do not react, my friend. Keep your focus forward."

67

A rush of adrenaline had given John the power for his attempted escape. Yet now, he barely had the strength to walk. When the gate cleared the opening, Frederick held on to John's waist, and they stepped through and into the light of the day.

Sunlight battered John and stopped him where he stood. He brought his hand up to shield his eyes. Frederick guided him over to the shade of an outer wall.

Grief tore a fissure in John's soul as he thought about losing his beloved Hannah.

"Oh, Frederick, how much more will God ask of me? I have born prison all this time. Must the Lord take Hannah, as well? I fear 'tis more than I can bear."

"Much has been asked of you, John. You must bear it with dignity and be strong for your family."

"I fear my strength has left me, Frederick."

"You must dig deep and find the strength. Hannah needs you. Your children need you."

"You speak the truth." A heavy sigh escaped John's lips. His children must see their father as a sound man, strong and sure of his faith in God.

Frederick said, "You have been in Newgate for over a year, John. I hesitate to tell you this, but you're dirty and unclean. You need to bathe and shave."

John groaned at the thought, though he knew Frederick spoke the truth.

His friend continued. "In the carriage, I have a change of clothes for you to wear. However, I'm afraid you're going to have to shave your head and beard to rid you of the lice. I brought one of my extra wigs so you can cover your shaved head."

John lifted his hands and turned them over, noting the grime which covered his skin. His clothing was tattered and filthy. He placed his palms on his hair, letting them slide down over his face and beard.

"Pray tell, will I ever be clean again?"

"I'll take you to a bathhouse, and you can clean yourself there."

"Nay, I cannot bear that, I desire to go to the Thames."

"What? The Thames?"

"Aye, I must rinse myself in the river. I am too filthy for a bathhouse. They would never let me through the door."

"Nay, John. It is not a good idea. The month is May, and the water will be quite cold."

"I will be fine. I know a place not too far from here where stairs run down into the water. I can sit on the steps and rinse myself there. Mayhap then I can use your horse trough for a final cleanse with soapy water."

Frederick let out a heavy sigh. "Very well, if that is your desire."

He guided John to the carriage where his footman awaited them. "This is my footman, Digory. You may direct him to the stairs of which you speak."

John turned his attention to the footman. "Not too far away are the Horseshoe Stairs."

"I know them well," Digory replied.

Digory took one of John's arms and Frederick the other while John tried to hoist himself onto the carriage step. His strength failed. Frederick caught him and pushed him up into the bench seat. Frederick followed him up, taking the bench opposite.

The carriage swayed at the weight of the footman climbing up to his seat. Frederick tapped his cane on the ceiling, the footman cracked the whip, and the carriage jolted forward.

Hard wheels bobbled over cobblestone streets and jarred John's bones. Freedom, albeit temporary, eased the pain. A sense of relief washed over him when the river came into view. Home was on the other side and within his grasp.

Upon their arrival at the stairs, the footman pulled to the side of the street. Frederick exited the carriage and turned to help John down. Digory climbed from his seat, pulled a blanket from the trunk, and passed it onto Frederick.

"Thank you, Digory," said Frederick. "Watch the carriage. We shan't be long."

They made their way across the street. Stone steps started at street level and descended into the water. There were several such stairways along the river to aid in boarding ships and boats along the length of the Thames.

John leaned on Frederick, and together they descended the steps toward water level. The Horseshoe stairs were in a quiet location and would afford John the privacy he desired.

"Frederick, please wait for me here, there is no need for you to get wet. I will go the rest of the way and rinse some of the filth from my body."

Frederick hunkered down on a step a few feet from the water's edge and averted his eyes. John continued to the water's edge, where he removed his shirt and pants and laid them on the steps behind him.

He sat upon a step and scooted forward until he could put his legs into the water. The first touch of the icy water brought a gasp from John.

"God's truth! The water is chilly." He heard Frederick chuckle behind him.

John began to splash water onto his arms, but it made little difference in the grime, which seemed to be painted onto his body. He scooted down a few more steps and turned to face the stairs. With a rush of bravery, he held onto the step and scrunched down, dunking himself under the surface.

Bursting out of the water, he lunged forward and grasped the steps once again.

Frederick let out a great guffaw. "Hoy! A bit colder than you first thought?"

John sent him what he hoped was a strong, scathing look. He kneeled and once again braved the water, this time a little more gingerly. As his body grew accustomed to the chilly water, he stepped down a few more steps. He dunked his head to scrub his face and hair, and, rising up, rubbed his arms and legs. When his energy was drained, he sat back on the steps.

"It's all the strength I have for now. I hope I have made some progress in removing the grime from my body."

He lifted his foot to the stair but, as he put his weight upon the step, his leg gave way. With a huge splash, he fell back into the water and was caught up in the current. Floundering against the pull of water, he struggled to keep his head above water, sputtering as fluid flowed into his mouth and nose.

John stroked against the river in an attempt to save himself, yet he was losing the battle. The witch of the water dragged him farther into the dark gulf of her domain. The gallows hadn't gotten him, though the river might well finish him off.

His body slipped farther into the current. Relief filled his soul as strong arms encircled him. Frederick spoke softly into his ear.

"I have you, John."

Supporting arms filled him with reassurance, and he leaned back against his friend. Frederick guided him to the side of the river and grabbed onto the rope of a boat moored against the wall.

"Hold tight, John. We will win this battle yet."

Frederick cried out to his footman. "Digory! Digory, come quickly!"

The beating of footsteps echoed from above. Digory peered over the top of the wall. Frederick waved a hand in the air. "We are down here, Digory. Get a rope and drop it down to us."

"I see you. Hold tight." His face disappeared. John and Frederick were alone in the river.

Frederick chuckled through chattering teeth. "I fear we both had a bath this day, John."

"I fear you are correct." John laughed along with him as he shivered in the cold water.

Digory reappeared at the wall. "I am here, m' lord, with the rope at your request."

"Very good, Digory. Drop it quickly."

Grabbing the rope, Frederick looped it around John's chest and tied a bowline knot, pulling it tight.

"We are ready, Digory—pull."

John felt the rope go taut. The loop slipped up his chest and lodged against his shoulder blades. He cried out in agony when he felt the full weight of his body being pulled against the rope.

"Be strong, John," said Frederick as he swam alongside him. "It will be but a short time."

John gritted his teeth and endured the biting rope. Rough hemp dug into his flesh. He tried to use his arms to swim, but the rope cut deeper into his skin. He moaned in agony.

Frederick said, "Be still, John. Let me help."

"Aye—I must." John stopped struggling and trusted his friend to save him. A great sense of relief came when he felt his legs bump into the submersed stairs. He brought his feet forward and crawled onto the step, relieving the tension of the rope. Frederick gave John a final push and joined him on the stairs.

John's chest heaved with his efforts to control the sharp intakes of air. He heard Frederick breathing in gasps, as well. Sometime during the commotion, Frederick's wig had come off, and now the sunlight shone on his shiny head. Exhausted, they both lay back on the steps.

Frederick said, "It seems my strength has not completely returned after my own stay in prison."

Digory came running down the stairs. "M' lord, how do you fare?"

"We fare well, though frozen. Bring more blankets."

Digory turned and headed back up the stairs. Frederick began to work the knot loose to free John from the painful leash.

Through chattering teeth, John said, "You have saved me once again, my friend."

"Nothing in comparison to the many times you've saved my soul. Now, let's remove this rope and get you home."

*****

Sunset was aglow in the west when the rag-tag occupants of the carriage saw Frederick's house appear before them.

The conveyance headed around the back and came to a stop in front of the carriage house. Digory climbed out and went around and opened the door, after which he assisted Frederick and John to the ground.

"I fear I am a poor host indeed to let you to clean up in the horse trough."

"Nay, Frederick, do not worry. I am grateful for all you have done for me. I am anxious to see my beautiful Hannah. Therefore, the horse trough will suffice."

"Very well. Go inside with my footman and he will help you. I will find Elsabeth and ask her to bring you some food." He turned and walked toward the main house.

Digory gestured toward the carriage house. "This way, m' lord."

John followed Digory inside, where he saw a large pile of straw against one wall. Without thinking, he walked toward the pile and flopped down upon it.

"I will get the fire going to heat some water for your bath. I will inform you when it is ready," said Digory.

John meant to say thank you but was asleep before he could reply.

Seven

LAMBETH

Rumbling along, jumping and jostling over cobblestones, the carriage rambled toward John's home. He wondered if his children would even recognize him. Would Hannah? He feared his current look was fairly startling.

"Do you think Hannah will even know me?" John said.

Frederick leaned forward and patted John on the knee. "You are pale and thin, but the same spirit shines in your eyes. Hannah will know the truth in them."

"I pray that is true."

The carriage continued to bump along. Newgate's stench was replaced with wood burning in hearths and gardens filled with flowers. The smells filled the countryside of Lambeth.

Frederick sat stiff and tall on the carriage bench, a coat stretched across his broad chest, his big meaty hands atop his cane. He swayed with the movement of the rocking transport. The ravages of prison were still etched into the lines of his face. John's heart broke for the many souls who suffered at the hands of Bishop Laud, all for the sake of religious freedom.

He sat opposite Frederick, the brown wig upon his head. The suit Frederick brought him was comfortable, though a little large. Anything was better than the lice-infested rags he'd worn over the last year.

He leaned back against the bench seat, clutching a blanket around his shoulders. Coldness began at the river and seemed a stubborn fellow indeed.

"How does the congregation fare, Frederick? Have more members left to join with the Baptists?"

"Other than those who left last year, the congregation has remained faithful to you. They long for your return."

The conveyance pulled to a stop in front of John's house. Soft light shone from the windows, which seemed to stare back at him. It didn't seem real.

Frederick alighted from the carriage. "Remain here, Digory." He turned to assist John.

John pulled the blanket from his shoulders and laid it on the seat beside him. Leaning forward, he took Frederick's hand and stepped to the ground. He adjusted his wig and pulled at his tie.

"Do not fret over what your family will see, John. You are still a comely man."

A low chuckle came from John. "Why, thank you, Frederick."

His friend clapped him on the shoulder, a smile stretched wide across his face. "I do what I can."

The stately Tudor house stood tall and proud before him. A deep sigh raised and lowered his shoulders. "I believe I am ready now."

He made his way to the door, lifted the latch, and quietly pushed it inward. A moment of weakness caught him off guard, and he leaned against the door jamb. He pulled fresh air into his lungs and stepped forward into the house.

The scene before him caused a surge of appreciation and thanksgiving to God.

His children sat in various places around the large hall. Barbara and Johnny had their backs against the wall near the fire, each with a book.

John's heart filled with love at the sight of his two deep thinkers engaged in their favorite passion—reading.

Jane sat in the smaller stuffed chair at the side of the hearth working on some embroidery. John stiffened at the sight of Edmund, Jane's young man, sitting on the floor at her feet, with his head resting against her leg.

He scanned the room, and his eyes came to rest on Samuel, Joseph, and little Benjamin playing marbles in the corner of the room to his right. His three youngest sons had grown a bit older but still held onto their childhood.

Thomas sat cross-legged on the floor, poring over an unrolled map spread on the ground. A few other rolled papers lay by his side. What map had Thomas so enthralled? John wasn't happy to note Thomas sat with his back to Jane and Edmund, seemingly unaware of their closeness.

He took a deep breath of frustration. Jane glanced up and surveyed the two men standing at the doorway. She put down her embroidery, arose from the chair, and walked toward them. Edmund jumped to his feet and clasped his hands at his back.

Jane stepped forward. "Frederick? Is that you?" Moving closer, Jane eyed John. He smiled to see her curious expression. "Ah, yes . . . it is you, but who is your companion?"

She cocked her head gently to the right and paused to stare at the thin man standing against the jamb, hands clasped in front of him. Her expression changed from confusion to recognition.

"Father! You are home."

John stumbled as she leaned into the hug, but felt the reassuring strength of Frederick's arm come around his waist. He pulled his oldest daughter tightly into his chest, breathing in the clean smell of her hair.

Ah . . . it was good to be home.

The commotion brought Thomas's attention out of the map. He jumped to his feet. Wooden floorboards groaned as he covered the distance to his father in three long strides. Thomas's strong arms pulled John in, and he squeezed Jane between the two of them. Jane yelped, and Thomas freed her.

"Father! We didn't realize you were coming home today," he said.

Before John could clear his throat to answer, Frederick quipped, "We thought to surprise you."

Johnny had let his book fall onto his lap and sat in silence. Barbara fairly flew to greet her father. The young boys left their game, sprang up, and rushed to his side. Tears filled John's eyes as their hands reached for him with love and affection.

"We have missed you so," said Barbara.

Samuel added, "You are finally home, Father." He reached his arms out toward John, who clasped his hand and pulled him in with the bodies already surrounding him.

Johnny remained by the fire, watching him. John signaled him to join the other children.

Frederick's warmth was of great comfort to John as he continued to offer his strength and support.

"My young ones, I love you so."

"We love you, Father," said Joseph.

He touched each one of his children, some by the tops of their heads while others were close enough to rub their arms.

"Children, I am so happy to be home. I have missed each one of you. Every night in prison, I have dreamed of this moment. However, I am only home for a short time. There is still a requirement for me to return to Newgate."

A collective sigh radiated from the group of siblings. "Oh, Father, how can it be so?" Johnny said.

"The Bishop has only granted a temporary pardon so I might see your mother. He demands I return to prison shortly." The dejected group sagged in disappointment, and John sensed their sorrow.

"I have the same displeasure at the thought. For now, I must beg your pardon." A forlorn smile touched his mouth. "I long to see your mother."

Johnny spoke. "She has been ill for some time now. She has needed you."

Jane glanced back at her brother. "Johnny, do not speak to Father so."

John smiled and patted Johnny's head. With regret, he disentangled himself from his children's loving arms. Hannah's pull was strong, and he longed to see her. The children stayed near him, clumped together as he made his way across the hall to the first story bedchamber.

Frederick reached out to them. "Children, I beg of you. Remain with me."

John glanced back at his friend. "Thank you, Frederick, for all you have done for me today. You are a true and loyal friend."

Frederick nodded and put his arms around the children. "Come, let us give your parents their time. It must be your bedtime, anyway. Your father will be here in the morning."

"Good night, Father," the children cried.

Jane turned back and put her arms around her father's chest. "I am so happy you are home. I love you."

John replied, "And I love you, darling daughter."

Edmund remained by the hearth. John noted the questioning and eager appearance on Edmund's face. John smiled, fairly sure he knew what Edmund wanted.

"Edmund? Might there be something you have to say to me?"

"Aye, sir. Knowing this is a difficult time for you, I thank you for hearing me out. Perchance might I have your permission to court Jane? I do love her and long to be with her."

John sighed in exhaustion. He scanned Edmund up and down. He'd previously heard of the Fairfax family. They were a respectable family with strong land holdings. Edmund would be a good match for his daughter. He also understood young love, and he knew Jane would never let him rest until his blessing had been given.

"Very well, Edmund. You have permission to court my daughter. I expect you to be good and kind to her, and to treat her with respect and love."

"That, I will. In gratitude, I thank you for an audience at this difficult time. Good eventide to you, Reverend."

The floorboards creaked as Edmund walked across the room. He stopped to cup Jane's chin in his hand. A broad smile crossed his daughter's face, the look of love strong in her eyes.

Edmund moved to the door and pulled it open. Turning back to nod at John, he stepped out into the night.

Jane flew to her father and threw her arms around him. "Thank you so much, Father. You have made me joyful this night."

"I hope he will bring you happiness, Janey."

"I know he will, Father."

John turned his attention to his other children. "I love each of you, my wonderful children. I will see you all in the morning."

He stepped through the doorway with a last smile before he pushed the door closed with a soft click.

John turned into the room. A candle burned in a holder on the bedstead. Its light cast a glow over Hannah's face. John watched her for a few moments. She had lost quite a bit of weight, and her skin had a yellow cast. His beloved wife was a shadow of her former self. She had wasted away while he sat in that infernal prison.

A soft moan escaped Hannah's lips. John went to her side and sat on the edge of the bed.

Hannah turned her head, and her eyes found his. His love for her overwhelmed him. He stared back into the soft brown eyes he'd always loved. Gently, she raised a hand to his arm and peered up at him. "Can this be real? Are you truly home?"

"Yes, Hannah, I am home. How I have missed you." John placed a hand upon her cheek. "I have been so lonely without you."

"Oh, John, I cannot begin to express the joy I feel at your homecoming. I was afraid I might never again lay eyes upon you." Her eyes glistened with tears. "For, you see, my time on this earth grows short. The Lord calls me home."

"Please, don't say such things, Hannah. I cannot bear the thought."

John rested his head on her chest. One hand stroked her soft blonde hair while he felt her heart beat against his cheek.

He whispered, "I have longed to hold you by my side for so long now. May I lie beside you?"

"Nothing would bring me more joy."

John removed his wig and coat and laid them on the sideboard. He pulled the boots from his feet and dropped them to the floor.

Hannah shifted her body to make room for him. John lifted the covers and climbed into bed next to her, pulling the blankets over them both. He slipped his arm under her neck and brought her close so she could rest her head upon his chest. The warmth of her body flowed through him.

He casually stroked her hair while he chanted in her ear.

"All will be well, my love. I am here with you. I won't leave your side. I am here with you. Worry no longer, my sweet. I am here."

Midnight turned into morning while John lay holding his wife. He heard her uneven breath pulling in and out. Though he was exhausted, his mind would not allow him to sleep.

Time spent in prison had separated him from his family for more than a year already. How much longer would he be forced to wallow in Newgate? If he vowed his loyalty to the Church of England, he would be freed. But his beliefs and morals dictated otherwise.

Did he have the strength or the faith to go on? How could he ever live without Hannah? How would his children survive with no parents at home? He worried his congregation faltered without leadership. What would the next year hold for him?

These thoughts and more filled his mind through the long, dark hours of night.

Tomorrow was another day. Perhaps God had a new plan for him.

LAMBETH

Sun rays streaked through the window panes, glinting on flecks of dust floating in the room. John sat on the bench across from a sleeping Hannah, his loyal friend Frederick at his side. John waved his hand in the air, causing the dust to scatter from before him. The specks merely swirled away, only to come back and torment him all the more.

He gave the dust a few last swats and gave up the battle, resting his elbows on his knees. John watched Hannah's chest rise and fall with every tortured breath.

Dark circles had taken up permanent residence under his eyes. Worry filled his waking moments while she slipped away, little by little.

Frederick leaned forward and whispered to John. "It has been a fortnight and two since the date of your temporary liberty. I worry since you have not returned to prison, a warrant will be issued for your arrest."

"That worries me as well," said John.

"I'm distressed that you may truly have a trip to the gallows this time."

John knitted his brow as he intently watched Hannah's breathing. He realized she wanted him to commend her soul unto God, and it must happen before her passing, but not too much before.

"Hannah's time comes soon." John reached out to sweep the hair from her brow. "I cannot leave her."

She lay as still as a rose petal floating upon the ocean. Her breath rose and fell with each swell of water.

John looked over to his friend. "I'm concerned about you as well, Frederick. I don't want the law to come down upon you because of my late return. I still recall what Jervis threatened at the prison."

"Oh, that dreadful little man, he's all bluff. He has no power to sentence me to prison. Worry not for me, John."

Frederick leaned back and patted John's leg. "I have procured another audience with the bishop. I will implore him for an extension to your liberty. I hope he will understand and allow you time enough for her funeral."

"Thank you, my friend."

Sweat trickled down the side of John's face and onto his jawline. Using his shirtsleeve, he wiped it away. He would only leave Hannah's side when necessary. Food held no appeal to him, and he hadn't eaten in a day or two. His own body was growing weaker. Still, he was apprehensive about leaving her.

Though Jane had protested, John allowed Doctor Mead to perform another bloodletting. The doctor didn't understand why the bloodlettings weren't pulling the infection from her body. He explained to John about Hannah needing to repent of her sins so she could be cured. John stopped him before he could spit out any more of those vile accusations.

He had tried everything he could to save her. He ached to save her. He begged God to save her. Yet, Hannah grew weaker every day.

With a soft sigh, Frederick laid a hand on John's shoulder. "You must allow Jane to bring you some food. Your weakened state from prison has left you vulnerable to illness."

Without looking up, John said, "Very well, she may bring me some pottage."

"I will let her know." Frederick rose to leave. "Elsabeth will continue to help Jane in acquiring food. We will watch over your children while you are watching over Hannah, and after your return to Newgate as well. Do not worry over them."

Hannah let out a soft moan. John rushed to her side. "Hannah, I am here." He took her hands in his and brought them to his mouth, touching them tenderly with his lips.

Floorboards creaked as Frederick stepped through the door. In a soft voice, he said, "Take care, my friend."

John's attention was brought to Hannah as she began to moan. She thrashed her head back and forth, struggling against the bedclothes. John climbed into the bed beside her. He took her in his arms, pulled her close, and began humming the tune of a favorite song.

The sound calmed Hannah, and she settled into his embrace. He recalled some words to the song and sang the haunting melody.

> *Other refuge have I none,*
> *Hangs my helpless soul on Thee;*
> *Leave, oh! Leave me not alone,*
> *Still support and comfort me.*

Day crept into evening as John continued his vigil. Jane slipped in with the supper tray, placing it on the sideboard.

"Father, I have brought your supper."

John glanced up at her. "That is fine. I will eat later." She turned and crept back through the door, bringing it to a soft close.

Stroking Hannah's hair, John wondered how he would survive without her. She had been his loving companion for twenty-three years.

When they'd first learned Bishop Laud had issued the warrant for his arrest, she'd reminded him of his calling. She spoke of the responsibilities to his own conscience, to his congregation, and to

God. She encouraged him to stay devoted to his faith and purpose. She told John God would provide a way for him to preach in the method true to his heart.

Now, God was taking his beautiful wife. John had given up so much to stay faithful to Him. What more did He want from him?

Hannah stirred and her eyes slipped open, though only a little. Glancing in John's direction, she focused on something beyond his shoulder. His heart leapt in his chest. Was this her time? Those familiar icy fingers clawed at his heart. The fissure grew larger as they tore at him.

"I am here," said John.

She moved her lips. John bent forward to put his ear near Hannah's mouth and strained to hear her soft voice. The words, *I go soon*, filtered through her lips.

Frigid fingers scratched at his soul. He whispered, "Oh, Hannah."

Her eyes slid closed, and she eased back into her troubled slumber. Slowly, he pulled his arm from under her neck, drew the covers back, and sat up on the edge of the bed. He pulled the blankets up to Hannah's neck and tucked them around her shoulders.

Something within whispered her time was at hand. Jagged sobs caught in his throat, but he clenched his jaw and gulped them back down. Air itself seemed to fight against him. He let his head fall into his hands.

O God, I have come to accept my beloved—my soulmate—my wife—is going to be taken from me. I don't understand why, but I have come to accept it. Now I ask of Thee, I beg of Thee, make her passing less painful.

Head in his hands, his breath coming in gasps, he struggled for control.

The time to perform last rites had arrived. He'd been dreading this moment since Frederick first retrieved him from Newgate and informed him of her wish. Though it tormented him to do so, he must fulfill her request.

Easing up from the bed, he went to the sideboard and retrieved his Bible. He remembered the many nights they had spent reading scriptural passages by the fire.

He knelt at Hannah's bedside and took one of her hands while clutching his Bible in the other. He bowed his head and began to pray.

"Almighty God, unto whom our hearts belong, and from whom no secrets are hidden, I pray to Thee, cleanse this soul by the inspiration of Thy Holy Spirit. I ask Thee, take this special spirit unto Thee, to be Thine own, that she may be saved through Thy Son, even Jesus Christ, our Lord and Redeemer. I ask Thee to take her quickly to ease her suffering. I now commend her soul unto Thee, through His Holy Name. Amen."

John laid his head on the side of the bed. He pulled Hannah's hand closer to his cheek. He thought about their many happy years of marriage. Her gentle spirit brought him comfort, though she still slept.

After a time, he stood and returned the Bible to the sideboard. He lifted the covers and crawled back into bed with her. Pulling blankets over the two of them, he drew her into his arms.

Never had he known a love so deep, or possessed a want so great, as what he had for Hannah. The day they met was the beginning of an adventure he had hoped would never end.

The ending was cruel, sorrowful, and lonely.

Grief felt heavy and darkened his mind. He watched the evening sky pass by his window. The moon slowly slipped into its heavenly place, and stars grew bright in the expanse of night.

*****

The morning cock crowed a somber greeting and woke John from his fitful slumber. He lifted his head and groaned in pain, turning it from side to side while his neck complained of its torture. Summoning all the strength within him, he lifted the covers and sat up on the side of the bed, letting his feet fall to the cold, wooden floor.

The morning chill chased a shiver up his legs and across his back. He rubbed his hands up and down each arm, scrubbing the chill away.

Reaching back, he began to tuck the blankets around Hannah, but realized something was wrong.

Her breath appeared too still, too quiet.

Every nerve ending came alive. Though he knew her time had been close, each part of his body grieved to realize it had arrived.

He stroked her arm. "Oh, my dear Hannah . . ."

Peace lay upon her face. He watched her closely but could not deny what he knew to be true. She'd slipped away from him while he slept by her side.

A deep, soulful cry stumbled from his lips. His shoulders shook with pain as misery passed across his back. He glared upward with teeth clinched, grinding them crosswise against one another, his hands clutching at the bedclothes.

How am I to go on? How am I to live without her?

He stroked Hannah's cheek. Tears slipped down his face, and he swiped at them with his fingers.

"Hannah, my beloved, I miss you already."

Painful sobs caught in his throat. His soul groaned in agony. He brought the blanket to his mouth and bit down with all his might, until he was finally able to rein in his emotions. He drew his hands down his face and neck as he lowered his head.

Hannah had been a kind, caring, and loving mother to their children. They had conversed about each of their children over the past few days. Now, he was left alone to tell them their mother was gone.

Turning back to watch his wife, he spoke to her. "Jane will be here to remind me of you. You both have such beautiful, wavy blonde hair with the same deep brown eyes. You will always exist through her, through all of our children."

He knew only the shell of his wife remained, for her spirit had moved on. He touched a finger to her chin and traced her jawline. "I will meet you again in Heaven. For now, rest, my love." He drew the blanket, bit by bit, over her face until she was gone from his view.

He needed time to strengthen his spirit before facing the children. He crossed to the bench and sat down, trying to find the courage essential to confront them with his news. The length of time he sat on the bench was only manifest when his muscles began to groan in protest. With a deep sigh, he arose, stretched at the waist a few times, and headed out to the hall.

His children slept together, clustered near the hearth. The room had gone cold sometime in the night. He moved to the hearth, where he found the fire fork leaning nearby. He used it to push at the darkened, smoldering pieces of wood until they sparked and began to glow. Several pieces of wood lay in the wood box. He selected a few to arrange overtop the embers and nudged at a small flame.

Thomas arose from his slumber. "Oh, Father, you have left the bedchamber." He rubbed at his eyes. "It can only mean she is truly gone."

John considered Thomas and nodded. He turned his attention back to the fire and stabbed at the wood a bit longer. When satisfied, he leaned the fire fork against the hearth.

He folded his body into the large padded chair near to the fire. He prayed the flames would drive the chill from his soul.

Thomas began to nudge each of his children. "Awaken, our father is here."

One by one the children arose, stretching their arms and rubbing their eyes. They turned toward John as though waiting for him to speak.

He considered each child, one after another, and knew he must be strong for them. He called upon courage stirring deep within his being.

Courage he'd gained in prison and through Hannah's final days. Courage he must rely on to get him through these dark days. The very soul of courage he needed to guide him through the difficult times ahead.

"My sweet children." He rubbed a hand over his eyes and down his chin. "It pains me to utter these words."

Control was slipping away. He stopped and pulled it back in. "Last night . . . your mother's suffering came to an end . . . our Lord God has called her home."

"Oh, Father!" Jane buried her face in her hands.

Thomas stood and paced back and forth across the hall. "First, my father is taken. Now, my mother must be taken as well? What more does God want from us?"

"Thom, please come and sit by me."

"Nay, Father. I cannot." Thomas headed to the hearth, turning his back to John. He lifted his hands to warm them by the fire.

A slow sigh came from John. His poor Thomas. So much had fallen on his shoulders of late.

John motioned for the other children to gather round his knees.

"My dearest children, your mother loved you from the depths of her soul. It grieved her deeply to know she wouldn't be here for you. She spoke of you many times over these past few weeks."

He regarded his eldest. "Thom, she told me she was heartbroken to know she wouldn't be here when you meet your future mate, for she sensed it will be soon." Thomas stiffened his shoulders and turned away from him.

Jane let out a moan which tugged at John's heart and brought his attention to her. He reached forward and wiped a tear from her cheek. "Janey, she was grateful for the tender care you have given her and how close you've become over the past months." Jane laid her head on his knee, and he ran his fingers down her hair.

Glancing toward Johnny, he said, "Johnny, she was sad she would not see you graduate from college, for she knew it was your greatest desire." Johnny stared off toward the fire.

He leaned toward Barbara and touched her cheek. "Barby, she longed to watch you grow into young womanhood. She always said a young woman hides within you, and someday you will find her." A smile tugged at the corner of Barbara's lips.

He reached down and ruffled the hair of both Samuel and Joseph. "Sammy and Joss, she was proud of the good, strong boys you've become, and so desired to be here when you grow into men." The boys looked at one another. Samuel teasingly pushed his shoulder into Joseph, and they both smiled up at their father.

John lifted Little Benjamin onto his knee. "Little Benny, she told me I should never let your young mind forget who she was. She was your mother, and she loved you dearly." He tucked Benjamin into his chest and rocked back and forth.

Thomas remained facing the hearth with his back to the group.

"Thom, please, come and sit with us."

"Nay, Father."

"Very well, but please remember, your mother would never want her passing to burn a hole in your spirit."

Silence coming from the hearth fairly screamed at John. His son struggled under the weight of grief. The day would soon come when John needed Thomas even more. Would his young shoulders be able to bear the burden?

Only the future would tell.

LAMBETH

Memories of Newgate tore at John and scorched a pit in his soul. He opened the front door and viewed a morning filled with daylight, which shone bright and unclouded, in contrast to his feelings of gloom and despair. Still deficient in strength, he faltered as he stepped through the doorway. Nevertheless, the reverend rolled his shoulders back and stood tall. He hoped to survive prison and someday be returned to his family.

John adjusted the brown wig covering his shaved head. Tugging at his waistcoat, he folded a new woolen cloak over his arm.

Frederick's carriage sat ready upon the lane in front of the Lothropp house. It appeared to John as though they were about to have a day on the town. Digory was at his post, ready to assist someone into the transport.

Sunlight glistened off the shiny white exterior of the conveyance. Two dapple grays stood patiently awaiting further instructions from their driver. It gave the impression of a cheery situation, yet John was anything but cheery.

Merely two days had passed since his beautiful wife Hannah had been laid to rest. The children had been by his side throughout.

Frederick and Elsabeth offered their love and support, as well as many friends and parishioners who had come to pay their final respects.

On this sunny but dismal day, he must return to Newgate. Back into the filth and misery of Satan's own abode. How he would handle it, he knew not. He only knew that he must.

Heat beat down on him. He pulled a kerchief from his pocket to wipe his brow. His children stood in a tight group, apprehension spread across their faces. Frederick stood off to one side, ready to offer support when needed.

John steeled himself against the onslaught of emotions which flooded every part of his body. He must say goodbye to his children once again and head back to the nightmare he'd been living in for over a year. The nightmare he prayed would end before his body succumbed to the daily torture of prison.

With a feigned smile, he turned to face his family. "I will be home again soon, my precious children. Frederick is going to meet with the Bishop to discuss my final release. I believe he will afford me liberty, once he has learned of your mother's passing."

Thomas came forward and took his father's hand. "I will watch over the family while you are away. You need not worry over them."

"I entrust them to you, my son."

Thomas stood tall and stoic. John reached up and wiped the teardrop which had found its way onto Thomas's cheek. He pulled Thomas into his arms and pushed back the tears fighting his own emotions.

"Oh, my boy, you are a good son. You fill my shoes well."

"I do my best, Father."

John gave him a final squeeze and whispered in his ear, "I am thankful you finally brought Emma to meet me before I return to Newgate. I understand why you kept her from the family for so long, and why you desired to protect her from the trials we've been facing. She seems like a good woman, Thom. Take care not to lose her."

"Thank you, Father, I will," Thomas whispered back.

Using the kerchief to mop across his brow, John pulled it down over his face to subtly catch the lone tear which had escaped his resolve.

Thomas stepped away, rolled his shoulders back, and held himself erect. Such a strong young man he'd become.

"Children, I must take my leave now, though I am sad to do so. Please come and let me have a last look at you before I go."

Jane ran forward and embraced her father, hiding her face in his shoulder. "Oh, Father, I cannot bear to see you go." Her body shook against his chest.

John held her close, letting his fingers trail the length of her long blonde hair. "Jane, my dear, I am so grateful for the care you have given your mother these many months. Beyond doubt, you made her last days more comfortable and peaceful."

He drew back from the embrace, his hand coming to rest upon her cheek. "I love you, my sweet girl."

The other children surrounded him, and one by one, he touched them and shared his love for each one. He strove to memorize their faces so when he lay in his prison cell he might search his memory and see them in his mind's eye.

"Oh, my lovely children. Always remember, I love you."

Their voices chimed together in a chorus of "I love you, Father."

Frederick placed a hand on John's shoulder. "I fear the time has come for us to go."

"Aye, I do believe it to be so."

Digory opened the door and stood at the ready. John raised his hand in a sad goodbye to his children. With the aid of Digory's proffered hand, he lifted himself onto the step and crawled inside, pushing against the bag of supplies Frederick had brought for him. He took the seat facing the rear of the carriage, folding the cloak over his lap.

Frederick leaned into the carriage. "Nay, John, please take the preferred seat, which faces forward."

"Thank you, my friend, but I do not desire to see where I am headed, but from whence I've come."

Little Benjamin pushed through the group and clambered into the carriage, throwing himself at John.

"Oh, Papa! Don't go."

John pulled Benjamin into his arms. His small cries were muffled by the cloth of John's shirt.

Thomas came forward and tapped Benjamin on the shoulder. "Come with me, Benny, and let our father go where he must."

John's heart broke into little pieces as Benjamin was pulled into the outstretched arms of his brother. His youngest son held onto his brother, wrapping thin legs around his waist. Benjamin buried his face into his big brother's chest, and John's heart broke a little more.

The fissure in John's soul grew wide with torment. He turned his head away, lest his children notice the agony written upon his face.

Frederick heaved his body up the steps, taking the opposite bench. He settled in and tapped his cane against the ceiling. John heard the crack of a whip and felt the horses pull forward. He bolstered his courage to give the children a final wave and smile of encouragement.

Thomas stood behind the group, holding Benny, whose face was buried in his neck. Jane's shoulders shook as she held her hand aloft in a forlorn wave, her arm around Barbara's shoulder, who also wept. Johnny's face was stern and held a look of accusation. Samuel and Joseph stood to Thom's right, faces wet with tears. The scene filled John with sorrow and apprehension. He kept his eyes on the group as they grew smaller and smaller.

The transport continued down the lane as they started on their way to Newgate. John pulled in from the window and leaned back upon the tufted leather seat, wondering at the twists his life had taken over the last few years. He had once believed his path lay smoothly before him. Now, the future brought uncertainty and trepidation.

*****

The sun sat low on the horizon, casting an orange glow across the carriage while it made its way down the street. The conveyance swayed back and forth, lulling John into a state of false rest. His mind remained focused on memories of his children.

Frederick interrupted John's reflections. "It seems the old gate appears before us."

John regarded his friend's comment. "It is a sight I'd hoped to never see again."

Digory guided the carriage to the side of the building. Death, and the sickening smell of human waste, filled the air. John sat upon the seat, trying to summon the courage to disembark and step back into a world of stink and despair.

He pulled the wig from his head and rubbed a hand over the stubble which had grown since he'd come home. Laying the wig upon the seat, he picked up the cloak and bag of supplies, looking over at the stone archway.

"Such a constant smell that seeps into my soul and fills me with disgust."

"I am sorry, John. I will do all within my power to procure your release."

John reached over and patted his friend on the knee. "I know you will, my friend."

Frederick caught up John's hand and clasped it within his own. "I hurt to watch you return to this hellhole."

John squeezed Frederick's hand and pleaded, "Take care of my family."

With a last glance, he turned and stepped out of the carriage. The reverend pulled the new woolen cloak around his shoulders, bringing the clasp together at his neck.

John said, "I cannot thank you enough for all you have done for me. I wouldn't have survived without you."

"I am glad to help whenever you need me. You are my closest friend."

John's arms encircled his friend, patting him on the shoulder. Frederick clapped him on the back in return. John pulled the kerchief from his pocket and held it over his nose in an effort to suppress the stink. Frederick did the same.

The old Roman gate stood tall and imposing. With a desperate sigh, John stepped forward, his companion following close behind. Upon arrival at the iron bars, Frederick lowered his kerchief and called into the darkness. "To anyone who is there, we seek entrance into Newgate."

John heard the sound of something being dragged across the stone floor. A voice mumbled and cursed. With some clattering and clanging of chains, the gate began its upward journey. It wobbled back and forth in front of John's face before it came to a stop high above his head.

A familiar sound echoed from the darkness—a sound John had come to dread over the past year.

Thud, clomp. Thud, clomp.

John and Frederick stepped under the gate and into the darkness of the waiting area. The abhorrent sound of a mucus-infested cough filled John's mind. Before his eyes had adjusted to the gloomy interior, he felt the spray of Jervis's spittle mist over his face. His body flinched, and the fiendish chill he had left behind entered him once again.

"Jus' who 'ave we 'ere?" Jervis stepped into the light, and John noted the Keeper was just as ugly as he'd ever been. "Be tha' ye, Lothropp?"

"Aye, it is me. I have returned after my pardon." John wiped the moisture from his face and held the kerchief over his nose once again.

"Well, ye are back at last." His voice held a condescending tone, which inferred a certain degree of supremacy. "Ye are late with yer return."

"The delay was a necessary obligation."

Jervis used his arm to wipe the eternal river of drool than ran from his mouth. "Tha' be nothin' t' me, ye will get yer due."

Leaning onto his crutch, he reached forward and pointed his finger at John. "Do ye have some coins t' pay fer yer return?"

"Aye, we do," said Frederick.

"Tha' be two shillin' t' ge' through th' gate, two t' ge' past th' door . . . and two more cause o' yer lateness, Lothropp." He turned his palm out toward Frederick, waiting for the coins.

Frederick glowered at Jervis before he reached into his waistband to retrieve his purse. He counted out six shillings. John noted the Keeper's gnarled hand as the coins were placed thereon.

Jervis snapped his hand closed around the money and glanced over to the reverend. "I will take ye t' yer new home now, Lothropp."

"What? My new home? Will I not return to the same cell?"

"Ye lost tha' right when ye stayed out past yer time."

Jervis tramped to the thick oak door and pulled it open. The hinges creaked and groaned, revealing a place where the sun struggled to shine. The Keeper retrieved his lantern from a ledge next to the door and turned the wick up. Light spread through the portal and partway down the passageway, but was quickly swallowed up by darkness living inside the prison.

He held the lantern high, and John realized two other gaolers stood against the wall near the gate mechanism. The larger one stepped forward. He gave John a push toward the door. The door that led back into perdition—back into the sickening insides of Newgate.

Unnerved, John turned toward Frederick. Memories of being inside the prison brought renewed fear to his soul. He wanted to take in every bit of his friend before he disappeared from view.

Jervis gave Frederick a forbidding look and pointed to the gate. "Ye be leavin' now." The Keeper signaled the smaller gaoler to lower the gate. John heard wheels being turned as the gate slowly descended.

Frederick hurried to step through the arch, then turned to watch the descending gate. "John, I will do what I can. Rest your faith in God, and He will provide a way."

The Keeper shoved John past the door. The large gaoler stepped in behind him. John glanced over his shoulder as the door closed and Frederick disappeared from view.

"He cannot save ye, Lothropp. Ye be in my realm now," said Jervis.

Dread carved a new path through John's nerves. The shadows of Newgate closed in around him. Only the lantern's glow kept darkness at bay.

They passed deeper into the innards of the old prison. Cold, dank air cast its chilly tendrils over John's skin. An angry chorus of the damned and forgotten bounced across stones and echoed down the passageway. Cries slipped through the door grates and pierced his soul.

John stumbled along, his feet slipping over slimy stones as they wound their way through the halls of the prison. Thick smells of ammonia burned his nostrils and watered his eyes. He held tightly to his cloak, the itchy wool almost a welcome friend now, the muslin bag tucked securely against his side.

After a miserable journey down long, dark corridors, the group came to a stop in front of a thick wooden door. Jervis pushed a rusty key into the lock and scraped it against the tumblers. Grabbing the handle, he pulled—but the door would not move.

"Blast! The door be stuck."

The larger man said, "Step aside and let me have a go at it."

He pushed his hair back behind his ears, grasped the handle, and pulled. His face flushed red and sweat beaded up on his wide forehead. The door would not budge. He used his considerable size and slammed into the door. He jerked the handle toward him, yet still, it did not move. He kicked at the bottom hinge and pounded at the top hinge.

Panting, grunting, pulling.

Rusty hinges groaned in protest. The door began to creak open.

Jervis held his lantern into the room so John could see his new cell. A loud cackle filled the air. "Tha' be yer home now, Lothropp."

The larger man shoved John toward the opening. "You'll not be alone fer long. Your furry friends'll find you soon enough."

John bent over and stepped through the opening. The room was about five feet deep, and he doubted it was wider than he was tall. The ceiling was low, so he remained bent over.

There was no grate in the wall to give him light or air. No grate in the door to give him sound. No bed to lie upon. No cellmates to befriend him. Merely a tiny room with a filthy, stone floor and four cold stone walls.

"Why must this be, Jervis?"

His answer came as the door began to scrape closed. Mucus bubbled up in the keeper's throat, and he spat it upon the ground.

"Ye thought I would take pity on ye fer th' loss o' yer kin, yer wife? Ye thought to be special, an important reverend? Well, I be th' important one about this here place. I be th' head Keeper, and what I say, goes. Ye do not make th' rules, it be me. Ye returned late, and now ye will pay."

The lantern's light fled as the door closed solidly upon its hinges. John was left in utter darkness.

Alone.

Deep in the bowels of Newgate.

RIVER THAMES

Moonlight played across small ripples on the slow-moving river. Thomas set his sculling oars in the dark water and felt a deep ache in his shoulders. He pulled back to propel his long, narrow wherry boat away from the stone stairs and into the flow of the river. Working the river was dangerous, yet Thomas felt confident in his ability to maneuver the lengthy, pointed bow of the wherry through the heavily congested traffic of the Thames.

It had been a hard day of hauling people up and downriver. His body ached and his stomach growled, triggering images of hot pottage and the goal of bedding down for the night.

A gentle breeze flowed across the river and brought the subtle sound of a voice calling out, "Waterman, waterman!"

Thomas's heart sank with the thought of paddling another fare to some unknown location. However, he knew he must take every opportunity to earn money in support of his family. He pressed his oars firmly into the water to stop the boat's forward momentum, and then in opposite directions, turning his boat to face the stairs.

A man ran along the river walk waving a hand in the air. Thomas set his oars into the water once again and rowed back to the stairs.

The man stood at the top of the steps and leaned forward, taking in deep breaths. "Thank you for answering my call." He pulled in a few more gulps of air. "My name is Barnaby. My family disembarked from a sailing vessel, and we are in need of a wherry to carry us home."

The man then pointed down the walk, where Thomas noticed a woman and two children hurriedly making their way toward him. Barnaby continued, "I have my family and luggage with me. Might I prevail upon you to ferry us to Wapping? I will pay extra for the late hour and the trip upriver, in addition to helping with my trunks."

Thomas winced at the extra work rowing a family upriver would entail. Yet he could not sacrifice the opportunity to add to his coffers, nor did he want to leave this family in peril.

"Very well, m' lord, let me tie up my boat and I will help."

"Thank you, young man, it is greatly appreciated."

Thomas grabbed a loop at the end of the rope and stood, reaching out for a ring embedded into the wall. He pushed the loop through the metal ring, twisted it around the rope and yanked it back through the loop, deftly tying his favorite hitch knot. He grabbed an oar from inside the boat and stepped over the side, landing on the wooden dock extending from the bottom stone step. Barnaby had already headed up the stairs. Thomas followed on his heels.

Upon reaching the top, Thomas lifted his cap and nodded to the woman. "Ma'am," he said. Two young girls held onto her, fear and exhaustion on their faces.

He smiled at the trio and said, "Good evening, my name is Thom. I will get you home post-haste. For now, it would be safer for you to wait at the bottom of the steps."

"It is a good thought." Barnaby offered an arm to his wife and guided his family down the stairs. Once the family was settled into the shadows, he returned and proceeded down the river walk with Thomas.

Barnaby said, "Why do you bring an oar with you onto land?"

"The hour is late. Oft times ruffians roam these streets. It is merely a precaution."

"Good thought, Thom. I cannot thank you enough for answering my call. I had been searching for a waterman at each of the stairs. I knew the hour was late and feared all had gone home for the night."

"I was on my way home, for sure. I barely heard you calling. If I'd gotten much farther, I wouldn't have heard at all."

"When I saw you pushing off from the steps I felt my stomach sink. I had made arrangements for a carriage to take us home, however, none arrived. I feared we'd have to sleep in some tavern this night, or maybe even on the streets."

"Well, then, I am glad to be of service, m' lord."

"The trunks are up the walk a bit farther." He pointed down the street a ways.

Thomas stared in the direction Barnaby had indicated. A trunk and several bags were stacked against a building. A few youths picked through the items.

Barnaby called out, "Hey, you there! Step away from those items." He began to run toward the youth.

Thomas rushed forward with Barnaby, hoping the boys would scatter, but to no avail. As they reached the miscreants, the tallest boy, clearly their leader, stepped up with a scowl on his face.

"These bags are abandoned and fair-game," he said.

Barnaby rose to his full height, which wasn't quite as tall as the boy. Thomas knew he must strengthen the situation. He squared his shoulders and hoisted the wooden oar high over his right side. Undeterred, Thomas fixed him with a fierce stare. "You boys move along. These items do not belong to you."

The leader stared up the length of the oar. Thomas noted a flicker of concern on his face. Thomas advanced closer, coming nose to nose with the youth. He repeated, "You boys move along. These items do not belong to you."

The boy held Thomas's gaze for a few moments before he turned back to his cronies and bobbed his head to the right. "Let's go, men. It seems these things are not abandoned, after all."

They turned and headed down the walk and off into the city. Thomas leaned toward Barnaby. "I'm amazed those boys backed off as quickly as they did. Things could have gotten ugly."

Barnaby smiled at him. "It surely was your frightening look. Your line of work must have allowed you to hone it to perfection."

Thomas grinned. "Not only that, but a young man hankers after my sister, and I've had many occasions to practice the look on him."

Barnaby clapped him on the shoulder. "It's clear I found the right man to help me this night."

"Let's make haste to get these things onto the wherry and take your family home."

Thomas grabbed the trunk by the handle and hoisted it onto his back. He gripped the leather straps of a few bags and lifted them as well. Barnaby collected the remaining bags. With the luggage gathered, they made for the stairs.

Thomas asked, "From whence have you sailed?"

"We have come from the New World."

Thomas felt his heart skip a beat. "The New World? What is it like?"

"It is a wild and untamed wilderness. There is land as far as you can see, and way beyond. The native people are unique and live a different life than you could ever imagine. Many are friendly and have developed relations with those in Plymouth and the surrounding townships. However, many tribes are savage and fight against those trying to settle the land, and even other indigenous tribes."

"The thought of the New World fills me with excitement, and I long to see it for myself."

"Perhaps you will one day. There are many opportunities for strong young men such as yourself. I own a shipping company, and we are always in search of help."

Excitement filled Thomas's soul. If only he could reach out and grab this opportunity. But he had promised to watch over the family while his father was away. He felt disappointment flow into his body.

"Nay, I am sad to say I cannot. My father is presently indisposed, and I promised to watch over and provide for the family while he is away. I must stay in England for now."

"Well, when you are released from your promise, please contact me, and I'll arrange for a job on one of my ships."

"I am truly grateful, m' lord. I will do as you suggest."

Thomas continued with Barnaby until they arrived back at the stairs. The mother waited below with the children, each girl clinched a side of the mother's skirts.

They made their way down the steps, where Thomas nodded to the wife and smiled at the girls. Stepping onto his wherry, he laid the bags along the inner sides of the boat. He loaded the trunk into the center of the boat, resting it upon the bottom.

"M' lord, if you would like to assist your family onto the boat, you may leave the remaining items on the steps, and I will load them up. You may take the padded seat aft with your daughters, and your wife can take the bench seat directly in front of them. It will help balance the wherry."

"Thank you, Thom." Barnaby left his bags on the dock and stepped onto the boat to help his family.

Thomas took the remaining bags and loaded them between the forward and middle plank seat. He stepped to the bow and went to work untying the knot. He coiled the rope into the boat and turned to sit on the plank seat at the bow.

"Are you ready to proceed, m' lord?"

Barnaby turned toward his wife and said, "Are you well established, dear?"

His wife sat upon the seat facing Barnaby. She said, "I am set, if you will keep the girls safe with you."

Barnaby sat between his two daughters. He laid one arm around each girl and drew them to his sides.

"Aye, we are ready now, Thom."

Thomas pressed an oar against the bottom step, pushing the boat out into the river. He slipped both oars into the forward U-shaped oarlocks and bore down on them, propelling the boat into the middle of the river. He drove his oars in deeper and the sharp bow cut through the water, beginning the journey upriver toward the Wapping stairs.

Though the flow of the Thames was slow, Thomas still felt a burning in his shoulders as he continued to push the wherry upriver. Sweat built up on his forehead. He took a moment to press each side of his face against his shoulder to wipe it away while continuing to drive the boat forward.

A soft breeze blew across the river and flowed over Thomas's head, giving him some respite against the balmy night air. It cooled him, and he was grateful for the relief while he continued to dig his oars into the water.

Barnaby held onto his two daughters. One lay across his lap and had fallen asleep, while the other rested her head upon his shoulder. His wife sat upright with her eyes closed, her head swaying with the movement of the boat. Thomas watched them and wondered what it had been like to cross the waters of the great ocean. They had been to the New World! How he longed to undertake such an adventure. Perhaps one day.

Stars twinkled and moonlight shone, helping Thomas make out some of the landmarks along the river. He considered the young family and wondered about his own future. He felt a deep longing to see the world and explore new locations, perhaps to even discover a place never before seen by man. Yet the contemplation of a wife and children of his own filled his heart with joy. Perhaps he could have both.

A voice brought him from his thoughts. "I recognize the look in your eyes."

Thomas pulled from his reflections and noted Barnaby's stare.

The man continued, "It is the look of a true adventurer. I repeat my earlier offer. There is a job waiting for you when the time is right."

"I am truly grateful and I hope the day does come. I do wonder what this world has to offer."

"Oh, it has a lot to offer, young man, things beyond your wildest imaginings."

Thomas envisioned stepping onto an ocean ship and setting sail for some exotic location. A quiver ran through him, and the sense of adventure delighted his soul. Someday he would set sail on a new quest. For now, his wherry and this family were his top priority.

The sway of the boat soothed the weary travelers, whose heads lolled forward in sleep. Barnaby remained alert, watching over his family. Crossing the great ocean must have brought sheer exhaustion to them. He continued to push through the water as he methodically made his way upriver to Wapping.

The city gave way to a more industrial area where shipping companies abounded. He realized why Barnaby lived in this part of the country and wondered where his shipping offices might be located.

He glanced over his right shoulder. The Wapping stairs were close. He slipped the left oar into the water and, in a sweeping motion, guided the boat to the end of the steps.

Thomas eased the craft to the stairs, careful not to bump the wooden sides against the rock. He tied off onto one of the rings. Barnaby raised his head and glanced around.

"At long last, we have arrived," he said.

The others awoke, and Barnaby helped them off the wherry and up the steps to the street. Thomas began unloading the trunk and hauling it to street level. After the family had been settled at the top, Barnaby returned to help Thomas with the remaining bags.

Barnaby said, "My shipping offices are a few doors down. Would you please help me take the baggage there? I'll send a wagon for them in the morning."

"I'm happy to help, m' lord."

Thomas hoisted the trunk onto his back once again. He leaned down to grasp some of the bags while Barnaby gathered the remaining ones. They walked down the street past a few office fronts before they came to a building with a hanging sign made of wood, on which a sailing vessel was carved.

Barnaby stopped at the door. "This is it. You may leave the bags here. I will load them into the building. Many thanks to you for your help this night. You went above and beyond."

"I am happy I was there when you needed someone."

Barnaby reached into his pocket and pulled out his leather purse. He rifled around inside for a moment and handed Thomas three shillings.

"Nay, m' lord, this is too much. The normal fare is eight pence for this distance, with another four pence for going upriver. The total would be twelve pence, which makes only one shilling." Thomas took two of the shillings and held them out to Barnaby.

"Thom, you have far surpassed the worth of a normal fare. I insist you keep the shillings for the extra work you did in helping me this night. You didn't have an obligation to help with the baggage either here or in London. And your help with those ruffians was most certainly what caused them to back down. Please keep it, son."

A lump formed in Thomas's throat. He stared toward the ground, running his foot back and forth across the cobblestones. The extra money would mean so much for his family.

He pulled his gaze back up to Barnaby and said, "Thank you, m' lord, my family will benefit greatly because of your generosity."

"You more than earned it, my boy. I need to get my family home, it is but a short walking distance from here." Barnaby reached into his doublet breast pocket and pulled out a card, handing it to Thomas.

"When you are ready to work for me, please come to my offices. There will be a job waiting for you."

A flutter of excitement filled Thomas. "Indeed, I am grateful and will do as you suggest."

Barnaby patted Thomas on the shoulder. "Good bye for now. We will meet again someday."

Thomas smiled and nodded. He turned and headed back down the stairs, once again climbing aboard the wherry. He pulled the knot free of the metal ring and used an oar to push away. This time he sat amidships and used the center oarlocks. As the boat slipped into the flow of the Thames, he urged his oars into the water and headed for home.

Peering over his shoulder, Thomas saw the silhouette of Barnaby against the moonlight. He pushed one oar onto the edge of the boat and waved to the man who might hold an exciting future for Thomas in his hands. Barnaby waved back as he walked down the lane toward his family.

The motion of the river caused the end of the oar to tip back into the water. Thomas reached out and grabbed it.

A new energy flowed into his rowing, and he struck both oars into the water, pushing harder. He knew he must shoot the bridge before he could get back to his home dock, where he'd be able to tie up his wherry for the night. Though shooting the bridge could be great fun, at night it was much more treacherous, and he must use caution.

There was a part of Thomas who loved England. The moon shone brightly in the night sky. Thomas watched the countryside pass him on either side of the river. The bustle of London brought its own rewards and pitfalls. While he enjoyed much of what the large city had to offer, he also knew crime, brutality, and filth abounded everywhere. At least his family had been able to live a fairly peaceful life in Lambeth. Up until his father had been arrested.

If not for the sound of water lapping against the wooden sides of the boat, this night might be called silent. The oars soundlessly propelled him forward, and the river lulled him into a sense of peace. He let himself slide into the rhythm of rowing while he pulled and lifted, pulled and lifted.

Starboard, the London cityscape began to reveal itself. He glanced back over his shoulder and saw the great bridge not too far off. It was time to line up his boat between the pilings toward the bank side, where the current was slower than on the wall side.

When the bridge loomed large before him, he pulled in the oars and laid one inside the boat. The other he carried with him as he made his way aft. Stepping over the plank seats, he stopped in front of the padded seat. He leaned into it to use it for leverage and slipped the oar into the stern oarlock to use as a rudder.

The water churned under him. He braced his feet and stood with his left shoulder facing the bow. His wrists pressed back and forth on the oar, carving a figure eight pattern in the water. Pushing and pulling, he sculled his wherry toward the arch. The bow began to rise up, and the calm river churned into great swells.

He chose his favorite arch and aimed the wherry toward the inverted V made by water sweeping between the pilings. The long, pointed bow rose higher, and Thomas leaned his body forward for balance as he worked to keep the boat from capsizing.

Water propelled him forward through the arch. He felt a whoosh and knew he'd hit the sweet spot in the center of the swells. The wherry skimmed along the surface of the water and rode the churning wave through the arch. One last rise of the bow, and the boat slanted forward, coming down a wall of water.

The boat came out to a smoother, more even current on the ocean side of the bridge. Thomas felt his heart thudding in his chest. No matter how often he'd shot the bridge, it was always a bit harrowing. Usually, his passengers chose to disembark the wherry and walk around the bridge, meeting him on the other side. However, there were always a few brave souls willing to shoot the bridge with him.

He pulled the oar from the lock and returned to his seat amidships, facing stern. He thrust both oars into the water once again and continued to row his way downriver.

Bankside passed by at his right. It was a place where he'd ferried many passengers heading to the theater district. He knew he'd soon travel around the long bend in the Thames and be able to see Lambeth.

A slow current pulled the boat along. He relaxed his oars against the inside of the craft and let the current carry him. It had been a long, hard day, and the ache in his upper back warned him of a painful night's sleep.

When his home dock neared, he slipped his oars back into the water and rowed closer to the planked wooden dock. High tide meant he could row right up to the mooring.

He maneuvered the boat around a few other wherries already tied down for the night until he found a place to tie up his own craft. Standing, he stepped onto the dock, grabbed the end of the rope, and pulled the boat in tighter, tying off on a cleat.

A dirt lane ran alongside the bank. He trekked up to it, turned right, and started for home. Water lapped against mud along the riverbank, and Thomas paced his steps with the sound. A few shops dotted the lane.

He strained his eyes in the darkening night, alert for any danger. A woman appeared from behind a tree and strolled down the lane toward him.

Thomas approached her and noted how the breeze wafted long ringlet curls away from her beautiful face. Moonlight shone across alabaster skin, revealing full lips which held a charming smile. Coming to a stop in front of the woman, he contemplated deep, dark eyes and was transfixed by a subtle gaze.

Drawn in by the intensity and beauty of the girl, he brought his lips down to rest upon hers. Her touch was warm as she deepened the kiss and brought her arms around his neck. Thomas pulled her in close and savored the sweet taste of her.

Pulling away, he watched her eyes. "What has brought a proper young girl out on a night such as this?"

"The answer is simple enough—I have missed you, my dear Thom."

A wide smile passed across his face, and Thomas pulled her back into his arms. "I have missed you as well, Emma. However," he pulled away from her again, "I do not understand how your father would ever allow you to come out here. Though he has given our courtship his blessing, this is not a safe or respectable place for you after dark."

"He thinks I am abed for the night."

Thomas fixed her with a stern gaze. "Emma, it is not right and proper for you to do such a thing."

"Right and proper? Why is it a man can come and go as he pleases, yet a woman must worry over what is right and proper?" A quiet giggle emerged from an impish smile. "Besides, I was careful and hid behind the great oak. The risk was worth it to see you." She touched a finger to his chin. "If only for a twinkling."

"It has been a long time since last I've seen you, and I have most certainly missed you, however, I must escort you home, straight away."

"I figured you to say such a thing. For now, can we enjoy these few moments together?"

Thomas pulled Emma's hand into the crook of his arm and turned down the lane toward her cottage. "Please vow to me you will never do this again. I will worry about you every night as I work."

"I do make the vow to you, my sweet protector."

He longed for the day when he might introduce her to his family. However, the day wasn't quite yet. Their relationship must remain a secret for the time being. His family was struggling with so much, and he needed to stay focused on protecting and supporting them. Or was there another reason for his delay in introducing her? She was a forward-thinking woman with new ideas. How would his family react to her?

For the moment, he wasn't going to fret. Thomas put his arm around Emma and guided her down the lane. She leaned her head into his shoulder. It didn't bother him to take the long way home tonight.

"Oh, Thom, it is so good to see you tonight."

"And you as well, my dear one."

The warmth of Emma calmed his troubled mind and filled his heart with love.

A shimmery moon slowly slipped down the night sky, heading toward the west side of London.

Eleven

LAMBETH

The house stood quiet, as if holding its breath. Jane sat upon the small stuffed chair near the hearth, using the firelight to shine upon her embroidery. In spite of this, she simply could not concentrate on the stitches. A note she'd received from Edmund a few days past had asked if he could visit on this night. She'd sent a note in the affirmative, and now she anxiously awaited his arrival.

Winter hovered over the city. Icy roads afflicted people passing through London, which had prevented Edmund from traveling. Tonight, there was a reprieve from the cold and ice.

Jane awaited his arrival with mixed emotions in her heart. Feelings of eagerness were jumbled with a certain level of apprehension. Warmth from the fire felt hot against her skin as she sat by the hearth.

Thomas worked on the river almost every night, which afforded Jane and Edmund the opportunity to have a few unchaperoned, unsanctioned moments together. The children were abed upstairs. Jane was alone awaiting her love.

A few taps on the door sent her heart beating and blood rushing to her face. She dropped her embroidery into a basket on the floor and started for the thick oak door. Another knock sent her scurrying to answer, for she didn't want the children to awaken. She opened the door to gaze upon her dearest waiting on the other side.

A thick wool coat stretched around his broad chest. She noted the woolen scarf she'd knitted for him wrapped loosely around his neck.

Her heart fluttered deep within. She stood rooted to the spot. Staring at Edmund, she took in every inch of his strong, masculine body and good looks.

"Jane? May I come in?"

Embarrassed to be caught staring, she stepped back and motioned for him to enter. He moved through the opening and began to unbutton his coat.

Nervously, Jane stood by as he entered her home. She knew her father would not approve of his presence here tonight. A knot grew in her stomach, knowing Thomas would promptly throw Edmund out if he were to come home and find him here.

Her tongue ran over lips, dry from anxiety. She noted the thickness of his neck when he removed the scarf. Brown hair curled over his collar and escaped the ribbon with which he'd tied it back.

Edmund's hand grazed across her arm as he pulled off the coat. The spark of something new, something she hadn't felt before, tinged her chest. Was it nerves, or was there more? Edmund secured both items over large wooden pegs on the wall. He turned toward her, and she felt a brief moment of apprehension.

She longed to have Edmund's arms around her. Such a longing allowed her to push convention aside and arrange for him to be in her home—while Thomas was away.

Edmund smiled down and placed an arm around her shoulders, guiding her to the hearth. Sweat broke out across her forehead, and she reached up to dab it away with her fingertips.

Earlier, she had laid out a blanket, a plate of tarts, and two cups of ale near the hearth. Edmund lowered himself to the blanket and reached up to pull Jane down with him.

She adjusted her dress around her and gave her heart a moment to stop pounding. Pulling in a deep breath, she glanced toward the man she loved.

A flicker of firelight shimmered over his wavy brown hair and swept upward to spark a glow in his sea-blue eyes. She touched her palm against his cheek and felt the bristle of his beard as she stroked her fingers down his strong jaw line. Emotions churning deep within her core caused a rush of blood to surge up to her face.

She pulled her eyes down, only to find them coming back up to rest on his lips—full lips she longed to bring close to her own.

Jane's face flushed even deeper, and she drew her eyes away. Nerves jangled within her.

Was the fire causing her flushed and clammy feelings? Or was it the discomfort of knowing she was going against her father's wishes?

Or was it the man sitting next to her?

She began to fiddle with the edge of the blanket. Did she dare stare into those blue eyes again?

"My dearest Jane," Edmund began as he pulled her hands into his chest, bringing her in closer. "Your beauty has inspired me to write a sonnet, which I have dedicated to you."

Her eyes flew up in anticipation. "A sonnet? Oh, I beg of you, speak it to me."

Edmund brought his hand up and cupped her face within his soft, gentle palm. He fixed his eyes upon hers, and she felt a tremor pass down her spine. In a soft, deep voice, he began his sonnet.

"*Lying upon a field of verdant green, I yielded to slumber's seductive voice. Drifting e'er downwards I beheld a scene of such loveliness, my heart did rejoice!*"

Jane closed her eyes as his fingers slid into her hair and glided down the length of it, coming to rest at her waist.

Edmund drew her even closer, his warm breath upon her face. "*On the field 'fore me a girl clad in white, her golden hair shimmering sunlit rays, face of Troy's Helen with eyes dark as night, piercing my soul and capturing my gaze.*"

Heat rose in her body, like the swirl of hot wind on a summer day. Edmund tucked two fingers under her chin and pulled her face toward his. Jane felt herself being drawn in by the depth of his gaze. Her skin flushed with pleasure.

His thumb gently rubbed across her full, tender lips, his mouth moving ever closer to hers. *"Her slender body arched up to the sky, a vision of soaring ere taking flight. To meet her embrace I wanted to fly, to feel of her grace and taste of her light."*

She focused on Edmund's eyes, not wanting to miss one word of his beautiful sonnet, but her gaze pulled back to his lips, so close to her own. His breath was warm upon them, as he spoke the last words to her. *"Rising up, I heard the songbird's refrain and, waking, whispered, 'My beloved Jane.'"*

She closed her eyes and gently parted her lips, waiting for the touch of his mouth. She felt his soft lips meet hers. A shimmer passed through her body. Never had she experienced anything as sweet and perfect as his gentle touch.

Edmund moved his mouth across hers and deepened the pressure. A flutter arose in her middle and infused her with desire.

Jane moaned as Edmund slowly released the pressure on her lips. He pulled back and brought both hands up to cup her face between them.

"Oh, my dearest Jane, how long I have waited for this moment."

He lowered his face again, and Jane closed her eyes in anticipation. She felt the soft touch of his lips. Oh, the sweet sensation it brought! Her world spiraled around her.

As he deepened the kiss, his arms encircled her waist and pulled her even closer. She ran her hands over broad shoulders, reaching around his back to rub across taut muscles. The movement of Edmund's lips brought a pleasant sensation deep within her body.

Jane reveled in this new feeling. She wished this moment would never end. Yet she knew it must—or there might be no end tonight. Slowly, she drew back. It was almost painful to draw her lips from his.

She pulled away, gazing up at him. His face held an expression she had never before imagined.

Was it the look of love—or desire?

Edmund said, "Why do you pull away from me, my love?" There was an air of frustration in his eyes.

"I don't want to. However, I must. We cannot allow ourselves the pardon of becoming too intimate."

He sighed deeply, shifted his weight, and leaned back. He bade her into his arms and brought her to lie back against his chest.

Jane said, "Oh, Edmund, the sonnet is so beautiful. Could I have it written down, so I might hold it close forever?"

"I have already written it down for you. I brought it with me and will bestow it upon you when I leave tonight."

She rested her head against his shoulder. His strong arms held her close, bringing security and peace to her soul.

"How I wish this night could go on and on," said Jane.

"I desire the same thing, my love. Mayhap the day will actually come when I can make you mine. I fear with your father being in prison things have become quite problematic."

"I feel such frustration over the situation." Jane took in a deep breath and pushed a sigh past her lips. "We still await word from the bishop regarding a meeting about Father. It seems it will never happen. It has been months since our mother's death, and we want our father home again."

"I want that for you as well. However, and I'm sorry to say this Jane, I do not have confidence that your father will ever be released. Look how much time has passed, yet he still wallows in prison. It seems we will never have permission to wed."

Jane shifted around and turned her face toward his. She brought a hand up to his cheek and looked into his eyes. "We must never lose faith that my father will be released. Frederick works hard for us. Soon we will be granted an audience with the bishop."

Edmund pulled her back into his chest and circled his arms around her shoulders. His breath was on her neck as he whispered in her ear,

"I wish I had the faith that you do. Your pain and frustration brings me grief and I long to take it away."

"Every day, I pray Father will come home soon. I know that he will, Edmund."

Jane nestled her head against his shoulder. She lost herself in the security of his arms and the glimmer of firelight.

Oh, how she longed for the day when she could marry Edmund and they would become Lord and Lady Edmund Fairfax. When the day arrived, she would no longer have to bid him goodnight and watch him walk away from her.

Thoughts of Edmund and their future together filled her mind. Time passed by without her notice, and suddenly the sound of footsteps brought her alert. Leaning up from Edmund's shoulder, she stared at the door.

"Oh dear, it must be Thomas coming home from work. Quickly, sit in the chair."

He arose, and Jane pulled the blanket from the floor, laying it across the back of her chair. Edmund went to the larger stuffed chair, and Jane took the chair opposite him. She folded her hands in her lap, but rethought her position and quickly retrieved the embroidery from the basket on the floor. She lifted a finger to her lips to signal quiet.

Thomas stepped through the door and pulled off his coat. Her breath caught in her throat as she watched him turn toward the coat hooks and stop. He appeared to be staring at Edmund's coat.

Her brother turned his head into the room. Jane watched as he viewed the scene before him. She caught a glimpse of anger flash across his eyes.

She smiled stiffly and said, "Oh, Thomas, it is good to see you home safe."

A few quick strides and Thomas was standing between the two chairs staring from one person to the other. He caught sight of the tarts and ale and turned toward Edmund. Reaching forward, he grasped him by the shirtfront and pulled him to his feet.

"I cannot believe you have the gall to come into our home when I am not here to chaperone your visit. You well know the tenets of courting. You are not to be alone with my sister."

Edmund said, "It was a harmless visit, Thomas. There is nothing for you to worry over."

She listened to Edmund's words with concern. They were not the truth, but Jane was afraid to tell Thomas what had transpired here tonight. She'd stopped things before they went too far. However, she had encouraged Edmund to come here when Thomas was away. Now they were both in trouble.

Thomas stretched to his full height and stared Edmund straight in the eye. "No visit alone with my sister is ever harmless. You must leave this house at once."

Edmund glanced over to Jane. "Your guardian has arrived to inform us our night is over. I guess it's time for me to go."

He jerked his shirt from Thomas's grip. "Never fear, Thomas, I will leave. There is no foul done here this night," he said as he made his way to the door.

Jane followed him to the wooden pegs, where he retrieved his coat and scarf. She knew Thomas was upset, but she also wanted to say goodbye to Edmund. He pulled on his coat and reached into a pocket.

He brought Jane's hands up and pressed the paper into her palm, closing her fingers around it. Jane supposed it was the sonnet he'd written, and she smiled at the memory.

The sound of Thomas clearing his throat told her it was time to say goodbye. "I know, Brother," she said. "Let me have a moment."

Edmund buttoned his coat and wrapped the scarf around his neck. He leaned down and whispered in Jane's ear. "I will ache until I can set my eyes upon you once again. Fare thee well, my love."

He pulled the door open and stepped through. The night swallowed him up, and he was gone.

Jane pushed the door closed and turned back into the room. "Oh, Thomas . . . do you not have a care for me? It was a magical night, full of love and hope for a better future. Edmund helps me forget life is so difficult, if only for a little while."

"I do understand, Jane. Father left me to care for this family. If he were home, you know he too would have sent Edmund away."

He turned and headed up the stairs. "I love you, my sister. I will do all I can to allow you and Edmund time together. However, something still feels amiss with him, so please exercise caution. And even though Father did give his blessing on this courtship, you must still be mindful to only see Edmund when I am present. For now, I am exhausted and need to sleep."

"Thank you for understanding, Thomas. I will be more careful in the future."

Thomas continued up the stairs, and Jane turned back toward the fire. She sat down upon the small padded chair.

Logs had grown smaller and embers had turned gray. She loved Edmund dearly. Building a life with him brought a smile to her lips. It felt nice to ponder something good, if only for a moment. She leaned back into the chair, unfolding the piece of paper Edmund had given her. Edmund's beautiful sonnet was written across the page.

When is my life going to move on? I long to be Edmund's wife. It seems Father will never return so Edmund and I can marry.

I must not think such things! Father truly suffers in prison. How can I be so selfish?

Jane stood and folded the paper, tucking it into her skirt waistband. She retrieved the fire fork and pushed at the wood until the embers burned red and a small flame flickered brightly.

The tarts and ale had appeared delicious when she'd set them on a blanket in front of the hearth. Now, they held no appeal to her, and she placed them inside the cupboard.

Taking a candle from the mantle, she held it to a glowing ember until its wick took up the flame. It danced and sputtered, struggling to live in the damp air of Lambeth. She shivered and retrieved the blanket, wrapping it around her like a shawl.

Holding her hand around the candle to protect the flame, she headed to the stairs and took the first step up toward the room she shared with Barbara.

Edmund, what is to become of us? What does our future hold?

The flame swelled tall and luminous, its glow shining brightly against the darkness of the staircase. A slow smile tugged at the corners of her mouth. Thoughts of her magical night with Edmund filled her mind.

Tomorrow, oh tomorrow, may I hold my love, tomorrow.

NEWGATE PRISON

Darkness pervaded the air around John. He lay on his back with his eyes wide open, though he could see nothing. With no sunlight to gauge whether it was day or night, he wasn't sure how many days had passed since he'd been left in solitary.

Many of his waking moments were spent crawling the width and breadth of his tiny, cramped cell. In his mind's eye, he saw every nook and cranny.

There were two stones to the left of the cell door, yet on the right only one. The side walls were identically numbered with five stones along each side. The back wall had seven stones running its length. Each stone was stacked upward in an offset pattern which continued to the ceiling, which was made of thick wooden beams.

Stones making up the floor were unevenly placed with no apparent order, other than which ones fit where. He had found several shapes in the rocks—a horse's head, a large flower, the profile of a man with a large aquiline nose, to name a few.

John cleared his mind and, though he couldn't see the ceiling, he stared upward into the dark, visualizing the wooden beams running the length of his cell.

Many times, he'd felt pressure to pledge his allegiance to the Church of England, whereupon he could escape this hole and be returned to his family. Yet his heart warned him to remain true to who he was—taking the oath would be against his moral beliefs.

His mind struggled over the day he'd stood before the Court of the High Commission. As one of the worst days of his life, second only to the day Hannah had passed from this world, he couldn't let it go.

Bishop Laud had asked John if he were a minister, and John had answered in the affirmative. Bishop Laud asked John how he came to be a minister and by whom he was qualified. John explained he was a minister of the Gospel of Christ and the Lord had qualified him.

With scorn written on his face, Bishop Laud stared down at John and asked, "Will you lay your hand on the book and take the oath?"

John refused the oath and was immediately sentenced to Newgate. Yet, before he was taken from before the commissioners, he watched Bishop Laud and stated, "I desire that this other passage be remembered, that I dare not take this oath."

He could no more swear his loyalty to a church he felt had been torn from its noble ways and forced down a path of sacrilege and heresy than he could deny the love he had for his wife and children.

He rolled over onto his side and turned his thoughts away from his past, coming to focus on his present. There were Bible passages he knew well and could recite with ease. He had taken to narrating them over and over until eventually no thoughts passed through his mind. Being able to reside in a state of nothingness helped separate him from his current condition.

His mind had become adept at oblivion. It was simple to fall into such a state. To allow a constant state of waking stupor would surely take his sanity.

Newgate was filled with screams of tortured souls which constantly tore through the air. It mattered not if John pushed his palms against his ears to block the sound—the tortured cries of those desperate souls filled his mind.

He cried out and rose to his knees in supplication to the Lord.

Oh, my Beloved God. Those cries of pain fill me with despair.

My heart weakens in this prison, and I worry I have nothing left to give. How much longer until I am freed from this horrid place? My will to live attempts to take flight, and I fear for my soul.

John covered his face with his hands and leaned forward, his head coming to rest upon his legs.

I implore Thee, save me from this place or give me the strength to go on. I need to feel of Thy love, or I must surely die. If not myself would die, at the very least my soul would die.

He remembered times when darkness threatened to overcome him. It was then when he felt the Lord's presence in his cell, as though He sat cross-legged on the floor beside him. His comfort and peace kept John sane when he would rather be dead than alive. A silent prayer filled his mind.

I need Thee, oh, my God. Every day and every hour I need Thee. I come to Thee in a desperate state, and I need Thee now.

I plead with Thee for the courage and strength to go on. I plead with Thee to take this pain from me. Yet, in the end, I must do Thy will. I submit my life into Thy hands.

In the name of Thy Son, and my Most Beloved Savior, I close this prayer. Amen.

He must find the power to go on. He must maintain his mind and his sanity. He must stay strong enough to withstand this vile and desolate place.

He rolled onto his back and pulled the cloak up to his neck. The ache of Hannah's death felt the same today as the day she died. Torment filled his every waking thought as he lay alone in his tiny cell.

Hope of going home to his family was sometimes the only thing which kept John from losing his mind. Frederick had promised to watch over them and keep them safe until John returned. Still, he felt the ache it brought to his tortured soul. It pained him to be in this pit while his children struggled to survive in the lonely world.

John focused his thoughts toward his children. He brought each of their faces to mind.

Thomas had grown into a man, so strong and brave he'd become—working hard on the river and taking care of the family while John was away.

Jane was a beautiful young woman and looked so much like her mother. He noted her dark eyes and her long blonde hair pulled to the side in a bunch of ringlets.

His next son had never lost his zeal for learning, and John saw intelligence in young Johnny's eyes. Young Johnny—he was no longer a little boy, but a young man through and through.

Barbara, his little Tomboy, always climbing the trees. Hannah could never keep up with all the mending that came from Barbara's antics. But the girl had a sweet and loving heart, always reaching out to help another.

Samuel seemed to be a copy of Thomas, his spirit in constant search of the next great adventure. John wondered where those desires would take him.

Joseph followed after John's own heart. His love of God was evident in the way he listened with such intent while John read from the Holy Bible. A true and gentle soul was young Joseph.

Little Benjamin had been so small when John had been hauled away and he'd barely come to understand his youngest child. He longed for the day when he could spend the time necessary to truly come to know his little boy.

Baby Anne still brought a tortured smile to his lips. She was a beautiful little babe. Yet God had taken her back into His care. John wondered if she was with Hannah even now.

Pain tore at John as these thoughts ran through his mind. Though he was bodily trapped in this prison, he must not allow it to trap his heart and soul as well.

Footsteps echoed down the passageway near John's cell. He cocked one ear toward the cell door. The sound seemed evenly spread and not the lopsided clomp of Jervis. Was it one of the Keeper's cronies coming down the hall?

He pushed up into a sitting position. An ever-present ache in his back screamed after his long stretch in solitary.

Familiar sounds of a key scraped in the locking mechanism. The large oak door squealed on its hinges and opened out into the hall. John extended his arm to block the glare of a lantern held in the opening.

A voice spoke through the opening. "Lothropp, it is your time in the exercise yard. Arise and come forth."

John's heart lifted. Thank the Lord! He knew God had answered his prayer by bringing about this gift today.

"Aye, I'm coming," John called.

He pulled himself up from the stone floor until he teetered on his feet. His knees shook from the weight pressing down on them. For lack of headroom, he remained hunched over. John willed his feet to step forward, and slowly they obeyed. He hunched a bit farther to fit under the doorway, and once in the corridor, he stretched his body to its full height.

Relief filled his mind when he saw that the man who stood before him was the guard who had befriended him a few months past. "Fulke, my man. You are a good friend and an answer to my prayers this day."

Fulke lowered his voice. "Shh . . . keep your voice low, John. Remember, you must not speak to me thus in the presence of Jervis or the other gaolers. Jervis does not realize I bring you out to the yard, so keep your head down and your eyes averted to avoid notice."

"Aye, that I will do."

"Let's go."

Fulke pushed the door closed but didn't lock it. He turned back the way he'd come. John followed close behind. His legs trembled with the exertion he placed upon them, yet still he felt his soul lighten, knowing he would soon see the light of day.

He followed the gaoler through several hallways until they came to a door which led into the exercise yard. The yard lay in the middle of the prison, with hallways and cells surrounding it on all sides.

Fulke pushed a key into the lock and turned, pulling the door open into the passageway. He motioned for John to step through. He whispered, "Lothropp, remember, keep your head down and be quiet."

John nodded as he passed through the opening. A group of several men had formed a large circle and paced around the perimeter of the yard. Others were clustered in smaller groups, talking amongst themselves. John stepped into line with the men who walked, and one foot in front of the other he went, his eyes focused on the ground.

Shuffling along, he pressed onward in an attempt to work his stiff muscles. The desire to engage someone in conversation was great, but Fulke's warning of quiet still rang in his ears.

Instead, John focused on the outside air. Though still foul, it felt good to breathe air which hadn't spent years inside of Newgate. Fearing his legs would betray him at any moment, he again focused on merely putting one foot in front of the other.

The prison yard had no roof overhead and lay open to the elements. On this day, sunlight shone down on the inmates. Though the brightness hurt John's eyes, it was a welcome relief from the perpetual darkness of solitary.

Air in his lungs began to burn, and he knew it was time for a break. He scanned the yard and found one corner where no one rested. The line of men worked its way around until John was able to step out and make his way to the corner. Once there, he leaned back against the wall and closed his eyes for a momentary break from the light.

Warmth felt good upon his body, and he shifted his weight to get the complete effect. Being able to stand at his full height was a pleasant reward today. Though his legs wobbled and his knees shook, he remained upright. Nevertheless, he used the wall for support.

Heat was an appreciated benefit after living in stone-cold darkness for days . . . weeks . . . months—he knew not. He knew only that he was still alive.

He would not give into thoughts of misery and death. He must focus on thoughts of peace and tranquility. Someday, he would return home.

A sigh of gratification eased past his lips, and he fixated on the heat. He let the sun warm his body as thoughts of home warmed his soul.

A familiar voice broke through John's thoughts. "Well, well. Who do we have here?"

John stiffened as a chill raced up his body, stabbing painfully into his heart. He opened his eyes to look upon the face of Gryffyn Cane.

"What is it you want?" John was frustrated to have this man standing before him. No matter where John went, Gryffyn eventually followed.

"I'm amazed to see you out here, John Lothropp. I thought you were put in a hole and left to die."

"Well, you thought wrong. I'm still very much alive, and I plan to stay that way."

Gryffyn stepped toward John until only inches remained between them. He pushed his finger into John's chest and fixed him with a fiery gaze.

"We shall see, John, we shall see. I have more power and connections than you can ever imagine. If there's anything I can do about it, you will never again be set free to be with your family."

"If you have so much power, then why are you still in prison?"

"There are those who work on my release as we speak. Do not dare to think that I will be here for long."

"Gryffyn, I hope that is true, for the sake of your soul. But answer me this, why do you still hate me so? Have you not yet had your vengeance?"

"You know why! I hate you for all your blessings. You got everything while I got nothing. You still have a family and a home, but my only family died because of you."

Annoyance slipped into John's mind. "I worked hard to get what I have. You seem to suppose it came without effort. Anything worth having is not going to come easily."

Gryffyn took a step back but kept his eyes focused on John. "Please, spare me the sermon, John. We're not in church."

"No sermon, Gryffyn, just the facts. You must work hard for what you want. Nothing important has ever been gained without sacrifice. You must be strong and courageous to reach your dreams. It doesn't matter who you are, you have to accept that you're going to get hurt in the process. You have to be patient and work through the injuries."

Gryffyn met John's gaze. "It is bitter to see happiness through another's eyes. I had to sit back and watch while you were handed everything you'd ever hoped for."

John replied, "I can't imagine how you can possibly think such a thing. I spent years in school. Earning my place in the church was challenging and demanding. It even took good, hard work to win Hannah's affections. And our children came at great sacrifice to us both. Nothing in life comes without problems or heartaches. And now . . . Hannah has passed on from this world. Does that make you happy, Gryffyn?"

He watched Gryffyn's eyes flick away for an instant. There seemed to be a softening on the man's face, and John wondered if there was still kindness deep within his soul. Yet as quickly as the look came, it left again. His one-time friend moved closer and pressed his hand around John's throat, digging in with his thumb and fingers.

Gryffyn spat words at him. "You still have blessings, John. As for me, God took the only thing I ever loved—my mother. After she was gone, creditors took my ancestral home and lands. Now, I truly have nothing."

"Ah . . . now I understand why you landed in prison. You couldn't pay your creditors."

Gryffyn's eyes darkened with anger. "You know nothing of me, John Lothropp." With a final push against John's throat, Gryffyn turned and walked away.

John reached up to rub at his neck. The inmates had stopped what they were doing and watched the exchange between John and Gryffyn. Though a dull expression still covered their faces, they seemed interested in what transpired. He prayed the altercation with Gryffyn hadn't left a big impression on any man. Hopefully, Jervis would never learn of the situation—for retribution would be brutal.

Almost as one, the men turned to their previous undertakings. John stepped forward and fit himself into the line of men and began to move forward. He continued to pace around the yard, head down, eyes on the ground.

Time passed slowly in the Newgate yard. He began to wonder how long he'd been walking in a circle when he felt a nudge from someone behind him. He chose to ignore it, hoping the person would leave him be. Yet another nudge came, and he knew his hope was unfounded.

He turned slightly to see who'd jostled him. Twisting further around, he peered down into the smiling face of Tibbot. It lifted his soul to see his young friend, but he must exercise caution.

He grinned and signaled for Tibbot to stay quiet. As the circle of men came around to an empty place in the yard, he stepped out and pulled Tibbot with him. The young man threw his arms around the reverend's neck, and John felt him tremble against his chest.

Tibbot cried into shoulder. "Praise be! I thought you to be dead!"

John reached up to wipe away the boy's tears. "We must speak quietly."

Tibbot lifted a finger to his lips to show he understood.

John said, "Oh, how I have missed you, my boy." He studied Tibbot's face and saw clarity in his eyes and realized Tibbot had overcome his illness. "Praise the Lord, you have beaten the fever!"

"I was sure to be done in, but finally the fever broke, and I've gotten over it." He placed his hands on John's shoulders. "And you—I thought you were certainly headed to the gallows when they dragged you from our cell. How did you come to be here?"

"When they took me, I was able to return home for a short while. However, it was because my wife was ill, and unfortunately, she passed on while I was home."

"Oh, m' lord, I am sorry for you." Tibbot lowered his hands and stared toward the ground.

John tucked a hand under Tibbot's chin to lift his head and observe his friend's eyes.

"Thank you, Tibbot. It was a difficult time, to be sure. I was required to return here after she passed. I supposed I would be put back in my old cell with you. However, Jervis placed me in solitary because I was late on my return."

"That vile little man. He must work for the devil himself."

John laughed at Tibbot's response, and he raised his brows. "I have had such thoughts a time or two myself." It renewed John to be with his young friend.

Tibbot grinned at the reverend's admission. "How long have you been back, m' lord?"

"I have no perception of time's passage, since there aren't windows in my cell. How long does it feel since I left you?"

"It has been a few months, at least."

"That's nigh onto what I surmised. I don't know if Jervis will ever let me out of solitary."

A whistle shrilled across the yard. John and Tibbot turned toward the sound. Two gaolers stood at the door, each holding a lantern to light the hallways and a truncheon to keep the men in line.

One gaoler called out into the yard. "All ye men line up and make ready to go back to yer cells."

Inmates slowly made their way toward the door, lining up single file.

"Stay in line and follow me." The gaoler turned and passed through the door, inmates following behind. The second gaoler waited to bring up the rear.

John wasn't sure what to expect, since it was Fulke who had secreted him into the yard. He pulled Tibbot with him, and they merged into the column of men. He must obey this gaoler, or he might be found out.

John followed the men through the door and down the passageway. Gloom pervaded the length of the hall, except immediately around the lanterns. John prayed neither of the gaolers would observe a man who wasn't meant to be there.

The line of men funneled down the hall, pacing the man directly in front of them. John matched step with them, wondering what would happen when the gaolers became aware of the situation. Perhaps he could convince them he was intended to be there and they would merely return him to his cell.

He kept his head down but scanned his surroundings and watched for the route back to solitary. He remembered Fulke had left the door unlocked. Perhaps he could find his way back and slip into his cell unnoticed.

A soft glow radiated from a hallway intersection. Could it be Jervis? John felt his stomach tighten at the thought. He turned his head away from the light and stepped closer to the man in front of him.

Someone clenched his arm and wrenched him into the adjoining passageway, then pressed a hand over his mouth. A groan emitted from John's throat in response.

"Shh . . . it's me, Fulke. Keep your voice down, and I'll get you back to your cell."

Tibbot turned to glance his way. John waved him off, and Tibbot stepped forward to close the gap. The reverend's body relaxed against the barrel-chested man who held him while the procession of men disappeared down the hall.

The shuffle of footsteps ebbed away. John remained on alert, knowing full well they weren't out of trouble yet.

Fulke said, "I believe we can safely return to your cell now."

John spoke in a low voice. "I didn't know what to do when the men were lined up and told to leave the yard, so I fell in line with them."

"Forgive me, I was held up at the gate. I never thought to leave you in the yard for so long. Thankfully, it wasn't Jervis who came to get the men. We'll use back passages to get to your cell. Hopefully we won't come face to face with the Keeper."

Fulke turned and signaled for him to follow. John trailed behind the gaoler who had become his friend.

"Keep your footfalls light," Fulke said as he worked his way down the hall.

John slipped and stumbled over slimy stones which made up the floor. The gaoler guided him deep into the bowels of Newgate and down halls he'd never seen. Eventually, John stood in front of the thick oak door which led to his cell.

The gaoler said, "We must thank God we weren't found out by Jervis."

John reached up and clasped Fulke's shoulder. "Thank you, my friend. You have made my life a little easier today."

Fulke pulled the door open, and John lowered his head to step through, back into the hellhole that was his lot in life. Turning, he watched his ally slowly disappear as the door closed on squeaky hinges. He heard Fulke's key scrape in the mechanism. Walls closed in on him once again.

John searched around until he found his sleeping area. Lowering himself to the ground, he curled into a ball atop the straw, pulling the cloak over his shoulders and up onto his head.

He prayed, thanking God for the blessing of his time in the yard. Even though he'd had an encounter with the hatefulness of Gryffyn, he was still thankful he'd gotten a small break from solitary.

It was an added pleasure to see Tibbot. John thanked God Tibbot had gotten over the gaol fever which had plagued him for so long. Oh, how he missed the boy!

The reverend quietly closed his prayer, thankful he and Fulke made it back without incident.

Sleep's fingers tugged at him, and slowly the world began to fall away. As the last bit of consciousness was about to slip past his mind, a creature crawled up his leg and onto his back. It continued onto his shoulder and came to a stop on his head.

John slipped his hand out from under his cloak and up toward his neck. The small animal was foremost in his mind as he snapped his hand up and grabbed the rat. Loud squeals filled the cell. John pushed the cloak back from his head and sat up, still clutching the grimy vermin in his hand.

Plagued by rats since he'd entered Newgate, one by one he'd cleared his cell of the filthy varmints. Yet, here was a brave new rat attempting to invade his space. It would not do. He rolled up onto his knees and crawled his way to the door.

The rat continued to squeal in his hand. John ran his other hand down the wooden door until he found the opening at the bottom. He pushed his hand, rat and all, through the opening. With a flick of his wrist, he sent the rat sailing down the hallway.

"And stay out!"

John crawled back to his bed and lay upon the straw, pulling the cloak up over his shoulders and head once again. His eyes slowly closed, and he knew he must remember to be hopeful. He must remember to be faithful. And he must remember God watched over him.

He must find it in his soul to forgive the man who hated him enough to betray him to the bishop. The man who had facilitated his arrest and landed him in jail. The man who had been his friend but was now his enemy.

Gryffyn Cane.

LAMBETH

Howling winds raged through the streets and brought eerie sounds into the house. Jane was uneasy as she sat in a small wooden chair by the hearth. She worked her embroidery needle through a piece of linen held in her lap. Her mother was gone and her father was back in prison. Every creak and groan in the house gave the impression it mourned along with her.

Thomas lay supine on the floor. Today was a much appreciated break from his grueling work on the river. Little brothers, Joseph and Benjamin, lay alongside him. Big brother's strong arms held them close as the little boys' chests rose and fell in slumber.

Johnny had taken a book into the garden to read while Barbara and Samuel had sullenly withdrawn to other parts of the house.

Fire crackled and interrupted Jane's thoughts. She was distressed to see the many mistakes she'd made in her embroidery work. Vines rambled in the wrong direction, overlapping a small bird she'd so painstakingly worked while at her mother's bedside.

"Drat . . . I've made a mess and worked terrible stitches into this embroidery. I'd planned to use it as a collar for my blue dress. This is the last thing Mother and I worked on before she passed. Now I have ruined it."

A deep sigh issued from Thomas. "Mayhap Elsabeth can help you."

Jane let her hands drop into her lap. She checked whether the little boys were still asleep. Speaking quietly, she said to Thomas, "Oh, Thom, what are we to do? With Father gone again, I fear we cannot care for the children much longer. How will we provide for them? Our garden is sparse, and it seems only the weeds will grow. Though Mother did teach me to garden, I fear I cannot produce the food we need."

Turning his head toward her, he said. "I will help when I can, but I must work the river. We need every bit of money I can earn." He rolled his head back toward the fire, resentment on his face.

Jane struggled to keep her frustrations about their current situation under control.

Did Father allow devotion to God to come before devotion to his family? How long would the bishop make him pay?

Oh, she must stop! She quickly reminded herself that father suffered far more than she did. His example of strength and courage meant she must do the same. Yet, she didn't feel strong or courageous— she merely felt lost.

She stretched her foot forward and tapped her toes on Thomas's arm. "Thom, will we be able to survive this trial?"

He turned his scowl toward her. "Father cares naught for *our* needs. Once again, I do not understand why he doesn't simply vow his allegiance to the Church and get out of that infernal prison."

She studied her brother's angry expression. "You understand he cannot, for it would be a lie. It is hard, but we must support our father."

Little Benjamin shifted his weight, and Thomas let him settle back into his chest. He lowered his voice and continued. "What is Father gaining from being in such a wretched place? We are left to fend for ourselves and take care of the younger children. I do not know how much more I can bear."

Jane worried the cloth in her hands. She felt disloyal about her anger toward their father. "We cannot let ourselves be disheartened with Father, or with his choice to follow God in the way he feels is correct. He is brave to stand up for his beliefs, even though it landed him in prison. He has shown true courage, and we must find a way to do the same."

"I understand your words." Thomas fixed her with a disheartened look. "I do believe our father is brave for what he is doing."

Jane brought her embroidery into the firelight. She studied the stitches, and a solution to her mistakes came to mind. "Think about it, Thom." She lowered the fabric to her lap. "The true test of courage is showing bravery in the face of fear. When we do what we must to overcome our fears, we gain strength to tackle the next challenge. There are few people who will change the world, but we can each make changes in our own small worlds. And if we do so, we will gain more courage than we ever thought possible."

*****

A few days had passed since Jane and Thomas reaffirmed their need to stay strong and hold the family together. Jane stirred a pot of stew hanging from the large iron bracket hinged over the open hearth. Using an iron spoon, she dug deep into the pot, bringing some meat up from the bottom.

She'd used some potatoes, as well as a few carrots and onions from their diminishing garden. To that she'd added the lamb Temperance Allen, a member of her father's congregation, had brought over. It was a nice change from the same old pottage they'd been eating every day.

Using the pot pusher, she moved the bracket into position over the fire. She sat back and watched the flames. Her eyes followed them as they sparked and sputtered within the hearth.

Thomas worked long hours on the river. Most days, she and the children were in bed before he returned home late at night. When she arose in the morning to prepare porridge for the children, only a rumpled blanket on his cot confirmed he'd been home at all. Being the sole caretaker of the younger children, day in and day out, kept Jane trapped in a situation which brought great loneliness to her heart.

Oh, how she longed to see Edmund. She missed strolling along the river with him and watching the boats flowing with the current or bucking against the wind. However, she found it difficult to find time for him with the responsibility she had of acting as mother to her younger siblings. She longed to be free again.

A loud thumping brought Jane back from her thoughts. Someone knocked upon the entry door. She arose to answer the knock and see who'd braved this chilly autumn day. Lifting the latch, she felt the wind pushing inward against the door. She held it tightly and eased it open, only to look into the smiling faces of Frederick and Elsabeth Pemberton.

Elsabeth's smile warmed the heart. Her full lips turned up at the corners, carrying the smile to her soft green eyes. The poor woman's skirts blew sideways while she grasped her bonnet to protect it from the blustering afternoon wind.

Frederick's smile seemed a bit less tender. He struggled with the need to lean on his cane, grip his hat, and keep his cloak from taking flight.

Jane stepped back. "Oh my—please enter quickly, lest you blow away."

"Thank you, my dear," said Frederick. He tucked his cane under one arm and leaned down to pick up two muslin bags lying at his feet. He waited as Elsabeth stepped through the door. He followed, his cloak blowing out behind him.

Jane closed the door against the chilly wind while Elsabeth made her way quickly to the hearth and turned her back to the fire.

Frederick hauled the two heavy bags to the cupboard near the hearth and placed them upon the ground. "We have brought some fresh supplies for you and the children."

Jane's heart felt deep gratitude for their kindness. "Thank you so much. I fear what life would be like without your aid and support."

He leaned his cane against the round hall table, removed his capotain hat, and set it upon the table. The hat, with its tall conical crown rounded at the top and narrow brim, was quite fashionable for the day.

He made his way to the hearth. "It isn't much, but it's all we have right now. However, many things in our garden will be ready soon, and we'll bring more." He lifted his meaty hands to the fire, alternating between rubbing them back and forth and holding them up to the flames.

Jane motioned for them to sit. "May I take your cloaks?" Frederick had shaved his beard into a Vandyke, so popular for the day.

Elsabeth muttered, "Thank you, but today the wind seems to draw every bit of warmth from me, so I will keep mine."

Frederick rubbed his hands up and down his arms. "And I will keep mine, as well."

Elsabeth sat upon the proffered chair and asked, "Now, my dear, how are you? Does Thomas still work the river? Has Barbara been able to pull from her despair? How is Johnny? Has he accepted his father's return to prison? Poor Samuel, Joseph, and Benjamin—Frederick told me how they cried when your father climbed into the carriage, how do they—"

"My dear wife! You must give her a chance to respond before asking another question," Frederick said.

Elsabeth smiled and held her hand up toward Frederick. "Very well."

Jane laughed and said, "We do as well as can be expected, given the circumstances we presently face. Thank you for asking, Elsabeth."

Frederick appeared downcast and said, "I'm sorry for being harsh, Elsabeth."

"You are quite forgiven, my husband," she said, smiling.

Frederick retrieved a chair and pulled it close to Jane, where he sat upon it. "We have been overly anxious regarding all of you. Forgive us—it has been a while since our last visit. Now, I believe we bring a bit of good news."

He smiled and continued. "The former Bishop of London, William Laud, who was responsible for your father's imprisonment, has been enthroned as the Archbishop of Canterbury."

Jane lifted her brows and watched Frederick, wondering why he thought this would be good news to her.

Frederick said, "That is not the good news I came to impart. His appointment to Archbishop left an opening in London, which was filled by William Juxon. While Laud was Bishop of London, there was no hope of your father's release. However, now that Bishop Juxon holds the position, I do believe if I present your family's case to him, mayhap he will release your father from prison."

The power of Frederick's words filled Jane with optimism. Her heart lifted with hope of her father's freedom.

Frederick pulled Jane's hands into his own. "We will need your help if we are to succeed. I will argue the case by explaining your mother has died and your father has been returned to prison, which makes you children wards of the church. However, if the Bishop were to release him, that would no longer be the case."

Jane's chin fell to her chest. She and Thomas worked hard to care for the children. The thought of being wards of the church was disheartening.

"Thomas and I do our best to survive. The Allens have given us some lamb today, which I'm sure the children will be happy to have in the pot tonight."

Pulling free of Frederick's hands, she turned towards Elsabeth. "I have wanted to ask for your help in the garden."

Elsabeth said, "It would be an honor, my dear, I would love to come and help. When would you like to begin? In fact, I can come over tomorrow. Although, there's not too much we can do until the spring. And please forgive us for not coming sooner. Frederick's imprisonment left us bereft of time and supplies, but we have recovered somewhat and will now be able to help you more."

Frederick glanced from one woman to the other. "Ladies, please allow me to go on before I lose to more talk of gardens."

Elsabeth smiled warmly and waved her hand at him, signaling for him to continue.

"It's important for all of the Lothropp children to appear before the bishop. He may come to understand you are young and in need of parental leadership. He may also want to question some of you."

Jane rubbed her hands up and down her thighs. "I am nervous to do such a thing."

"Do not be fearful, I will be there to speak for the family. Bishop Juxon is a fair man. I believe upon hearing your case, he will show mercy."

"It does sound promising," Jane said.

"Elsabeth will also accompany us so she might help with the children and give you comfort. There are many preparations to make. We must take our leave now. The ride home is long, and the day grows colder with each passing minute."

Fetching his capotain hat and cane from the table, Frederick arose and made for the door, but Elsabeth remained in the chair and appeared reluctant to give up her warm place by the fire.

Frederick returned to take his wife's arm and help her to her feet. She said, "Nay, the fire beckons me to stay, Husband."

"It calls to me, as well. Yet, we have much to do this day, and the storm grows in power."

"Very well, I will leave the comfort of the fire for you, my husband."

Frederick placed the hat on his head, pushing it down firmly as they headed to the door. He turned to Jane and said, "I bid you adieu, until next time."

"Good morrow, and thank you for all you do to help us."

Jane lifted the latch and pulled open the door. The couple braved the storm and made their departure. The Pemberton's carriage was parked on the lane. Both horses stood with heads toward the ground, facing into the wind. Digory leaned against the side of the carriage. Once Jane's visitors were in the carriage, she waved and pushed the door closed.

The hearth would warm her. She hurried over and lifted hands to the flames. An audience with the Bishop of London! What a frightening thought. Each day brought her a new challenge.

Would life ever be as simple and sweet as the days when Father had been curate?

Her father being taken away to prison—seeing him return a ghost of his former self—seeing her mother waste away and die—observing her father step back into the carriage and return to prison—those were the memories which pressed on her young mind.

She must turn those thoughts away. She must let her heart sing with the idea of her father's release. She must let her mind lift with the notion of what her future might hold.

She must let her soul breathe once again.

Fourteen

LAMBETH

Sunlight shone directly overhead, signaling midday. Jane, Barbara, and Johnny stood by the carriage with Frederick and Elsabeth Pemberton. Digory sat atop. Master Allen's carriage sat behind the Pemberton's, and he stood at the door.

Thomas leaned his head through the door of the Lothropp home, calling out to his brothers. "Come quickly, boys, we are waiting for you." He turned back to the carriages and said, "I don't know what could have happened to them."

"I'll go find them," said Jane. She moved to the house and stepped into the hall. "Sam? Joss? Benny? Where have you gone?"

No sound came from within the house. She walked through the house and listened. The faint sound of muffled voices caught her attention.

Hair from three little heads poked over the top of the dish cabinet. Jane felt a chuckle growing at the back of her throat. "Oh, come now, boys, I see your three little heads above the cabinet. You can't hide any better? Please come out."

The boys worked their way forward to face their sister with heads bowed.

"Why were you hiding?" asked Jane.

Samuel said, "We are afraid to go before the bishop."

Jane rubbed a hand across his head. "It is scary. I'm afraid too! Yet we must do this for our father. Don't you miss him and want him home?"

"Aye," each boy sang out, as if one.

"Come on, let's go. We cannot be late."

Jane ushered the boys outside, saying, "At least the sun shines and brings cheer this day."

Elsabeth took charge of the young ones. "Come, boys, you may ride with me. It will be a great adventure." She guided them toward the carriage.

Jane called out to Elsabeth, "Do you want me to ride with you and help with the boys?"

She turned back to Jane. "We will be fine, do not worry."

"Very well," said Jane. "Signal us if you change your mind, and I can join you."

The younger boys followed Elsabeth and climbed into the Pemberton's carriage. Thomas, Jane, Johnny, and Barbara took Master Allen's carriage, with him sitting atop as the driver.

Off they went to meet the new Bishop of London. This day had been a long time coming. Thoughts of their father being granted liberty filled Jane with hope.

They bumped and jostled over the dirt road on their way to Stangate Horse Ferry, near Lambeth Palace. The Pembertons and the Allens had graciously provided the money necessary to cross over at the ferry instead of having to fight their way across the London Bridge, which could add hours to their journey.

Johnny and Barbara quickly went to sleep with the swaying of the carriage. The carriage bounced down the road and into a dip, sending Jane lurching forward. Thomas reached out and caught her before she landed on the floor in front of him.

"Thank you, Thom. I fear the floor would have been unpleasant." She smiled at her brother. Jane leaned back against the seat. Even though the carriage bounded over the road, her two younger siblings slept.

Sleep tugged at the corners of her mind, and she closed her eyes, enjoying a moment of quiet. Her moment was, however, short-lived, as she heard Thomas clear his throat.

"Jane, have you ever wondered if your feelings for Edmund have grown quickly because of the unrest in your life?"

Jane opened her eyes and sent her brother a withering look, hoping he would stop this conversation.

Unfazed, Thomas continued, "Mayhap because of the loss of our mother and father, you have a certain insecurity, which has then resulted in you reaching out to Edmund?"

"Oh, Thomas, do not worry so. My love for Edmund is real."

"I wonder if you will feel the same love for him when Father returns. How well do you know Edmund? He is somewhat of a mystery."

She was tired of Thomas questioning her relationship with Edmund. "He loves me and I love him."

"Be very careful, Jane. I feel there is something odd about him."

Jane turned her attention to the landscape out the window, dismissing any further talk. She knew Edmund loved her, yet she trusted her brother.

From the corner of her eye she spotted concern washing over her brother's face. A sickness grew in her stomach, but she pushed it down, not wanting to acknowledge the omen she felt growing deep within her soul.

The River Thames came into view, and Jane turned her attention to more pressing matters. Anxiety overwhelmed her when she saw the ferryboat, which seemed quite feeble. It didn't seem up to the task of carrying them across the river to Westminster.

The carriage stopped near the water, but the vibrations of travel still quivered in her bones. Master Allen climbed down and opened the door.

"Would you care to come out of the carriage, Jane?"

"Yes, thank you." Jane took his proffered hand and stepped down to the ground.

Thomas climbed out of the carriage and reached around to help Barbara. Johnny scrambled out after them.

The Pemberton's carriage swayed back and forth. Jane walked closer to check on the boys to be sure all was well. She peered in the window. The boys were wrestling with one another as Elsabeth sat back upon the bench.

"Boys, you must settle down," Jane called out.

Elsabeth chuckled. "It is no worry, Jane. They are merely anxious and this is how they express it."

Jane shrugged her shoulders. "Very well, but you may suffer for your decision later." She grinned and headed off toward the ferryboat.

Gazing across the river, Jane wondered about her father on the other side. She bent her head and closed her eyes, silently praying things would go well today and her father would soon be home.

She opened her eyes and found that Frederick and Digory had walked down to the water to speak with the ferryman. They soon returned and explained they would take one carriage across at a time, with respect to the weight of the carriages, the horses, and all the passengers.

Digory climbed back atop the carriage, while Frederick returned to his seat inside. The conveyance pulled forward, wobbling back and forth on its way toward the ramp. The thought of Elsabeth crossing the river with her three little brothers brought an impish smile to her lips. Frederick and Elsabeth had been blessed only with girls, now grown and married. Jane wondered how well her friend would fare being alone with three little boys.

Jane walked toward the water but kept an eye on the carriage while it slowly made its way down to the ferryboat. The sight of the ferryman guiding the horses down the ramp and onto the wooden conveyance brought apprehension to her mind. Her stomach tightened at the thought of crossing the river atop a ferry, replete with carriage, horses, and passengers. It would be her first time crossing on a ferry in such a manner.

Their carriage was secured to the planks, and they began their way across the river. The stress of the situation prompted her to return to the Allen's carriage and climb inside, hiding her face in her hands.

*****

Both carriages made it safely across the river. Jane leaned back against the seat. The rigors of the day overwhelmed body and soul, and her heavy eyelids closed in exhaustion. Yet, sleep stayed out of reach as thoughts of an impending meeting with the bishop filled her mind.

Frederick described Bishop Juxon as a kind, merciful man. Yet still, she felt apprehension within her. If the bishop did sign the order for her father's release, how long would it be until he came home?

She opened her eyes and noted St. Paul's Cathedral as it appeared over the buildings. Its high walls stood tall and imposing upon Ludgate Hill.

Newgate prison was not far from St. Paul's. It troubled Jane to be so close, knowing Father suffered and wasted away within its gates. Memories of how he appeared when he was home filled her mind. What must he be like now?

Both carriages arrived in front of the cathedral and came to a stop along the road. Jane leaned out the window to view the building. It stretched out from the sides of the tower. Its many arched windows lined each side. It was the longest building she had ever seen. Thoughts of stepping inside filled her with growing unease.

Master Allen climbed down and opened the door, reaching his hand forward to help Jane off the step. Her hand trembled as she reached forward to lay her palm in his.

Settle down, Jane.

Master Allen's gentle eyes brought her comfort. "Worry not, Jane. Bishop Juxon is nothing like Archbishop Laud."

She nodded her appreciation, and he helped her exit the carriage. Thomas followed and turned to assist Barbara. Johnny rambled out by himself. They all joined the younger boys at the Pemberton's carriage. Jane's siblings had become very quiet.

Frederick stepped to Jane's side and spoke to her in a soft voice. "Though the sun shines brightly in the sky, it seems a dark cloud has fallen upon the Lothropp children." He spoke so all the children could hear him. "I realize you are afraid, yet you must find your bravery to visit the bishop and help your father's case. Lift your heads high and make ready to seek your father's liberty."

Thomas stepped forward and turned toward the group. Jane looked from sibling to sibling, and gradually each child lifted their eyes and watched their oldest brother.

"Frederick is correct. We must be brave for our father. Trust in the Lord and know that He will help us today."

Jane struggled to find her smile. Elsabeth joined her and whispered in her ear. "Jane, stand tall, the young children see you as a mother. You must act the part." Jane glanced toward Elsabeth and drew strength from her smile.

"Thank you for being here, Elsa. It means so much to me, to all of us." Jane took a few deep breaths and dug deep in her soul for the strength she hoped was there. "The time has come for us to meet the bishop. Lift your eyes to God and keep a prayer in your souls. We must have faith that his heart will be softened towards our father."

Thomas stretched his hand out toward Benjamin, who grasped it. Joseph reached up to take his other hand. Thomas had begun to look and act in many ways like their father.

A soft smile spread over Thomas's face. "Let us stand tall today. We are the children of John Lothropp. Be brave for him now, as he is brave for God."

Jane heard a snuffle. Frederick used a kerchief to wipe his face. "Oh, children, when your father is home, I will tell him of this day. He will find great joy in knowing of your bravery for his cause, and for the support of one another as well."

He patted little Benjamin on the head. "Even you, little one, even you have been brave." He gestured his hand toward the church. "Follow me, and let's go see the bishop."

Jane took Barbara's hand, and they shooed the children forward, following Frederick and Elsabeth to the entrance of the church. Master Allen and Digory stayed behind with the carriages.

They approached the large double doors of the cathedral, with their arched stained-glass windows and the beautiful stonework. Frederick stepped forward and pulled the doors open, allowing the group to enter the building.

The windows shone a rainbow of colors across the floor. Jane struggled in the dim interior and stopped a moment so her eyes might adjust to the shadows of the church.

She pulled in a long breath of air. Frederick led them through the church toward the vestry, where they would conduct their audience with the bishop.

Jane's stomach lurched and roiled. She said a silent prayer asking for the strength and daring she needed to face a man of such power.

Please God, let me find the courage deep within me, the courage I long for, the courage I need.

The vestry door stood ajar. Frederick lifted his hands to stop the group. "Please wait here a moment." He stepped inside the room. There was a mumble of voices, then he returned to stand before them.

"I have spoken with the bishop and asked how he would like to proceed. He has chairs for each of you to sit upon. I need you to enter quietly and sit down. I will speak your case to him. Please keep still while I speak so as not to offend him. If he has questions, please answer with respect." He paused, scanning down the line, watching each child. "Are you ready?" Several heads nodded up and down at once. "Very well, let's go in. Start with Thom. Enter in age order and take your seat. Elsa, forgive me, my dear, but you must wait out here."

Jane gave Elsabeth a glance of thanks and returned her attention to Frederick. He stepped back into the vestry, followed by Thomas. She moved toward the doorway, and all attempts at courage abandoned her.

Her eyes watched Thomas's back as she shadowed him into the room. Johnny came through the door, trailed by Barbara, Samuel, Joseph, and little Benjamin. They all took their seats.

Frederick moved to the front of the room. Jane couldn't bring herself to see the man who held the fate of her father in his hands. She heard Frederick speak.

"Your Grace, I thank thee for thy kindness in accepting an audience with us this day . . ."

He continued talking, and Jane took the opportunity to still her heart and summon her courage.

Some of Frederick's remarks registered in her mind as he continued to speak. ". . . their mother passed away, and their father was required to return to prison. I have brought the Lothropp children here today so you might meet them and hear of their sufferings since they have become wards of the church and been left with no parental supervision."

Summoning whatever strength she could find, she lifted her eyes so she might observe the bishop. She began at the base of his robes, beautiful white robes of the finest silk she'd ever seen. A scrolling floral motif continued up the front of the gown. She let her eyes flow upward to note large flowing sleeves and a broad gold collar.

Look farther, Jane. See the face of the man who holds your father's life in his hands.

Her eyes continued up the collar to a neck which sagged with age and hung from a rounded chin; next was a nose, long and narrow. Fear kept her from seeking out the eyes—those windows into his mind and soul. With all the courage she could find within herself, she gradually stole a peek. As she locked onto the bishop's bright blue eyes, she felt the answer ripple through her.

She knew the fate of her father.

NEWGATE PRISON

John lay on his right side, befuddled. He'd been pulled awake by sounds and light coming through the slot at the base of his cell door. He brought his hand up to shield his eyes as he strained to hear the mutterings of two men out in the passageway.

"Do ye think he still be livn'?" one man said.

"Hard t'say. I ain' seen 'im move, hide ner hair," said the other.

"Nor I. He be a wily one though—and right fearsome too."

"Ye are scared as an ol' wench. Get back while I ha' me a look."

John lay on his right side and listened as the two men squabbled. How long he had been lying on the stone floor, he did not know. Time had ceased to matter. The sun never graced his cell, for it could not penetrate the thick stones walls. He heaved a great sigh as he thought about his current predicament.

"Thar, did ye see? He be movin' a bit," said the second man.

"Ye think so?" replied the first.

"What is it you men want from me?" John said.

He heard some mutterings and a scuffle on the other side of the door. A bowl came through the slot, followed by footsteps running down the hallway. Bit by bit, the light was swallowed up by the inner recesses of the prison.

"Worse than the vermin that scurry through these walls," muttered John.

He brought his left hand down, pressed it against the stone floor, and began to push himself up. Rising a bit, he put his right hand underneath himself and rolled up into a sitting position. The exertion caused some dizziness, so he took several slow breaths until it passed. He sat, scratching at his beard.

It troubled him, not understanding how long it had been since Hannah's death. Most days, the pain felt raw as the day she died. Other times he could barely remember having been home.

No word had come from Frederick regarding the petition for John's release. Jervis could be behind such a thing. One relied upon the man's good nature to get items and information from the outside. John knew just how poor the good nature of Jervis could be.

The path to the door was as familiar to John as the course of the River Thames. He rolled over onto all fours. His fingers played across the floor until they found a groove in the stone. Crawling along, he followed the furrow until he came upon a soup bowl. Both hands cradled the bowl as he brought it to his mouth. Conscious of each sip, he drank the water soup through cracked and swollen lips.

He sucked at the last bit of liquid, licking around the edges and into the bottom to get any bits of bread stuck onto the bowl. Once this routine was complete, he reached out and felt for the door. He ran his fingers down an oak plank until he found the opening at the base. Lowering the bowl to the ground, he pushed it through the slot and out into the passageway.

His fingers rooted around the stone until he found the groove in the floor once again, which he tracked back to his sleeping spot. John rummaged around until he came upon the pile of straw he'd used to make his bed. He arranged it back into a column, plumping it as much as damp, moldy straw could be plumped.

The muslin bag was molded into a ball. He lay down upon the straw, his head coming to rest on his makeshift pillow. He drew his woolen cloak over his body.

Sleep was his saving grace, and a good friend in this hellish place. Time was nothing to John. Night was all that existed for him.

Before he would allow himself to fall back into a fitful sleep, since it was all he knew, he conjured the beautiful face of Hannah. He would not allow her memory to fade, nor forget the love he felt for her.

Next to his mind came Thomas, now taller than he, with long legs and a broad chest. His steel blue eyes held no malice, and his handsome face commanded attention wherever he went. There was beautiful Jane, so much like Hannah. John wondered if young Edmund was still courting her.

He continued to imagine the faces of his children. Baby Anne, already called to heaven, Johnny, Barbara, and his three youngest sons, Samuel, Joseph, and Little Benjamin. As their faces flowed through his mind, his lids became heavy and he fell into a slumber, which so aptly gave him the release he needed from perpetual darkness.

*****

A creaking sound penetrated John's mind. Unable to fully awaken, he listened as the sound grew louder still. His cell door creaked on its hinges and swung open. Bright light pierced through closed lids, compelling him to open his eyes. He lifted his hands to shield them.

Someone called from the light. "My friend, where are you? 'Tis Frederick."

While continuing to shield his eyes, John lifted his head.

A man stepped in front of the lantern's light. "Pray forgive me, John, for the light shining in your eyes."

"Can it be? Are you Frederick? Or is this a vain apparition?"

Frederick bent down and stepped into the cell. He went to John and rubbed his hand over his shoulder. "Nay, not an apparition. I have come to take you home. You have been freed!"

"Freed? Nay, this must be a dream."

"'Tis not a dream, John—'tis reality. You are finally free, after two long years."

John pressed his palm against the floor and pushed himself up into a sitting position. "Hope of freedom had nearly fled from me."

"Praise be to God. He inspired Bishop Juxon to have mercy on you and your children." Frederick went around behind John to help him arise. "And now, you are going home!"

"Home. The mere thought of it is wonderful. God did not forget me."

"Nay, He did not, my friend. Now come, let's get you home to your children." Frederick reached under John's arms and began pulling him up. It had been a long time since last John stood. Neither man could stand to his full height in the cell. They did as best they could in the small space. John's legs trembled with the exertion, and he teetered.

Frederick took hold of John's elbow with his left hand while he wrapped his right arm around John's waist. "Lean on me, and I will assist you."

Light from the keeper's lantern shone in the doorway. John could smell Jervis's stink even before he heard his labored breathing.

The two men worked their way out of the cell and into the passageway. John attempted to straighten up but needed the assistance of his friend to accomplish the task. Finally, standing as best he could, John viewed the ugly face of the Keeper.

Jervis leaned heavily onto his crutch as he reached up and wiped the spit which drizzled down his chin. He jabbed his finger at John.

"Don't ye be thinkin' ye 'ave seen th' last o' me. Ye will surely be back, and when ye are—I will be waitin' fer ye."

John squared his shoulders and stood a little taller. He stared down at Jervis. "I pray it never happens."

Jervis stared into the reverend's eyes, took a step back, and raised his lantern high. Turning, he headed down the passageway. The sound of Jervis's gait nettled John's mind.

Thud, clomp. Thud, clomp.

Frederick said, "We'd best follow him so we don't lose our way."

John stumbled along, clinging to his friend's arm. Solitary confinement had taken his last bit of strength.

The narrow corridor seemed to go on for eternity. John held onto Frederick, and the two friends made their way through the long dark passageways, pressing ever onward toward the far-off gate. Once there, he'd be free of the forced hell of these past two years.

They turned a corner, and sunlight spilled down the long hallway. Patterns bounced across the stone floor. A rat scurried past and disappeared into a small hole at the base of the wall—a wall forever wet from the fog which regularly occupied London. John clung to Frederick as they made their way down the passageway.

Fulke stood at the end of the hall and held open the immense outer door. The door which once barred his escape was now his passage to freedom.

A smile spread across the face of the gaoler who had befriended him. John paused in front of Fulke and returned the smile. Gratitude filled every part of his being. He wouldn't have survived solitary without his help.

Fulke's eyes glistened with unshed tears. "Fare thee well, John Lothropp." He stood aside to allow John and Frederick to step through the doorway.

"Fare thee well, Fulke, my man."

Sunlight beat through the gate opening and shone into the holding area. Another gaoler stood off to the side of the cross-thatched metal gate.

Jervis clomped through the door. "Hrrump . . . you bunch o' jackanapes still make me sick." He pushed the door closed and inserted a key into the huge iron lock. The scraping sound it made brought a chill to John's spine. It slowly worked its way up his neck and over his scalp, quickly sending shivers throughout his body.

The Keeper called out to the man standing near the gate, "Raise th' gate."

John tightened his grip on Frederick. "I am ready to leave this place once and for all."

Frederick handed Jervis the last two shillings needed to pass under the gate.

John moved forward and stepped through the opening for the last time. He shielded his eyes from the brightness of the noonday sun. A soft breeze danced across his skin.

The stink of Newgate flowed from the edifice and found its way to the outside world.

Yet, the air smelled sweet—it was the sweet smell of freedom.

Frederick took one of John's arms and guided him toward the carriage. Digory hastened over and took his other arm.

John said, "This looks to be the last of Newgate for me, Digory."

"Aye, that it does, Reverend, that it does."

The two men helped him into the carriage and onto the bench seat. Frederick spread a woolen blanket over him and took the seat opposite. Digory took his seat atop the carriage.

"I fear I must brave another trip to the Thames before returning home, Frederick."

"Aye, John, I greatly fear another trip to the Thames, as well, especially after our last visit."

Even through his exhaustion, John chuckled. "What an unsettling experience, indeed, and not one I would like to repeat. I will not underestimate my weakness this time."

Frederick's shoulders shook with laughter. He gave the carriage ceiling a few taps with his cane, and they were off—the final journey from Newgate.

"I made the necessary arrangements with Elsabeth before coming to retrieve you. She has a bath and some dinner waiting."

"That sounds delightful."

*****

The carriage rocked over the cobblestone roads. John's body swayed with the movement. Though he was eager for his home to come into view, his eyes were heavy and stayed closed most of the journey.

He was anxious to be home with his children. This would be the last time he would allow himself to be taken from them. There must be another way to worship God according to the tenet of his own conscience. He must find the way.

Frederick's words broke his reverie. "We have arrived at your home, John."

Pulled from his thoughts, John opened his eyes to the beautiful sight of his home standing among the willow and oak trees.

Frederick leaned forward. "Let me step down first so I can assist you."

He alighted from the carriage as Digory climbed down and came around to help. Frederick and Digory each reached up, and John took hold of their hands. He placed one foot on the carriage step and let his other foot come down upon the sod. It felt good to have Lambeth earth beneath his feet once again.

The sweet smell of Hannah's lavender filled his senses. A momentary glance at her country garden, and he knew home was standing right before him. John half expected to see Hannah step out from the garden and welcome him home, like she had done so many times in the past.

Frederick and Digory each took one of John's arms. Step by step, John made his way toward the house.

The front door flew open, and Jane ran from the house, calling over her shoulder, "Father is home! Come quickly, children."

Thomas filled the doorway, and next came the younger children. They ran out of the house and circled around John, calling out their greetings.

Frederick said, "Children, the sight of your father is good, though you can tell he is in a weakened state. We must take him to his bedchamber at once."

"Here, Frederick, I can help Father into the house," Thomas said. He stepped forward and put his arm around his father's waist.

"Thank you, Thomas, we could use the help," said Frederick.

Thomas took John's hand and guided it around his shoulders as the other arm held onto his waist. He took the weight of John's body upon his own.

John felt the force of home and loved-ones course through his body. Healing could now commence. "I am grateful for the help, Thom. I am so happy to be home. I love you, my children."

Jane retreated, saying, "Come, children, let us move away and allow our father access to the house."

He moved toward the door. "Home . . . it does not seem real."

Thomas said, "It is real, Father, you are home at long last. We have dearly missed you."

The group headed to the entry door, with John leaning heavily on his oldest son.

They stepped through the portal. John was met with the smell of beeswax candles and the crackle of fire in the hearth. He stopped cold, as thoughts of Hannah burst upon his mind. Tears stung his eyes, and the truth of her death slammed into his chest. Though he knew she was gone, he had tried to push those thoughts into the deep recesses of his mind. Now, he stood here in the house she loved so dearly, realizing she would never again grace its halls.

"Father? How do you fare?" Thomas said.

A sigh escaped John's lips as he lowered his head and steeled himself against despair.

"I fare well enough, Son." John gave him a squeeze. "Please help me to my bedchamber."

Forcing thoughts of Hannah from his mind, John stepped forward. Though still filled with a sense of dread, he headed toward the room he had shared with his beloved.

Barbara rushed to open the door, stepping aside to allow Thomas and their father to enter. They edged their way through the door. Frederick and the other children followed close behind. Thomas helped John sit upon the mattress.

John allowed the bed to take his full weight, and it creaked in response. The sound induced the memory of Hannah dressed in her bedclothes and reclining upon the mattress. It was going to be lonely without her.

Frederick said, "John, do you want help changing for bed?"

"Truthfully, I'll sleep in what I'm wearing. I fear I am too weak to change, yet again."

"As you wish. Come, children, your father needs to lay down and rest."

Benjamin called out, "I didn't get a chance to embrace him!"

"Come here, little one, and let me hold you." John stretched his hands forward.

Benjamin ran into John's arms and knocked him back, flat onto the bed. Even in his weakened state, John laughed and held onto Benjamin.

"Whoa, children, your father is weak, you must be careful. You may hug him tomorrow," said Frederick.

"Nay, Frederick. I cannot bear to sleep without having held each of my children."

"Very well. Be careful, children."

Frederick helped John into a sitting position. The children came forward one by one, each giving their father a gentle embrace. When hugs had been given all around, he shooed the children from the room. John swayed with exhaustion from the day's events. Frederick pulled the bedclothes back, and John lay upon the mattress.

Though John's eyes were already closed, he heard the words of his dear friend.

"I will come on the morrow and see how you fare, John."

"Aye, that is . . ." John's words trailed off as he fell into a deep slumber. Such a slumber as he had not felt in more than two years.

The slumber of a free man.

RIVER THAMES

Mist prevented the evening sun from reaching into the darker regions of London, making it difficult to see. Normally, Thomas would call out for another fare from his wherry or from the dock. However, tonight he moved up onto Thames Street to ply his services there.

"Come this way for the strongest waterman on the Thames!" he shouted into the crowd.

"Nay, this way!" another young man hollered, pushing Thomas to the side.

Thomas shoved past the boy, as well as a few others, making his way onto the street. He continued to holler into the fog, hoping to obtain another fare.

"Come join me on the fastest wherry in London!" he called out.

"You there, I am in need the fastest wherry in London,"

Thomas turned toward the sound and saw a portly, older gentleman emerging from the mist. He held a finger up to Thomas while he stopped to wheeze breath into his lungs.

"Pray, let me catch my breath for a moment." The man struggled through several more inhalations. "Are you the man who claims to have the fastest wherry in London?"

"Aye, that's me."

"I am with three others. We need to be ferried over to the theaters at Bankside," he explained.

"I can ferry you to Bankside. The fare is one pence each to cross the river. If there are three others, it would be a fourpenny bit for all of you to cross."

"I know the fare to cross the river, waterman, and you can trust me when I say there are three others," the man said.

Three figures emerged from the fog. A woman of large stature wore a hat with plumages which swept across the top of her head and over one eye. She constantly batted at them, but the fog had soaked the feathers, and they continued to fall back onto her face.

The second woman stood much taller than her male companion and held onto his arm as she picked her way over the slippery cobblestones while he did his best to keep her upright. Both women wore jewels at their ears and necks.

Once the other three had arrived at Thomas's location, the second man stopped and looked him up and down. "Is this the waterman who will take us over to Bankside?"

The first man replied, "Aye, this be him."

"Let's make haste, young man," he said to Thomas.

The men each had collar ruffs, which must have looked dandy when the night had begun; however, the starch had been soaked by the fog, and they lay in limp masses upon their cloaks. Both women's dresses dragged along the ground, dirt clinging to the hemlines.

Thomas smiled at the two couples. Undoubtedly, they had begun the evening magnificently appareled. The mist had ruined their appearance. He often wondered what compelled the people of London to wear such ridiculous dress, just to be in fashion. His family had opted for simple, less burdensome attire.

He turned to hide the smile playing upon his face. "Please follow me. It would behoove you to stay near me and in a tight bunch. There are many who would have your jewels for themselves this night."

The women pulled their cloaks tightly around their necks, and each man put an arm around his partner. They pressed forward in the crowd and tucked in near Thomas. It was clear the crowd surrounding the dock concerned them.

Thomas reached the top of the stairs and turned back to make sure the four were still with him. "This way," he said, as he headed down the steps toward his wherry.

He continued to push past several other watermen who were calling after their own fares. Thankful to finally reach the bottom step, he moved onto the dock jutting into the river. This was a favorite dock of the watermen, and Thomas had procured many fares by plying his services here. The watermen were an unruly, rowdy bunch. He tried to keep himself separated from the worst of the lot.

"My wherry is right here," Thomas said as he signaled to the group.

The men came forward and began to help the women into the boat while Thomas stepped to the bow to untie the rope from the cleat.

The taller woman was fairly agile. She took the proffered arm of her companion and stepped easily into the wherry, where she sat upon the padded bench seat at the stern.

The larger woman struggled to lift her skirts and step into the craft. Her foot didn't quite make it over the side, and she pressed it upon the edge of the boat. The wherry began to tip toward her. Thomas rushed forward to step aboard and steady the craft. He turned back to assist the woman to the aft padded seat to join her friend.

He asked the two men, "Do you need a hand to board?"

The larger man leaned forward. "Move aside. We are fine on our own."

"As you desire," replied Thomas, stepping back onto the dock. The two men climbed aboard and sat amidships upon the plank seat, facing the women.

Thomas pulled the rope free and coiled it into the bow. He took the forward plank seat, and retrieved one of the oars. He used the oar to carefully push away and guide his boat between the many wherries tied up at the dock. The long, narrow structure of the craft helped him slip between the other boats without too much ado.

Once they were free of the busy dock area, he retrieved the other oar and slipped them both into the forward oarlocks. Facing aft, he rowed the craft into open water. The journey to the other side wasn't far and wouldn't be difficult; however, he must use caution with so much fog.

He could acquire a new fare on the other side, since many people thronged to the theaters. Or even to the bear gardens, where, for some reason which Thomas could not understand, peasants and gentry alike enjoyed the arenas where large dogs were pitted against a single bear.

He let himself settle into the rhythm of rowing, and his thoughts began to drift toward memories of Emma. He pulled on the oars and forgot about the mist for a moment while he lifted and pulled his way across the river. A shout from behind snapped him out of his thoughts.

"Ho there! Watch me side, Thom, ye come close to me wherry," cried Humphrey, or Humph, as they called him.

Thomas was bearing down on another wherry. He pulled hard on the right oar, and the two boats skimmed past each other.

"Hoy, sorry, my man, I failed to see you there."

Humph laughed. "Learn to guide ye craft, my friend, or I won't be forgiving next time around."

Thomas smiled and nodded to his friend. "And you'd best watch your back, or I will steal a fare from under your nose."

"Ha, tha' be the day, Thom." Humphrey pressed his oars into the water and guided his wherry toward the dock.

"That'll be a good day, indeed," Thomas called out. Humph was one of the few friends he had on the river. Most watermen were crude and hardened and didn't care to make friends.

The larger man had turned to watch the close encounter. "Waterman! Please watch your rowing. You almost caused a collision."

"Aye," was all Thomas could reply. He swept his oars into the water and continued across the river. It was a busy night, and Thomas must not let his guard down again.

168

The women passengers fluffed their hair and adjusted their clothing, primping for their night in the theater district. They paid him no mind, which was nothing new to Thomas.

Bankside came into view. Pulling in one oar, he used the other to maneuver between the many boats already tied up. He noted an empty slot between two other crafts, and he slipped his wherry between them, coming to rest against the dock.

The man who'd arranged the trip turned to Thomas. "We do not need assistance. Hold your craft against the dock, and we'll disembark on our own." He stepped from the boat and assisted his female partner. The other man did the same.

"Here is your fourpenny bit." The larger man held out the coin without looking down. Thomas quickly reached for it before it was dropped into the water. The four walked down the dock, never glancing back.

Thomas sat in his boat, watching those he'd ferried over. He chuckled at the mess their haughty attire had become. Yet, they still walked proud, as if they were dressed like the King. He bristled at the way they'd treated him, as though he were a peasant and not worthy of their consideration.

Their days would be filled with ease and comfort, in sharp contrast to his own hardworking days. He longed to take Emma to the theater. What theater would they seek out? The Swan? The Globe? Perhaps, the Rose? What play would they see? He had no idea what currently played at the theaters. It was of no benefit to think such things. He couldn't spare even a penny for entertainment these days.

He grabbed the rope and stood ready to tie up and search for another fare. At the end of the dock, a tall, slender man stood with his back facing Thomas. The length and cut of his blonde hair made the fellow seem to be Edmund. The man turned to stare down the street. Thomas watched him. Yes, it was Edmund.

"Edmund, Edmund!" Thomas hastily waved his hands in the air. "Over here."

A wide smile spread across Edmund's face. Thomas smiled and waved higher. "Hey, oh!" he called out.

Edmund's smile broadened, and he waved higher. It was then Thomas realized Edmund didn't wave to him, but to someone down the lane. He followed the path of Edmund's gaze, and noticed he waved to a beautiful young woman, dressed in rich blue satin. Thomas watched in disbelief as the two came together.

Edmund offered the beauty his arm, and she tucked her hand into it. He leaned down and said something only she could hear. The woman threw her head back in laughter, laying a hand upon his chest.

Stunned, Thomas lowered his hands. Edmund planted a kiss upon the woman's lips, put an arm around her shoulders, and headed off toward the theater district.

There was something about Edmund which had always bothered Thomas, but he'd never been able to catch a hold of it. Edmund seemed like a gentleman. Their father had given permission for the courtship of Edmund and Jane, yet now, Thomas saw there was more to Edmund than he had ever imagined. He would have to speak with his father.

What about Jane? He must find a way to help Jane with Edmund's broken promise to her, but most importantly, he must find a way to help with her broken heart.

He must return home immediately to warn Jane. Stepping back into the boat, he threw in the rope, grabbed the oars, and quickly hauled them over the side. He cut them into the water with no care of what he hit or who he angered.

Consumed by thoughts of his sister and the pain she would have learning of Edmund's betrayal, Thomas continued to paddle toward his home dock. He dodged several wherries and other craft scurrying about the river on this busy evening.

He rounded the long bend in the river and his home dock come into view. Digging in with his oars, he pressed forward.

Dig deeper, Thomas, you must find Jane.

He felt the burn in his shoulders. He pushed the wherry hard and aimed toward the side of the river. Plowing through the water, he pressed forward until he bumped the boat against the side of the dock. He jumped from the boat with rope in hand, tied off on a cleat, and ran toward home.

Thoughts jumbled in his mind as he paced his breathing with his footfalls, pushing his way through pedestrians along the walk. When he came to the little lane leading to his house, he turned left and continued on.

The Tudor house he called home came into view. He picked up his pace and ran to the door, lifted the latch, and pushed inward in one smooth step.

He rushed into the hall and stopped at the hearth. Leaning forward, he gasped air into his lungs. Jane was not in the hall. A fire burned in the hearth and filled the room with warmth, too much warmth for Thomas. He headed back out the door and breathed in the sweet air of Lambeth. He wondered where she had taken herself. As his breathing slowed, he contemplated her location. Had she told him of an outing she was taking today? Mayhap she was in the garden.

Making his way around the north side of the house, he trotted to the back in search of Jane. She was not in the garden. Where had she gotten herself this evening?

Thomas grabbed a chair, sat down, and leaned back. He pulled in soothing breaths of air and closed his eyes. How was he going to tell Jane of Edmund's betrayal? She would surely be outraged and demand their courtship immediately cease.

A cool breeze fluttered through the willows. He lay back against the chair and closed his eyes, resting from his long run home. He longed for Jane to return so he might speak with her. Worried he had come home prematurely and given up additional fares for the evening, Thomas began to fret about her absence.

Jane—where are you?

As Thomas contemplated heading back out to the river in search of more fares, he heard the sound of voices wafting across the breeze.

He jumped to his feet and ran around to the front of the house. Jane and the three youngest boys walked toward the house, laughing and singing a song he recognized from bedtime rituals.

"Jane . . . Jane." He waved frantically as he ran toward the group.

"Oh, Thomas, you have returned early today. I do not have supper ready quite yet."

"Worry not, Jane. I must speak with you right away."

"What troubles you, Brother?"

"I beg of you, some time alone. Let's go to the garden."

"Boys, please go inside, Thomas and I will be in soon."

Samuel called out, "I will beat you both to the door!"

"Not if I get there first," cried Joseph. The boys took off running toward the house, with little Benjamin bringing up the rear.

"Quickly, Jane, lest I burst from the need to speak."

"Oh my, Thom, you are frightening me now."

"Hurry, let's go back to the garden."

Thomas and Jane made their way around the house. He guided her to one of the chairs, and he took the other.

His sister had become a dear friend, and he dug for the strength to tell her what he'd seen. She seemed fragile, but in reality, he had seen her show great strength and courage through the past two years.

"Thom, I am growing more nervous by the moment. Pray tell what you came to say."

"Jane, I'm not sure how to tell you this, so I will just say it. I ferried a group to the theater district tonight, and afterward I planned to seek out another fare." He lowered his gaze to the ground. Could he bring himself to say the words? Raising his head, he met his sister's worried stare.

"I stepped from my wherry to tie off on a—"

"Oh, Thom, please. Get to the gist of the tale."

He fretted over what he must tell her. Unable to sit any longer, he rose from the chair and began to pace in front of her.

"Thomas, I beg of you, stop your pacing and tell me."

"Very well. I saw Edmund standing down at the end of the dock. I supposed he saw me as well, but I soon realized he stared toward someone else." Thomas pulled in a slow breath of air. "It was a woman, Jane."

He watched his sister to gauge her reaction.

"Oh, Thom, you worry over nothing. It was most likely his sister, or mayhap a cousin."

"Nay, it was not. I watched him kiss her on the lips, and pull her to his arms, only to escort her towards the theater district."

"Thomas—I am sure you are mistaken. It must have been his sister or a cousin, and he must have kissed her on the cheek. Edmund would never betray me with another woman. We are officially courting."

"I am not mistaken." He watched Jane and thought about what to say next. Should he vow his undying protection to her? Or should he act more as a confidante and offer her comfort?

"Thom, Edmund loves me. I have no doubt."

"Mayhap Edmund loves to be with you because you are beautiful."

"Thomas! Do not speak such things of my intended. I do not appreciate you alarming me this way."

"Jane, you cannot continue your courtship with him."

"I can—and I will. You may have your worries about him. However, I trust and believe in him. I plan to be his wife."

"Nay, you must end this courtship right away."

"Thomas, you are not Father. He has returned home and is now responsible for my courtship. I appreciate your concern for me. Nevertheless, I have no intention of ending my relationship with Edmund. Please do not talk to Father regarding this. He is still weak and needs his rest."

Jane arose and stomped toward the front of the house. Thomas sat in stunned silence.

He thought back over events of the night and began to question what he had witnessed. Did he see what he supposed? Did Edmund kiss the woman on her lips? Or was Jane correct and it was on the cheek? It had been foggy at Bankeside. Perhaps his vision had been compromised.

Nonetheless, there was still something off about Edmund. He would watch him closely to judge if he was a good man who truly loved Jane, or whether he was just a man who needed many women to feed his own self-serving ego.

Time would tell.

LAMBETH

John reveled in the pleasing warmth on this rare day of sunshine in Lambeth. He sat in the garden and enjoyed a rest while awaiting word of supper. Cold's icy fingers had slowly eased their grip on him in the days since his long-awaited liberty from prison. Heat infused every joint in his aching body and brought him a sense of well-being he hadn't felt in years.

A lark sang its lovely tune high in the willow trees. Tall branches swayed in the gentle breeze, bringing the scent of Hannah's herb and flower gardens through the air and into his mind. He closed his eyes and let the peaceful warmth of the garden bring rest to his weary soul.

A voice brought John from his brief respite. "Never before have I beheld a more peaceful scene."

John opened his eyes and turned his head to note his friend Frederick standing at the other side of the garden, his tall capotain hat sitting jauntily upon his head.

"Well, that was so, yet the spell has been broken." John smiled and waved Frederick over. He heard a deep chuckle rumble from Frederick's chest as his friend covered the ground between them.

Frederick removed his hat and set it upon a small round table. "It appears the sun has scrubbed the last bit of Newgate from you."

"Sunshine does much to mend an ailing body. Jane and Barbara have been tending to me as well. How do you fare, my friend?"

"I am as well as can be expected. It is good to see you growing stronger. However, I must confess I come with a purpose greater than merely a friendly visit. I have a prospect for your future."

"A prospect? What sort of prospect?"

Frederick pulled a chair closer to John and emitted a low groan while easing himself down. With a deep chuckle, he said, "It gets more difficult to move with each passing day. We grow old, do we not?"

"Aye, that we do. Time spent in prison has been unkind to us both. I fear our years grow even shorter. Now, curiosity has gotten the best of me. Pray tell, what did you come here to say?"

Frederick wiped a hand across his face and heaved a sigh. "Concern for you has me at odds with the request. Though there is a great need, I worry for your welfare."

"I have much faith in you, my friend. I understand you would ask nothing onerous of me."

Frederick watched the ground and rubbed a hand across his brow. "The church elders have prevailed upon me to ask about your possible return to the position as their minister."

John pulled in a slow breath. He longed to teach the word of God once again. However, it was still illegal for him to do so in this country. On the other hand, many in the congregation had remained loyal to him throughout his time at Newgate, and they awaited his return. He also worried what dangers rejoining the congregation might bring to his family, yet he must somehow provide for them. Would they support a decision for him to preach again?

Frederick continued, "Mayhap talk of 'nothing onerous' was too soon?"

"Mayhap, indeed. What does it entail?"

"They desire you to reorganize the congregation and teach them more of the Bible and God's ways. They have enough money in the

176

coffers to use as a donation for your services and to provide for your needs."

"I must admit, I do long to meet with the congregation and, yes, I need help providing for my family's needs. My foremost concern persists. It remains illegal to hold a meeting outside the Church of England."

"Aye, that is true, John. Yet, it is not illegal for a group of friends and family to meet together in common love and understanding, even if talk of God comes as a result of the gathering. It is also not illegal for friends to donate money to care for a friend's needs, especially when such a friend has recently been released from prison."

John considered the man who had become his confidante and counselor. "Perchance, do you remember there were enemies of the Jews who tried to keep them from rebuilding the temple at Jerusalem?" Frederick nodded his head.

John continued, "Nehemiah armed them and said, '*And I looked, and rose up, and said unto the nobles, and to the rulers, and to the rest of the people, Be not ye afraid of them: remember the Lord, which is great and terrible, and fight for your brethren, your sons, and your daughters, your wives, and your houses.*'" [iii]

"We are indeed in a fight for our religious freedoms," said Frederick.

John pulled in a deep breath and said, "Aye, that we are. I would consider meeting with the elders to further discuss the congregation."

"To be sure, they will be thrilled. I will pass this information along to them and arrange a meeting."

"Discretion is a must."

"I will do so cautiously, so as not to bring anything to the attention of Archbishop Laud."

John closed his eyes and rested against the back of the chair. "Frederick, do you ever wonder if the King will allow us the freedom to worship God the way our hearts believe to be true?"

Frederick thought for a moment. "I fear that will require a new king."

The lark's song brought John's attention to the trees once again. He turned his attention to the high branches where they sang. "I have recently been pondering the New World. Many have found refuge there in New England. Mayhap it is worth considering."

"An interesting thought, indeed." A gust of wind blew across the garden. Frederick tugged at his wig, adjusting it on his head. "I have heard much about New England as an option for religious freedom. Yet, it is a wild place and does not have much to offer in the way of civilization."

"Still, I feel it warrants further consideration."

"I concur, John. There are those with information regarding this. I will speak to them and see what I can learn."

"Thank you for seeking out the particulars. I'll await further information before I draw any conclusions."

"It is good, John, I will take my leave now. Enjoy the sunshine while you can." Frederick arose to go.

John watched the man who was his dearest friend. "I still cannot believe I am rightly free. Nothing can truly express my thanks for your efforts to procure my liberty."

"My friend, while I do understand and appreciate your gratitude, you do not need to continue in your thanksgiving. You saved my soul from condemnation when you taught me the ways of the Lord. It was little I did, in comparison."

John bore down on the emotions threatening to overwhelm him. He leaned forward and pressed against the chair and began to rise.

Frederick rubbed a hand across John's shoulder. "Nay, my friend, stay where you are. Rest and get well. I will take my leave now."

John lay back against the chair and smiled at his friend. "I am happy to stay where I am. I will be interested in what you learn from the elders, as well as what information you find regarding New England."

"I will learn what I can." Frederick arose and retrieved his hat from the table and placed it upon his head.

"Until next time."

John watched him as he made his way across the garden and disappeared around the corner of the house. He settled back into the chair and closed his eyes, reveling in the heat of the day.

Contemplations of resuming with the congregation filled his mind. While preaching the word of God had been his lifelong purpose, he must also keep the needs of his family foremost in his mind. No decision would be made without their input and support.

The sound of footfalls brought John out of his thoughts, and he wondered what Frederick had forgotten.

"You have brought me enough worry for one day."

"Of what do you speak, Father? I bring you only good tidings."

John snickered, and opened his eyes to look into the smiling face of his eldest son.

"Ah, it is you, my boy. I thought it was Frederick come back to pester me a while longer."

"I passed him just now as he came around the house." Thomas stood near the chair that had recently been vacated by Frederick. "I came to say, Jane has our supper ready, and she asked me to retrieve you."

"Aye, those are good tidings indeed. I am ready to sup."

John slid himself to the end of the seat and pressed against the arms of the chair. He began to rise, but lost strength and lay back against the seat.

"Let me help you, Father." Thomas held his hands out toward John, who reached up and clasped them.

"Are you prepared to rise?" Thomas said.

"I believe so."

John tightened his grip and was pulled up and held in place by Thomas, who had been but a thin and wiry youth when John was first hauled away, and was now a strong, robust young man. So much had changed while he'd wasted away in Newgate.

"Are you able to walk on your own, Father, or do you need an arm?"

"I do believe I came make it, and it will aid in strengthening me. Though having you near is good, Thom."

179

*****

Sunlight filtered through the bedchamber window, setting off patterns of light dancing across the wall. Gauzy curtains billowed into the room from the small opening at the sill. John lay upon the bed in his room, mulling over the past few weeks.

He pondered the consequence of his decision to rejoin the congregation. Emotions fought against one another while he tussled with the notion of preaching outside the Church. It was still illegal in the eyes of the King.

For now, John believed God wanted him to return to the congregation and lead them once again. Thoughts of whether or not directing the Independents was truly his lot in life regularly trickled through his mind. He felt perhaps God had additional plans for him. Until the time when God enlightened him to go in another direction, John would rejoin the Independents.

He arose from the bed and went to a bowl of water sitting atop the sideboard. Reaching both hands into the liquid, he leaned down and splashed it upon his face, washing the night from his eyes. A small towel lay to the side of the bowl, and he used it to dry off.

Fabric billowed across his arm and drew his attention to the window. He strode over and pushed the fabric aside to open the window further so he might gaze across the landscape of Lambeth.

Many of the people living down these lanes were members of the Independent congregation. They had fought a hard battle against the tyranny of the King. He could not let them down now.

He turned back into the room and went to the trunk which housed much of his clothing. Riffling through pants, shirts, and undergarments, he found the clothing he'd previously worn as reverend of the Independent congregation, and he pulled them from the trunk to arrange them upon the bed.

John tugged his sleeping shirt off and laid it on the bed. He gripped the linen shirt and drew it over his head and down around his chest.

He sat and pulled white stockings onto his feet, then his black breeches. He rose to his feet and secured them at his waist.

Lifting the brocade waistcoat from the bed, he slipped his arms through the openings and pulled it forward, buttoning it closed. He drew on the long black coat and reached into the coat sleeves to pull the lace shirt cuffs down around his wrists.

His fingers rubbed over the fine embroidery which Hannah had so lovingly worked on his coat. It edged the front and wound around the neckline and cuffs. The image of her beautiful face flooded his mind, and he stopped a moment to relish her memory.

The lace cravat lay on the bed, and he tied it around his neck, with its lace fluffed onto his chest. He sat and pulled on his shoes, buckling them at each side.

Rubbing a hand across his head, he realized there was no need to comb his closely cropped hair. He'd begun to grow in his beard, but he enjoyed life without long hair or a wig. Perhaps he'd keep it short from now on.

He was dressed and ready for his first day back with his congregation.

The Bible, of which he'd regularly read for comfort since Hannah's death, sat upon the sideboard and to the side of the water bowl. He arose and went to it, letting his fingers rub across the leather cover. Every space in this room held remembrances of her.

John took hold of the Bible and held it to his chest. Kneeling down on one knee, he bowed his head and gave thanks to God for this opportunity to return to what he loved, preaching His word. He wrestled with thoughts of the New World and asked God for direction. He began to close his prayer with pleadings for the safety and welfare of his children. And lastly, he asked for the pain and loss of his beloved wife to fade, but he never wanted her memory to die.

Rising, he strode across the room and, grasping the handle, he pulled the door inward. The great hall lay before him. A warm fire crackled in the hearth. Jane sat upon the small chair and worked her embroidery. She turned and watched John's eyes.

181

"Oh, Father, you look wonderful in your attire." She stood and laid the needlework on the chair and came toward him, her arms outstretched. A smile spread slowly across his face, and he pulled her into his arms. With those simple words, Jane showed her continued support of his decision to return to the congregation.

Today was the beginning of a new life for John. The beginning of a new life for his family. The beginning of a new life for them all.

LAMBETH

Dew borrowed light from the sunbeams of a new dawn, touching each flower and plant with the sparkle of morning light. John walked through Hannah's gardens, running his fingers over damp leaves and purple blossoms, leaving a shower of droplets in his wake.

Fruit trees mingled with blueberry, raspberry, and black currant bushes. Lavender, pinks, peonies, and foxgloves scented the air. Gentle blossoms of the lavender had been Hannah's favorite, not only because of medicinal purposes, but because of the fragrant aroma.

Herbs of all kinds ran along the borders of the garden, spilling out onto a gravel path dividing the beds into four squares, a center circle joining each square.

In days past, John frequently found Hannah in the gardens, where she'd lovingly nipped and trimmed her plants, until eventually she'd created the paradise which surrounded him today. Jane had learned well the art of gardening. Hannah's gardens had been saved from the brink of extinction.

A riot of scents filled the air and beckoned memories of Hannah's dark eyes and loving smile. Her image was so clear, he longed to reach out and run his fingers down her long blonde hair. The ache of her death still lingered inside of him, though the sting had begun to subside.

Lavender's strong aroma caught his attention. John pulled the scissors from his pocket, leaning down to cut a few stalks. He fancied vases of them in the hall. In addition, he enjoyed dried stalks in every room, where they could chase away the musty smell of winter.

In May, after he'd been released from prison, a bond had been issued requiring his presence at Trinity to officially pledge his loyalty to the Church. He had not appeared in answer to the bond. He would never again vow himself to the Church of England.

Gathering the lavender in his arms, he made his way around the side of the house and to the entry door. The heavy metal latch succumbed to his pressure, and he pushed the door inward. His children were scattered around the hall, and he thanked God he was home.

Jane sat upon the smaller stuffed chair next to an old oak table, near the hearth. Though it was morning, the few house windows shed little light inside. The table held a double candlestick, and she worked her embroidery in its dim light. Benjamin lay against her legs, snoring in slumber.

Thomas sat on the floor next to the table using the candlelight as he poured over one of his maps. Johnny sat beneath the window, his back leaning against the wall, engaged in his favorite distraction of reading. Barbara leaned over his shoulder, reading the same book. Samuel and Joseph played Naughts and Crosses with items they'd found around the house and in the garden.

One by one, the children became aware of him.

"Father?" asked Thomas. "Is there something you need right now?"

"Nay, Son. Before me in this room rests everything I presently need."

Jane smiled up to her father. "May I help you with the lavender?"

"Perchance, is there a pewter jug I might use?"

Jane gestured toward the kitchen area. "Aye, one sits upon the cupboard. Water is in the crock, as well." Jane laid her embroidery down on the table and stood. "Let me take care of those for you, Father."

"Thank you, my dear. I love the smell of your mother's lavender in the house." He placed the stalks into Jane's outstretched hands. "I will retire to my bed for a morning nap."

"What a splendid idea. When you arise, we can eat our midday meal."

John leaned to kiss her upon the cheek and withdrew to his bedchamber. Sunlight filtered through the small latticed window, sparkles bouncing across the floor. He stretched out on the bed, bringing his hand up to lie across his eyes.

Thoughts of his present reality rummaged through his mind. He understood his calling in life was to serve God. However, the laws of this land required loyalty to a church he no longer believed to be genuine in its teachings. What of his failure to appear before the courts? How long would he be able to evade Archbishop Laud's minions? If John continued with his congregation, he would remain in jeopardy of being arrested for the same crime, as well as for nonappearance at court.

England was his homeland, and he loved her. Qualms of self-exile brought anguish to his soul and worry to his mind.

Many before him had chosen such exile. Reports of Plymouth Colony in the Americas were encouraging, though the colonists had suffered great loss of human life the first year. They now had a thriving community which abided by a similar belief system to which John subscribed. They lived a peaceful life, out of view of the King and the Bishop.

If he were to choose migration to the Americas, how would he afford passage for his family? And what of his extended family who remained in England? Would he ever see them again?

Sleep threaded its way through his reflections and bid his eyes close in slumber. He felt its alluring call while worries over life faded away and led to its sweet release.

*****

A heavy thud jolted John from his nap and interrupted his peaceful lumber. He jumped from the bed, strode across the room, and stepped out into the hall to investigate the loud disturbance. The children stood facing the entry door, each bearing a look of concern on their face.

"Easy, children. Let me see who bothers us this day."

Thomas followed him across the room to the entry door. John lifted the latch and pulled the door open in one swift move.

Standing before him was Gryffyn Cane. John's head spun with thoughts.

How was this man here before him, and not still at Newgate? How had he managed such a quick release?

"Hello, John Lothropp," said his former friend.

"How came you to be here?" His mind reeled in frustration, and he waited for the answer.

Gryffyn Cane glowered down at John. "I told you I had connections. Someone paid my debts for me and I was released. It was a true friend who didn't want me rotting away in prison."

John's heart drummed in his chest. He thought he had been rid of Gryffyn Cane for good. Now he was here, once again. "Pray tell, why have you come?"

"I come here today so I can witness this." Gryffyn Cane stepped back and gestured to his right. A man had been standing behind Gryffyn.

The man stepped forward, holding a letter toward John. "I am a courier from the offices of the Most Reverend and Right Honorable Archbishop William Laud. I so deliver this summons for your appearance at the Palace of Westminster."

John took the letter and ran his finger over the wax seal of the High Commission which was pressed onto the paper.

Gryffyn Cane shoved his way in front of the courier. "I wanted to be present when the great John Lothropp received his summons to appear before Archbishop William Laud."

Thomas moved forward and through the doorway. "You had better leave these premises and never return."

Gryffyn Cane inclined away from Thomas and took a stride back.

John struggled with anxious breaths. He placed a hand on his son's arm. "Wait a moment, Thom. I have a question for him." He sucked in his breath and leveled a stare at Gryffyn Cane. "How did you come to know of this summons?"

Gryffyn Cane moved forward once again but slanted a wary glance toward Thomas. "I am the reason such a bond came to be. When we were both at Newgate, I warned you I had more power and connections than you could ever imagine. For now, I am satisfied to know you received this summons. For you see, John, you will pay for your crimes against the Church. You *will* be in prison before the end of the year."

"What gives you the right to decide whether or not I have committed crimes against the Church?"

Gryffyn Cane set his eyes upon John and stepped in closer. "I have personally witnessed gatherings where you preached the word of God to a group of people. It has been deemed illegal by our sovereign King and our honorable Archbishop. That makes it a treasonous crime against the country, as well as against the Church."

Being wary of this man who accused him of high treason, John studied him to see if anything remained of the person John had once called his friend. Anger and resentment still coursed through him for what he'd suffered over the past two years, but he pushed it aside and tried to understand.

"Gryffyn, I profess only to be a man of God. Therefore, I cannot understand what is truly in your heart. Only God can know your mind and what has actually possessed you to turn your hatred onto me. Certainly, it is not what you have told me regarding your mother. There is something much deeper and more sinister behind your actions."

He continued, "Most likely, I will never come to understand how a trusted friend, whom I greatly loved, could come to be the angry, bitter, twisted man I see before me. I hope someday you will genuinely come to understand the pain you have caused me and my family—my wife died, my children were left alone for two years. Not to mention, many of us suffered great hardship and misery in prison because of your traitorous act when you informed the Church of our whereabouts."

John stepped through the doorway and reached forward, but Gryffyn knocked his hands away. John forced himself to respire in slow, even breaths. When he felt in control of his anger, he leveled a stare at his tormentor.

"I will labor to wait at the throne of Grace for the time when I can forgive you for the egregious pain and suffering you have caused. At this moment, let me beseech and entreat you in the grace of the Lord to stop your battle against me and my family. By your jealousies and fears, you have inclined to secretly plot against me. Leave us be, and with greater expediency press forward in your own life. Take yourself away from this house and never cast a shadow upon these lands again."

Hatred and anger crossed over Gryffyn's face. He stretched forth his hands and lunged toward John, who drew up an arm in protection. Thomas dove at Gryffyn and tackled him to the ground.

John called out, "Nay, stop this at once."

Thomas rolled Gryffyn onto the grass and pressed a hand against his head, grinding the side of his face into the ground.

Gryffyn said, "Get off of me, you nasty little boy."

"I beg of you both, please stop and arise," said John.

Thomas released Gryffyn's head and stood, leaving him lying on the soil.

Gryffyn rose to his feet and spat dirt upon the ground. "You will pay for this."

John stood with his feet set apart, his open hands raised in a gesture of frustration.

"I have been overly patient with you up until now, Gryffyn. I am a man of God and do not want to be harsh with you. Yet you have given me no choice. Do not come near me again. Thomas, let us escort this man from our land."

John reached for Gryffyn's arm, but before he could seize it, Gryffyn jerked it free and pulled it back, preparing to strike. Thomas rushed in and seized the fist. John caught hold of the foul man's other arm. Together they dragged him backward down the walk.

Gryffyn twisted and fought against them. John pulled the gate open and sent Gryffyn flying backward through the opening. He came to rest on the gravel lane, landing on his backside.

John took a step through the gate and held up his index finger. "Now, listen to me when I say this. Step away from this family, this house, and this land. Never come here again, or a watchman will be called to arrest you for harassment and trespassing."

Gryffyn rolled onto one knee and pushed himself up from the ground. He brushed dirt from his pants and combed a hand through his straggly hair.

"I lowered myself to be your friend, *Reverend*—and I use that term loosely. What makes you think *you* are the one who is loved by God? Where is God? Is He here now? Does He protect you from the evils of this world? Clearly, the answer is no."

"God is forever present in the lives of one and all. If you do not feel close to Him, it is not He who moved away, but you. You have chosen to contend with me because I understand my place with God—and because I have a family."

Gryffyn lowered his head and scowled at John, spitting through his teeth as he spoke. "We are opponents, you and I. Which of us fights the good fight? To whom does God speak? You? Me? Why do you believe it is you, John? Because you say it is so? You contend against Him and lead people astray with your teachings."

Struggling with the evil he perceived in Gryffyn's eyes, John pulled in a few ragged breaths. "At one time, I regarded you as my friend. I should now be disheartened to ever see your face again. But yet, and here lies the stone by which I stumble, I am greatly pained because of your soul. In the end, I will pray God forgives you for the trespasses committed against me and my family."

"Surely you jest with your words. Are they meant to save my soul from everlasting hell and damnation? It is too late, I am already there. Why do you think I fight for the King and the Bishop? I wage the war against you, hoping to save my own soul."

The sound of footfalls upon gravel caught John's attention. He scanned down the lane and saw two watchmen moving swiftly in their direction. Thankfully, he and Thomas would have some help. The watchmen drew close, and John recognized the men who kept order in Lambeth.

"Your time here is over, Gryffyn Cane. I ask you to leave of your own volition right now, or I will be forced to bring those watchmen down upon you."

John called to the watchmen. "Sirs, if you please, may I speak with you a moment?"

The watchmen came to stand near John. The taller one said, "To be sure, Reverend, we are your most humble servants and here to offer aid."

John lifted his brows and turned toward Gryffyn. "The time has come for a choice. Will you go peacefully, or must I prevail upon these watchmen to escort you from my land?"

Gryffyn directed a hardened glare at John. "In reality, you are the one with a choice to make. The summons has been served. Either you can appear in court and pledge your loyalty to the church, or risk arrest, once again."

John turned to the watchmen. "It appears I do need your aid in ridding my land of this person."

"We are here to serve you, Reverend Lothropp."

Gryffyn spat upon the ground at John's feet. "I will go . . . *Reverend*. Yet, do not suppose for a moment that I am gone. When you least expect my return, there will I be."

A tremble ran the length of John's spine. He watched his former friend spin on his heels and tramp down the lane, the watchmen close behind. The courier ran in the opposite direction, and John didn't blame him.

"Do you see how Gryffyn's anger and resentment has warped his image of reality and brought about his own unhappiness?"

Thomas nodded, and John motioned him to follow as he turned back up the walk. "It is time we read the contents of the summons and determine the danger Gryffyn has, once again, induced into our lives."

The children remained clustered around the entry door.

"My dears, I beg of you forgiveness for what happened. How do you all fare?"

Jane said, "We are well. Mostly, we worry for you and Thom." She reached out to pass John the summons he had dropped in the scuffle.

"Ah . . . thank you, Jane." He smiled to each of his children. "Worry not for us, children. Perchance, might Thom and I have a moment longer? Thom and I need to take care of something, afterwards we will come back to have a family talk."

Jane shooed the children into the house. "We will await your return by the hearth, Father."

John signaled for Thomas to follow him again, as he led him away from the house, past the trees, and to a place where the sun shone its brightest. John read aloud the words written on the outside of the folded paper.

To John Lothropp at Lambeth be this delivered.

From the Court of the High Commission at the Palace of Westminster.

Breaking the wax seal, John opened the letter and continued reading aloud.

From his Honorable Archbishop William Laud, by the grace of God and the King of England, to John Lothropp.

John Lothropp is commanded to appear before the High Commission at the next court date to swear an oath of loyalty to the Church and to swear he will not appear at any conventicles. We must insist that you, as an enemy of us and them, appear and so swear to this commission.

And I, William Laud, Archbishop of Canterbury, at the request of the rest, have, for us and for them too who are here at Westminster, affix my seal on the twelfth day of the month of June, in the year of our Lord, one thousand six hundred and thirty-four.

The mere thought of once again appearing before William Laud infused his soul with anguish. Control slithered from his grasp, but he made every effort to drag it back.

Hope of remaining in England, in anticipation of the day when the King would reverse his decree regarding religious gatherings, was gone. Prison loomed over him once again.

"Thomas, this summons brings me to a topic I've pondered since I was released from prison."

"What do you mean, Father?"

John had considered multiple ways he could broach the subject with his family. He now felt being forthright with Thomas was the best way, given the circumstances. He turned to face his son, laid a hand on each shoulder, and stared him straight in the eyes.

"I believe the time has come for us to migrate to New England."

Thomas took a step backward, and John saw the overall shock which registered on his face.

"New England? Pray tell if you are flippant with me right now," said Thomas.

"Nay, I do not speak in jest."

Thomas rubbed a hand across his brow, pulling it down over his face and beard as he considered John's words. "You know how I have longed to sail the seas. I have dreamed of exploring new lands and meeting all manner of people. Even so, the thought of leaving our homeland forevermore is something I never considered."

"It is a disquieting thought. Yet, the time has come for us to renew our commitment and faith in Jesus Christ. We must stand for what is good and true in this world. We must go forward being stronger, nobler, and more courageous."

He continued, "Paul told the Ephesians, '*Put on the whole armour of God, that ye may be able to stand against the wiles of the devil. For we wrestle not against flesh and blood, but against principalities, against powers, against the rulers of the darkness of this world, against spiritual wickedness in high places.*'" [iv] We must stand tall for Jesus Christ."

John paused to gauge Thomas's feelings about the declaration. Deep emotions passed over his son's face.

"Father, I desire to stand tall for Jesus Christ as well."

"Your words fill my heart with love. I honor you for your faith and courage."

"Can we not leave England and migrate to Holland, where so many have previously gone? Many Englishmen live there, well beyond the King's reach."

John laid a hand on Thomas's shoulder and leaned into him. "Son, I was born an Englishman, and I will die an Englishman. I surmise New England is better than no England at all."

"Such a sentiment rings true with me as well. I will go with you to the New World, Father."

"I thank you for your faith and trust in me, Thom. Speedily, we must make arrangements for passage aboard a ship. It will be difficult because there are so many in our family. We must sell our possessions and gather the necessary funds to purchase provisions for the trip, as well as for survival once we arrive in the Americas. We must also procure the various documents we need to pass the port. I will speak with Frederick about his connections to the shipping industry."

"Father! I know someone who owns a shipping company. His name is Barnaby. I ferried him and his family home late one night. He offered me a job on one of his ships. Mayhap he can aid us."

"Wonderful! Will you take your wherry to Wapping and speak with him?"

"I will make haste, come morning."

Pride and gratitude filled John's heart. Where Thomas had once been a little boy looking to him for guidance, he now stood a man. Not in front of John, not behind John, but beside him—two men working as one for the common good of their family.

Time hastened ever onward, ticking toward the day a warrant would be issued for his arrest.

It was time to set sail for the New World.

LAMBETH

The river walk was awash with people pushing and jostling along the street. They crowded into different shops or around peddler's carts. The smell of raw meat, bread, and spices, along with overripe fruits and vegetables, filled the air. Thomas pushed his way through the throngs of people while scanning each shop and each peddler's cart.

A din of people hawked their wares and called out to would-be buyers, filling the air with a jangle of talk.

"Very fine stuffs in all quantities," said a tall, thin man. He manned a peddler cart filled with a variety of items from cloth to fine China, to scarves and fans.

"Do you lack cloth to sew your clothes?" called out a plump woman. She paced back and forth in front of a store where all types of fabrics were sold.

Thomas wasn't sure what he might find for Emma that would help him convince her of his plans for their future. Perhaps a brooch, a small necklace, or some earrings would do. His leather purse hung from his belt and held the bit of money he'd been able to set aside for such a purchase.

It wasn't much, but he hoped it would suffice. With all his heart, he longed to marry Emma. Today he'd set off on a mission to seek after her hand. First, he must find a gift with which to honor her. Second, he must ask her father's permission for betrothal to his only daughter.

When their father had expressed thoughts of migration, Thomas felt it was the correct choice for the family. Even so, he wanted Emma to come with him, and he hoped Emma's father would likewise join them in sailing to the New World.

A pungent peddler's cart filled with spices and herbs drove him quickly away from the area. Drawing in deep breathes of air, he was able to clear the cloying smells from his mind and continue his trek through the other shops along the river walk.

He hadn't much to offer to Emma. However, he planned to vigorously work in the New World to build a house for her—in preparation to building a new life *with* her.

Surely, she'd seen how dedicated a worker he was. He'd worked hard to grow his wherry business, and it was a big success. Thomas was leaving it for Johnny to take over to use in helping pay for his schooling.

Thomas was proud of his daring younger brother Johnny, who planned to stay behind in England and live with cousins so he might attend Oxford University, which was the same school their father had attended. As yet, there was no university in the New World.

A small shop, of which Thomas hadn't previously noticed, sat tucked between two others. He stepped inside and noted rows of shelving surrounding the small room.

Where most shops usually stocked a certain type of goods, this one was stuffed with all manner of trinkets, baubles, and household items. Smells of fragrant spices once again filled his nostrils, but this time the milder aromas did not overwhelm his senses.

The confusion of items in every nook and cranny of the shop exasperated him, and he turned to leave. It was certainly better when a shop sold one type of ware, like cloth or meat, rather than this chaotic mass of items.

As Thomas prepared to leave, he hesitated at the small open-air window next to the entry door. It held a few shelves of plumed hats and folds of fabric. The glint of something in the corner by the window caught the sunlight.

A small wooden box sat upon the wall shelf, just inside the window display. Stepping toward the box, he peeked inside. A simple gold poesy ring lay upon a small piece of linen.

The shopkeeper appeared and asked, "Is there something that might interest you, young man?"

"May I look closer at the little ring in the wooden box?"

The shopkeeper lifted the small box from the shelf and removed the ring, handing it to Thomas. "This is a pretty ring indeed. I have had it for many years. Sadly, a young man lost his wife shortly after their marriage, and he no longer wanted the ring which reminded him of her. Read what the inscription states."

Thomas held the gold band up to the sunlight streaming through the open window display. He rotated the gold band in his fingers while reading, My love, my life.

His heart leapt—perfect words to describe his feelings for Emma.

"What do you ask for such a ring?" Thomas said.

The shopkeeper held Thomas's gaze for quite some time before he spoke. "Tell me why you desire to have it."

Thomas thought about what future lay ahead for Emma and him. "Well, I soon go to the Americas with my family. I have loved only one young woman in my life. I hope to convince her to come with me. Even now, I go to ask her father for her hand in marriage. I am a simple man who has little to give—only my love and a hard-working soul. If I were able to offer her a ring like this one, perhaps her father would agree I am worthy of his daughter."

"Ah . . . to be young and in love again." The shopkeeper rubbed a hand across his bald head and held a few fingers over his mouth. He eyed Thomas for a moment. "I haven't yet felt the right man has come for this ring. Might you be the man I seek?"

"I hope to be . . . but I am of humble means."

The shopkeeper squinted down at the ring and rubbed fingers across his lips. He appeared reluctant to reveal the price.

A sigh swished out of the man, and he asked, "Can you afford a fourpenny bit, young man?"

"You would sell this to me for a fourpenny bit?"

"That I would."

Thomas reached for his leather purse and tugged it open. He worried the man might change his mind before he could pay. A fourpenny bit slipped into his fingers, and he hurriedly held it out to the shopkeeper.

"Thank you, kind sir. I have been looking for quite a while, hoping to find something beautiful which I could afford. I had about given up when I walked in here."

The shopkeeper held his palm toward Thomas, accepting the coin. "I'm glad I could be of help to you and your sweet love. I feel good knowing this little ring will be part of a new beginning for a nice young man such as yourself."

The shopkeeper retrieved the ring from Thomas, placed it in the box, and covered it with the lid. "May the Lord guide your steps as you seek out your true love—and her father." He brushed a hand across his eyes. He mumbled, "Go with God, young man."

"Thank you, kind sir. You have truly blessed my life with your generosity this day."

Thomas stepped out into the sunshine but stopped to turn back toward the shop. The man watched him from within. Thomas lifted his hand in a wave and smiled. The shopkeeper waved back, a forlorn expression upon his face. Why had he offered such a low price for the gold ring when he seemed reluctant to even let it go? Was he the man who'd lost his love?

Thomas squeezed the box in his palm. Never did he suppose he would find something so beautiful for his sweet Emma. He pulled open his leather purse and tucked the little box inside. Cinching it closed once again, he tucked it into his breeches for safety.

His pace quickened on his way down the river walk toward Emma's home. A soft breeze wafted across the river, bringing a late springtime chill to the air.

Thoughts of Emma filled his mind, and he rehearsed the words he'd speak to her father. He feared explaining he was leaving for the Americas would be the more difficult and problematic subject. However, the more he thought about it, asking for Emma's hand might prove to be more painful in the end.

Thomas had been able to contact Barnaby and work with him to procure passage to New England for his family, as well as thirty-two others from the congregation. If Emma's father were to say yes, Barnaby assured him they could acquire passage for two more.

Deep in thought about the task which lay before him, he continued down the street, not noticing those who bumped and jostled against him. Thomas dodged past several people until finally arriving at the lane leading toward Emma's home.

He knew of Emma's love for him and was certain she would say yes to marriage. However, he fretted about Abell Browne, her father. Though he'd given permission for their courtship, would he do the same when Thomas asked for her hand? And how would her father respond when Thomas asked if they might both migrate with him to New England?

Thomas spent most days working the river, and there had been only a few occasions for him to speak with Abell. Nevertheless, Emma had often told him stories about her father and their life together. Emma's mother had passed on soon after Emma's birth. Abell had alone raised Emma. Over time, Thomas had come to recognize Abell as a kind and caring man.

The beating of his heart increased with each footfall closer to the house. He prayed for the strength, and the correct words, to convey what was on his mind.

Emma's small cottage appeared before him, surrounded by a short picket fence. Opening the wooden gate, he stepped through and walked up the flowered path to the entry door.

Garnering all the bravery he could muster, he knocked on the door. He was afraid to ask the question on his mind for fear of what the answer might be.

It wasn't long before Emma pulled the door open. A bright smile spread across her face when she saw Thomas.

"Oh, Thom, I did not expect to see you this day." Stepping past the opening, she pulled the door closed behind her.

Thomas reached up and drew her into his embrace. The warmth of her body infused with his, and he breathed in the smell of her. How he loved this woman.

"Emma, I have come to speak with your father."

Emma pulled back quickly and stared at Thomas. "What? Why?"

"I cannot say right now. I must speak with him."

"Thom, you sound so serious. Pray tell what the matter is?"

"Nothing is the matter. I merely need to see him. Is he about?"

"Aye, he is. However, he has been feeling poorly of late."

Thomas knew his actions confused Emma and he wanted to explain. However, he didn't trust his ability to speak with her, and also her father, before he lost his nerve.

"Please, Emma, trust me. All is well. May I see your father now?"

Emma eyed him with a questioning stare. "As you wish, Thom, please come inside. I will tell him you are here."

He followed Emma into the dim interior of the house. Feeling his purse, he pulled it from his breeches waistband and fingered the shape of the small box inside. A flutter crossed his stomach, and he grasped the box.

"Please wait here while I go in and inform him of your presence."

Thomas thought about what Emma said. *Inform him of your presence.* It was so formal. He wished he could ease her concerns, but it would have to wait until after his visit with Abell Browne.

He stepped to the latticed front window, looking out but not really seeing. Nerves jangled up and down his spine. A voice spoke from behind him, and he jumped at the sound.

"My father will see you now. You may go in."

Thomas went to Emma and cupped her cheek, bringing her toward him. He spoke softly in her ear. "Emma, I love you, please trust me. I do something good."

He pulled back and studied her expression. The corners of her mouth turned up in a little smile. "I do trust you, Thom."

"Thank you, my sweet."

A soft peck on the lips was all he could muster. He turned away from Emma and stepped into Abell's bedchamber.

The room before him revealed an older, thin man lying upon a bed with covers pulled up to his chin. A single candle sat upon a table by the door and chased away some of the darkness which enshrouded the room.

"Please, Thomas, bring the candlestick over here so I might watch you while we talk," said Abell.

Retrieving the candlestick, Thomas stepped to a chair and pulled it up to the side of the bed, setting the candlestick on a table.

"Thank you for seeing me today. Emma said you've been feeling poorly. What ails you?"

"I do not know for sure. It came on quickly, but I cannot seem to shake it. Emma takes good care of me." He reached out and patted Thomas's leg. "I will be back on my feet in no time."

"I will pray for your quick recovery."

"Thank you, Thomas." A sly smile crept across Abell's face. "Now, lad, I know why you have come, so get on with it."

"Sir, . . . um . . . I . . . I . . ." All that practice, now he couldn't recall a single word.

A soft chuckle came from the bed, and Thomas noted a big smile on Abell's face. "You pine for my daughter to be your wife, do you not?"

"Aye, that I do."

"Out with it, boy. Ask for her hand."

"Um . . . yes, I . . . uh, I do want to ask for your daughter's hand."

Abell Browne smiled. "Now, that wasn't so hard, was it?"

201

Thomas laughed and knew he already loved this man. "Nay, it wasn't so hard after all. Mayhap because you did the asking for me?"

A raspy laugh filled the room. Abell reached up to clasp Thomas's hand and pull him in closer. "You take good care of her. She is my only family and the love of my life."

"Well, sir . . . that brings me to my next question. My family and I are currently preparing for migration to the New World."

Thomas watched Abell and acknowledged his concerned expression. "Worry not. I do not plan to take her away from you. My hope is you will both come with me to New England."

Abell took in a large breath, causing a coughing fit. He pointed Thomas to a water pitcher sitting on the little table by the door. Thomas filled a small pewter mug with water and took it back to Abell.

"Pray, forgive me, Thomas. You surprised me with your last comment. It is something to ponder. I have actually considered migration to the Americas myself. I would have to wait until I'm well enough to make the trip. When do you plan to leave?"

"We hope to set sail by August."

"That is just over a month away. I don't know if we can be prepared by then. Why do you go so quickly?"

"I don't know what Emma has told you about my family, but there is a matter of some urgency which compels us to leave as soon as possible."

"If I weren't so sick, I would say we would join you right away. However, there is no telling when I will be well enough for a trip across the ocean."

Thomas bowed his head. He'd finally worked up the courage to ask for Emma's hand, but frustration washed over him. He realized the answer was, *Not right now.*

"Raise up your head, young man. I am not saying no. I'm merely saying that I cannot make the voyage at this time. Emma can marry you, and you may take her to New England. I will join you later."

"If she were to go with me now, who would be here to care for you?"

"I would be here to care for myself."

"Nay, I cannot take her from you. I must go with my family now. Therefore, I will go ahead and build a house for the three of us. When you are well, you can both join me."

Abell studied Thomas for a moment. "You are a good lad. My Emma will do well to be married to you. I agree to the marriage, but there is one condition. You must take Emma with you now."

Thomas stood and paced across the room. Turning back toward Abell, he said, "I must regrettably deny your condition."

Abell rose up in the bed. Coughing overtook him for a moment. Thomas refilled the mug and brought it to Abell, who drank deeply of the water.

"Thank you, Thomas. It will take some time to gain my strength, sell off my possessions, and prepare for a journey across the ocean. I will join you both soon enough. You must do this for me, young man. I need to know Emma is being cared for."

Thomas stopped his pacing and thought about Abell's proposition. "If you feel it is best. Though, I worry to leave you alone here in England." He considered Abell and noted the resolve in his eyes. "I do agree to take her with me, but under protest."

"Protest understood." Peace rested upon Abell's face. He leaned back against his pillow. "You go to her now, Thomas. Make her a happy woman."

Thomas smiled down at Emma's sweet father. "You are a good father to Emma. She loves you so much. I look forward to the day when we will be a family, the three of us."

Abell watched Thomas and chuckled softly. "Aye, and maybe a few young ones added at a later date."

Thomas's face burned as though the midday sun shone down upon him. He made haste to the door, pulled it open, and stepped out into the hall. He could hear the laughter of Abell Browne coming from the bedchamber.

Emma sat upon a small wooden chair near the crackling fire, a quizzical air about her face.

Thomas grumbled, "Do not agonize over the laugh, it is nothing." The embarrassment of Abell's words still fresh in his mind, he pulled the door closed behind him. He went to Emma and kneeled down on the floor in front her. "My dear, I beg of you forgiveness for my unusual behavior. It does pain me to see your father so ill. Has he been sick long?" He reached up and took her hands into his.

"It came on suddenly, but it won't go away. He grows worse each day. I worry about him."

"I will pray his recovery comes soon."

If time were not a factor in asking for her hand, he would have better prepared for this day. "Emma, you know of my father's struggles in prison. We hoped the Archbishop would not continue in his rampage against religious dissenters; however, we have learned there is another bond being issued against my father. It seems the Archbishop will not leave him be. Ergo, we soon leave England for the Americas."

"Oh, Thomas."

He noted the sadness in Emma's eyes and hoped his next words would chase it away. He fiddled with the box until it opened and the ring lay within his fingers.

"Emma . . . I long for you to be my wife." He brought the ring from his purse and lifted her hand, placing it on her palm. "I searched the shops until I found the perfect thing to tie our love together forever."

She glanced down at the ring, and back up to Thomas. "I beg of you, my love, please do not do this."

"Will you read the inscription inside the ring?"

Emma held it up to the firelight. Thomas saw her lips say the words, *My love, my life.*

Sadness entered Emma's eyes. She regarded Thomas and shook her head no as a single tear slid down her face. A piece of his heart broke free and landed at his feet.

"Please, Emma, I cannot leave England without you. I beg of you, be my wife and travel with me."

Emma glanced down at the ring and back up at Thomas. She brushed the tear from her cheek.

"Oh, Thom, it is truly a beautiful ring, and I long to take it and to be your betrothed—but I cannot. My father is too ill, and I am the only one to care for him. I understand the urgency and need for your quick departure to the New World. Perchance, we might join you one day after Father is well. It would allow us time to make arrangements for our own migration."

"Nay, you see, I spoke with your father. We both agree you should come with me now, and he will join us later on. It has all been decided."

The air in the room seemed to stand still. Emma arose from the chair. "Please arise from the floor, Thom."

Thomas got to his feet, watching her. Emma took his hand and turned his palm up to place the ring thereon. "So the both of you decided, did you?" She closed his fingers over the ring and pushed his hand away, folding her arms across her chest. "I will decide what is best for me, not the two of you."

"I beg of you, Emma. Please hear me out. I did not mean to decide anything for you. I merely sought to ask your father for your hand and ask if you would both come with me to New England. However, he is too ill and chooses to remain in England until such time when he is well enough to join us. He explained he would not consent to the betrothal unless I took you with me. So, I agreed."

He waited for her to speak, but she stood and went to the small front window. Following her, he encircled his arms about her waist and pulled her toward him. Emma held herself unbendingly, staring away from him.

Though the space joining them was small, the rift between them was large. Thomas said, "I would never imagine to tell you what you must do, or where you must go. You are a strong and capable woman who can make choices regarding her own life."

Thomas felt her relax back against his chest, and he hoped she was beginning to come around. "I love you, Emma. You are all to me."

"Oh, Thom, I love you as well." She turned and laid her arms around his neck, her head coming to lie upon his chest.

"Does this mean you will consent be my wife one day?"

"I suppose it does, my love."

Thomas brought his hand up to stroke his fingers down the side of her cheek. Lifting her chin, he lowered his head until his lips softly touched hers. Drawing back, he saw the love reflecting in her dark eyes. Heart pounding against his chest, he brought his lips down to hers once again. The sweet taste of her mouth thrilled him, and he marveled at the love he felt for her—this beautiful woman who would soon be his wife.

He pulled from the kiss but held her close. "My love, my life."

"I share the sentiment, Thom." She laid her hand upon his chest again. "However, you must understand, I cannot come to New England with you at this time."

Thomas felt his heart sink. How could he leave for the New World without Emma by his side?

"I must admit, I held onto the hope that perchance you would come with me now. Nonetheless, this is what I feared when I saw the illness which affects your father. I understand why you must stay and care for him. My mother was ill for a long time, and she always needed Jane's help."

He cupped her face within his hands and noted her sorrowful eyes. "It does break my heart to leave you behind. You are a loyal daughter to your father and will do what's necessary to care for him. I understand; I try to be a good son and am obliged to aid my father as well. I cannot leave him to remove our family to a new land without the help of his eldest son. I must go with him."

Emma reached up to touch his cheek. The expression on her face broke Thomas's heart and he longed to fix things, but it was out of his hands. They each had an obligation to their fathers.

"Thom, I agree to be your wife someday, even though I may not see you for a long time. I do so long to marry you and will watch for that day with longing. I feel the pain of your departure already in my heart."

Her sorrow was visible, and it pained him to be the one who brought her so much sadness.

"You make me a happy man, indeed, that you agree to wear my ring and to someday be my wife."

He took the ring from her and placed it on a finger of her right hand, as was the custom. He yearned for the day when they would vow their lives to one another and he could move the ring to her left hand.

"I love you, Emma."

"I love you, as well, Thom."

In a few weeks' time, he would be sailing away with his family. Off to a new land where Indians roamed the forests and all manner of strangers settled the lands. For now, knowing Emma would someday be his wife would have to be enough for him.

He pulled her into his arms and held her tightly against his chest. Conflicting emotions clamored for space in his heart. One moment joy, the next sadness.

"The day will come when you and your father can both join me, but for now, I will write letters and send them back on any ship which returns to London. When I arrive in the New World, I will build a house for the three of us."

Thomas reached up to stroke Emma's soft brown hair. "A house I can add to as our family grows."

A smile tugged at Emma's lips, though Thomas noted it didn't go all the way to her eyes.

"I will write to you in return. I look forward to the day when I can send the letter saying my father is well, and we will soon be joining you in New England."

"Come, Emma, let's sit by the fire and dream of our future together." Thomas circled an arm around her waist and guided her to the hearth. She took the small wooden chair, and Thomas sat on the floor in front of her.

He laid his head upon her lap and watched the flames sputter and spark. One day soon he would be forced to leave her, but for now, he would absorb every moment of time with her.

For tomorrow he would prepare to set sail.

Twenty

LAMBETH

Jane fluffed her petticoats and sat upon one of two wooden chairs she'd carried out to the center circle of the garden. Floral scents mixed with herbal smells, and the aroma flitted upon the breeze.

Birds chirruped an anxious song at her appearance, and their uproar escalated her apprehension of Edmund's impending arrival.

It had been almost a year since they'd officially started courting, and she was sure a betrothal date was imminent. How she still dreamed of the day when they would be Lord and Lady Edmund Fairfax.

She drew the cloak tighter around her shoulders to ward off the cold, though it did little to ease the chill she felt in her heart over quandaries in her life.

More than a fortnight had passed since she'd sent an urgent note for Edmund to come to her. Bitter disappointment permeated her heart at his lack of response. Finally, this morning she had a message in return.

She inhaled the scent of her mother's beautiful herbs and flowers which spilled down the garden borders. The aroma brought peace to her troubled mind while she awaited Edmund's delayed arrival.

A cool breeze wafted across the landscape, raising hairs on her forearm in response. Did the cold air cause the sensation, or was it anxiety over what she was about to ask?

The archbishop's latest summons had sent the family into a whirlwind of selling their possessions and preparing for migration. She'd busied herself with organizing, packing, and cleaning, all the while planning how she might convince Edmund to join them on their migration to the New World.

Oh, when would he arrive?

Footfalls captured her attention, and she glanced up to observe her love coming across the gardens. Anxiety over the past few weeks of awaiting word from him slipped away, and she rushed into his arms.

"Oh, Edmund, at last you have come."

"The long delay was unfortunate. I have been detained with business obligations."

"What business would keep you from my urgent call? Could you not have sent a note sooner to ease my troubled mind?"

"Pray, forgive me, my love, for you see my attendance was also required at a few soirees."

"Soirees? When I needed you here?"

"I had no choice. Attendance at those types of events is necessary because I am a landowner." He leaned down and pressed a gentle kiss upon her lips. "At length I am here. What say you regarding the urgent need to talk?"

Irritation at Edmund's supposed obligations with business and soirees had always troubled Jane's mind. However, she pushed those thoughts away to focus on her current predicament.

"Very well, Edmund. I beg of you, please join me on the chairs. We can sit and have a nice talk." Jane took Edmund's arm and allowed him to guide her over to a chair. He grasped the other chair, turned it to face hers, and sat down.

"Now you have my curiosity piqued. Has one of the children been misbehaving? Or has Thomas become overbearing once again?"

Jane's brow furrowed at Edmund's comments. She let the cool air fill her lungs and felt a renewed energy. Reaching a hand forward, she laid it upon his knee.

"It is not the children, or issues with Thomas, which prompted my call. So much has happened since last I saw you. I regret to say, Father has received a summons to appear before the archbishop."

"Oh, my dear Jane, that is preposterous. Had I only understood the serious nature of your call, I would have come sooner. What will he do now?"

"It is that very thing which brought about the need for our conversation today."

"I have no connections to help you with the Bishop or the Church. Might there be some other thing I can do to aid you or your family?"

Jane leaned forward in her chair and took Edmund's hands. "Aye, there is, Edmund, my love."

She watched his eyes and gathered the courage to go on, realizing it was unfitting for a woman to speak the way she planned to speak this day. However, she was sure her current circumstances warranted such actions.

"Father has determined our family will migrate to New England."

"What say you? New England? But Jane—"

"I know, I know. It brings me dismay as well. Nonetheless, I have a plan."

Edmund leaned back in his chair, withdrawing his hands from Jane's grasp. "Pray tell, what might your plan be?"

Jane dug deep for the courage she needed to reveal her idea. Drawing in a strengthening breath, she watched Edmund for a reaction to what she was about to say.

She exhaled quickly and let the words rush out. "We can sign our marriage contract now, and you can join me in migration to the New World." A broad smile spread across her face.

Edmund's eyes altered from sweet and loving to arrogant and proud. Jane's stomach roiled inside of her as fear strolled up her back.

"Edmund?"

"You do ask much, my dear Jane. I could not give up what I have here in England to migrate across the ocean to such a wild land. I am a landowner here—I have money and status. I would be nothing in New England."

"Perchance I could stay in England with you and we could sign the marriage contract here? Edmund, we love each other. I cannot bear to be apart from you."

"I do love you, Jane. Yet much has happened with your family over the past many months. I had patiently waited for your father to return home so we could officially court. After a time, I began to realize that our marriage day would never come."

Jane's entire body flushed with the emotions of what she was hearing. Edmund leaned forward and took both her hands into his. The serious look on his face caused Jane even more consternation.

He continued, "Jane, I must now confess that feelings of love have grown within me for another. It is a girl I have known all my life and never realized I could love."

Jane yanked her hands from his hold. She gasped in the afternoon air as she leaned back into the chair. Was he really doing this? Who was this man who sat before her? She thought she had known him.

"Oh Jane, my love, what happened to us? I loved you from the first moment we met. I desired that one day you would be mine. Yet a series of events unfolded which neither of us could control. Your father left the church, and was later thrown into prison. Your family status changed, and now, because of my own family obligations, that makes it impossible for me to marry you. I had hoped to spend as much time together as we could before I had to—"

"I beg of you, stop talking, Edmund." Leaning further away from him, Jane crossed her hands over her chest and looked over to the man she'd thought was her friend, her protector, her future husband.

She rose from the chair and began pacing across the garden.

"When did your intentions for our marriage alter, Edmund?"

He rose and went to her. "I beg of you, try to understand." He struggled to draw her into his arms, but Jane tugged away from him. Then, she turned back to gauge his thoughts.

She said, "You failed to answer my question."

Edmund stared at her, his lips moving to form words, but nothing issued forth.

Hurt flashed within Jane like sun streaks across the river, ever changing as the water flowed toward the sea. She grappled with her emotions, as today they'd swung from one extreme to the other. One moment a bright gleam upon a swell, the next a dark void dipping below the surface.

She stopped to think and clear her head. Edmund seized upon the moment and drew her into his arms. The nearness of him was familiar, and she laid her head upon his chest. For a moment, her doubts and troubles began to melt into his strong arms.

No! She could not allow herself to be lulled back into a false sense of security. She pushed from his clutches and turned away from him. Anguish surged over her like brumes rolling in from the ocean, obscuring the love she thought she'd felt for him.

"What I hear you saying Edmund, is that you love me, but not enough to marry me. Very well, I release you from our courtship."

"Oh, Jane, do not do this. Certainly, time remains for us to be together before you sail away from me."

Jane's face burned with the hurt and anger of his betrayal. She whirled around, thrusting her arms toward him. "I have come to understand you this day. You view me as someone not good enough to marry. Now, you have the audacity to stand there and tell me you've found a woman who you deem fit for your status as a Fairfax—someone you profess to love more than me. Do you truly consider I would spend one more moment with you? Please leave my sight immediately."

Edmund reached out to Jane, attempting to draw her into his arms. Her hands fisted at her sides and she held her stance, while she regarded the man standing before her.

Thomas had been right about Edmund. It appeared he did have a woman on his arm that night. A woman he planned to marry. A woman who was not Jane.

She thought of the hours she'd spent memorizing the words of that sonnet, holding them close to her heart, saying them over and over at night when she lay in her bed.

"Please leave me, Edmund. I desire to be alone now."

"I will go, though it pains me to do so. I have greatly enjoyed our time together, my love."

"I dare say, do not address me that way again. You do not have the right."

Edmund remained where he was. Jane held her breath, waiting, until finally he turned and headed back the way he'd come.

She released a tense breath at his parting. Her heart broke a little more with every step he took across the garden. Edmund turned back to her, bowed, and walked out of her life forever.

A raw sense of anguish left her soul feeling wounded. She heard the song of a lark, though it brought her no joy. She turned back to the chair and sat upon it, staring over the tops of the lavender. The last few moments in time played across her mind.

Jane pressed two fingers against her temples. She remembered how Edmund stood tall and proud on their strolls along the river walk. Why hadn't she listened when Thomas had tried to warn her about Edmund? The pain of losing him would have been long gone by now.

Dropping her head into her hands, she felt the bite of his loss as tears stung her eyes. Edmund was the man with whom she'd thought to spend her life. Now he was gone.

A breeze wafted across the garden and brought with it the mist of another England fog. Sitting up, she tugged the cloak around her shoulders, using it to dab at her eyes. She reflected on her relationship with Edmund and realized she had too easily passed the reins of her life into his hands.

That could never happen again. A new beginning was before her. The thought of it frightened her, yet she felt a deep, soulful stirring from within. She must seek the hand of God and find the courage to move forward.

Onward to a new land—onward to a new life.

Twenty-One

LAMBETH

Sunlight angled through the front latticed window of the Lothrop home and shone across the wooden floor. Dust particles glistened and sparkled in the rays, like tiny fireflies flitting to and fro across an evening sky.

John scanned the empty hall and recalled his precious Hannah. Her spirit lingered within the walls and floors of their home. Memories of her cooking at the hearth, the giggles of children as they scampered around her, filled every space of the different rooms. All this and more brought pain and loss to his soul.

Never before had he seen the hearth appear as cold and uninviting as it did now, with no fire crackling within its stone framework.

The children stood in a circle with him, each holding hands with the next. Little Benjamin was to John's right, and Barbara to his left, then Samuel, Johnny, Jane, Joseph, and Thomas, who held onto Little Benjamin.

John looked from child to child and saw Hannah's features in so many of their faces. Memories of her must be fresh in their minds as well. They each struggled with leaving their home and crossing the great ocean to a new world.

His children stood firm with him, never breaking the family ties, as the fight for religious independence from the King and Archbishop raged ever onward. The fight would now take them away from their beloved homeland, to a rough territory vastly different from anything they'd ever known.

"Children, my love for you knows no bounds. We stand as one, united in a greater purpose than ourselves. Our souls are firmly linked forevermore. I pray that through His Grace, both by prayer and by practice, as we endeavor to lighten our burdens and take ourselves to a new land, we will find the peace and happiness we so desire."

Thomas turned to John. "We are with you, Father. We stand as a family united, faithful to one another."

John nodded to Thomas, and he glanced over at Johnny, whose head hung low. "Johnny, do not despair, education is important. We support your choice to remain in England and achieve your degree. One day soon, we will all be together."

Johnny squeezed his eyes shut, seeming to block out his pain. "Thank you, Father. It does feel as though I'm abandoning the ship, so to say."

Jane leaned into her brother. "Oh, Johnny, do not fret. We all love you and look toward the day when you do set sail on a ship and join us across the ocean."

Johnny's feeble smile told John of his pain at their parting. He inclined his head toward Johnny and smiled back at him. "We will always keep you in our hearts, and we pray for a quick reunion in the New World."

The children all nodded in agreement. John continued, "The time has come to say goodbye to our home. We must step outside and make our first footfalls towards a new life. Let us bow our heads in prayer before we go."

Each child closed their eyes and lowered their head. John examined the circle of his family, and his heart swelled with love for them. He closed his eyes and began the last prayer he would ever give in this home.

"Our most Glorious God, we come before Thee this day as we make ready for a voyage across the great ocean. We pray for Thy guiding hand to be upon us while we go forward to a new land, making a new beginning.

"We pray for our dear Johnny as he remains in England, that he will work tirelessly to gain his degree and once again join the family. We pray for Thy blessings to be upon him.

"We desire to further Thy glory and live in peace and prosperity in New England, where we can have the freedom to sing praises unto Thee, our God and Father. Please guide us with Thy Grace and attend us as we are upon the dangers of the sea. We ask Thy aid and protection as we strive to settle in a new land. We beg of Thee the peace and joy we so desire. Amen."

Glancing up from his prayer, John said, "Well, children, the time has come to make our way to the docks, where we have packed Thom's wherry with all our belongings. There we will meet his friend Humphrey, who has been guarding our belongings, and who has also brought his own wherry to help ferry us downriver to the harbor. Do you feel ready?"

The children chimed together, "Aye!"

"Take one last look around and meet in the front garden."

John broke his grip with Little Benjamin and Barbara and moved to the door. He stopped to turn back and noted the forlorn expressions on the faces of his children.

Leaving Hannah behind in English soil was difficult. Nevertheless, he knew she would always live in his heart.

John passed through the doorway and out into a bright, humid summer day. Frederick and Elsabeth had been waiting outside so John and his children might have a last moment together. John moved down the walkway and stopped to pull the little wooden gate open. He stepped through it for the last time.

With a heavy heart, he turned back toward the house where he had lived so happily with his growing family. Deep pain entered his soul. The weight of it sat upon his spirit.

219

Turning toward his friend, John said, "Frederick, I wonder if this overwhelming sadness will ever leave me."

"Aye, John, it will. The passage of time will heal your wounds."

"I must let the past lie where it is, live my life in the present, always looking towards the prospect of a bright new future. I have spent enough time dwelling on old pains and sorrows. It is time to leave them be and move in a forward direction."

Though the smile was forced, John let it sit upon his face nonetheless. One by one, the children stepped from the house and out into the sunshine. Thomas passed through the door last and reached back to pull it closed behind him.

With the same smile still frozen on his face, John said, "Come, children, let us make our way to the wherries now."

Reluctance was written on their faces. They slowly worked their way down the walk and through the gate. Once gathered, John pulled the gate closed, and they began their journey to the dock.

Trailing behind the group, Frederick and John walked in silence for a while. Jane, Barbara, and Elsabeth walked out in front of the group, the others spreading out as they headed down the lane.

Memories of John's sweet little Anne, who'd barely lived a year, came to his mind. It broke his heart to leave her behind, but he took comfort knowing Hannah remained in England as well. In another world, they would come together as one family in God, but for now he must move on with his life.

A scream rent the air. Jane pointed toward the dock.

"Father, the wherry—it is burning!"

John and Frederick rushed forward, with Thomas and Johnny falling in with them. Flames licked at their possessions and grew in intensity.

"What could have caused our belongings to catch fire?" John cried out.

Wooden planks shifted under his weight as he ran down the dock. He passed several other boats and continued to Thom's wherry. The sound of running feet followed behind.

Flames sputtered and grew, engulfing the trunks and bags they'd so carefully tied down to the boat. Thomas and Johnny ran past the wherry and jumped into the river. Flames licked and sputtered at the boat. Standing in the waist deep water, they slopped water onto rising flames.

John arrived and jumped into the water on the opposite side of the boat. He heard the splash as Frederick jumped in behind him. Their attempts at dousing the flames continued, until John realized their futile gestures would not suffice—the fire had already taken their belongings.

"Stop, men! It is useless to save our things, they are lost. We must do all we can to save the wherry for Johnny. Unfasten the ropes and pull everything into the river to douse the flames."

He began to tug at the scorched ropes, which broke free without too much effort. He pulled charred and burning items out of the boat and dropped them into the river. He felt the burn in his palms as he continued to tug items into the water.

Frederick jerked at some ropes, but they would not give way. John joined him in his efforts. Together they yanked on the ropes until they could free the burning bags and let them drop into the water.

John's shoulders and back screamed in pain, but he continued to work until the flames were mastered and the wherry was safe. Standing back, his heart fell as he surveyed the contents still left in the bottom of the boat.

There were bags of food and seeds they'd packed to give them a start in the New World. The bottom of the wherry sat full of water, encasing the remaining items. Everything was burned or ruined by water.

John sloshed his way back to the dock and felt the pain in his hands as he pushed up onto the planks. He sat on the edge of the dock and wondered how they would ever make the trip to New England at this time. They had nothing to help them survive an ocean voyage, and only the clothing they now wore.

Why had the wherry caught fire?

Frederick, Thomas, and Johnny climbed onto the dock, and all four men sat staring at what used to be their goods and luggage. Elsabeth and the children came up behind them and stood in silence, staring at the mess left by the fire.

John's palms were torn and blistered. "What am I to do now, Frederick? How can we make a voyage across the ocean when there is nothing left to feed us, no other clothing for us to wear or blankets to keep us warm? We will not survive."

As John watched the last prospect of a good life slowly being pulled down river, he felt the same descent into the hopelessness of perdition he had previously felt at Newgate. He leaned toward his friend so his sons might not hear him speak. "Frederick, I feel my life being pulled into hell once again."

Frederick whispered back to him, "John, I always say—if you find yourself plodding through hell, do not stop, but keep walking. Then you will come out the other side and can leave it well behind you."

John knew he must find the same strength he'd found in prison—the same strength which had given him comfort and helped him through his darkest hours.

He closed his eyes and said a silent prayer for the courage to go on.

All his hope had lain in migration. How would he accomplish such a thing now? Since he had not appeared in answer to the summons he'd received, a warrant would soon be issued for his arrest. If he stayed in England, he would surely land back in prison.

How would his children survive with no home, no provisions, and no father?

Perhaps, he could implore his extended family for a temporary place to stay while he and the children went into hiding. When enough money was earned, they could possibly fund another migration attempt.

He opened his eyes and turned to Frederick. "I fear my only choice is to prevail upon my extended family for food and shelter at this time. Frederick, you must lead the congregation to New England and help establish them at Plymouth Colony. We will remain here in England and join you at a later date."

"What say you? Nay, John. You cannot remain in England. Surely you will be found and thrown back into prison. Elsabeth and I have a wherry full of provisions, and we will gladly share with you. Others in the congregation will feel the same and want to help as well. With all of us pulling together, you and your family can make the journey to New England."

"For that, I am truly grateful. However, I fear the burden would be too great."

"Nay, it is not a burden, and we gladly offer our help. Humphrey's wherry is large. Between his wherry and ours, there will enough room to transport us all to the harbor. You can leave Thom's wherry here for Johnny to later retrieve. All will be well."

Alarm filled John's thoughts as Frederick said the name Humphrey. He hadn't thought about what had happened to Thomas's friend.

Where was he? He had been left at the dock to guard their belongings.

Turning toward Thomas, John said, "Thomas, where is Humphrey? We must find him immediately."

Thomas and Johnny jumped up and began to scan the dock. John pushed up on his hands, but cried out in pain. The burns he'd received from the fire covered his palms. He remained sitting but checked the dock for Thomas's friend. A body was lying upon the wooden planks at the far end of the dock.

"There," John called out, pointing, "I see him lying upon the dock."

"Father, you stay here. Johnny and I will see to him. Come on, let's go!"

John's two oldest boys ran down the dock to the body lying upon the wooden planks. Thomas leaned down and shook Humphrey's shoulder. The young man sat up and rubbed the back of his head.

A sigh of relief brushed past John's lips, and he silently thanked God the boy was still alive.

Troubling thoughts filled John's mind regarding the additional strain his family would have on the parishioners. He rubbed a hand across his brow and turned back toward Frederick.

"I am sincerely grateful for the offer of help. Let me mull on it for a bit. For now, I wonder about how this fire began. I cannot imagine anything we packed which might spark a flame and cause the fire to burn so quickly."

"John . . . I do believe the fire was set. I found evidence of what seemed to be dried grasses tucked under the ropes. It would have allowed the fire to grow fast and sure."

"Gryffyn Cane—it can be none other than him."

John twisted his body onto the dock and rolled onto his knees, being careful not to cause any further damage to his burned fingers and palms. He began to scan the surrounding area. If Gryffyn Cane was responsible for this damage, he would stay close by to witness the destruction. It would satisfy Gryffyn to not only to see the ruin of John's goods, but the ruin of John as well.

Thomas, Johnny, and Humphrey walked up the dock and came to stand by his side.

"Are you well, Humphrey?" asked John.

"Me head hurts at bit, yet, I am well. I beg of ye forgiveness. Some crazy bloke must 'ave sneaked up and got th' drop on me head." He stroked the back of his head in protest.

"I thank God you are alive, young man." John patted a hand upon his shoulder. "Thomas, Johnny, Frederick—we must search the area for Gryffyn Cane, for it can be none other than him who did this dastardly deed. Humphrey, will you stay here to watch over the women and children?"

"Aye, ye can leave it to me," he said.

"And Humphrey, please be cautious no one sneaks up on you again. The four of us will search the area for Gryffyn. Two of us should go one way and two the other."

Thomas stepped forward. "I will go with you, Father. Johnny can join Frederick."

"Very well, we'll head south."

"And we'll head north," said Frederick.

John and Thomas began to search the trees and shops along the river walk, checking every place they thought a man might be hiding. When they came up empty, they made the way back down the river walk. Thomas and Frederick walked towards them. Frederick had his arms outstretched as he shook his head in the negative.

John called out, "Perchance, I was wrong about Gryffyn staying behind to watch the carnage. Let's go talk to the others and decide what our plans will be."

His heart felt heavy as they headed back to the dock. He had a big decision before him. Should he remain in England? Or prevail upon friends for the support of his family?

John and the others headed down the wooden dock. They made their way past several other boats while heading back to the wherry.

A movement to the right caught John's attention. A skiff wobbled and banged against two wherries on each side. A man used an oar to push against the dock, causing the boat to float backward.

John recognized the face of his tormentor.

"Gryffyn Cane! I knew you must be behind this catastrophe. How could you have been so heartless? Why did you do it?"

Gryffyn held his balance against the wobbling boat and snarled at John. "Why? It was done for the mere purpose of bringing you to my level of destitution and despair. I have wallowed in the gloom of perdition alone. Now, you can join me in the darkness and feel the torture of my agony. Your anger has surely torn a hole in your spirit. Can you not feel the very gates of hell and eternal damnation clawing at your soul?"

"I do not feel the burning of hell coming after me. While at times I have given in to anger and despair, I have always pulled myself from its grip. My children, my friends, and my God give me the strength to stay away from such a place. While you continue your journey into damnation—we set our sights on Heaven."

Gryffyn shoved the oar into the water, driving the skiff back to the dock. "You will go into the filth of this river, as is your due for crimes against God." He leapt from the boat and lunged after John.

Frederick, Thomas, and Johnny grabbed Gryffyn before he could knock John off the dock and into the river.

John felt his anger rise, but he drove it back as best he could. He must not allow this man to cause him such negative emotions any longer.

"Stop this infernal struggling, Gryffyn! Why do you act like such a coward? Stand before me like a man."

John stood with his feet spread and shoulders squared, facing his accuser.

Gryffyn stopped thrashing and stood rigid, glaring at John while the three men continued to hold onto him. "How dare you say I am a coward? You are the one who feels you can hide from your sins in a new land."

"I go about doing good, trying to make a new life for my family and my friends. You go about doing harm to others in an effort to make yourself feel powerful during their weakest moments."

A sinister growl came from Gryffyn. Evil seemed to live in his eyes and give strength to his form. With arms outstretched toward John, Gryffyn yanked free of the men holding him and leapt forward.

A searing jolt of fear coursed down John's spine. He felt Gryffyn's hands clawing at his arms, and he reached up to push them away. Gryffyn shoved him toward the river.

With renewed strength, John twisted against Gryffyn's grip in an attempt to shake him off. He felt a marked shift in Gryffyn's body weight, and John used the momentum to twist away from the dock's edge and pull from Gryffyn's grasp.

The other men seized hold of Gryffyn once again, though they struggled to maintain their hold as the man flailed about.

As if Gryffyn Cane had a sinister legion of fiends giving him strength, he yanked free of the men, quickly sweeping a leg under Frederick. Gryffyn pushed the larger man into the two boys and knocked them all off balance. In a flash, he turned back toward John and lunged at him. John twisted to the side. Gryffyn's forward momentum carried his weight beyond John and down into the brown, muddy waters of the Thames.

Falling to his knees, John reached out for Gryffyn while calling to the others, "Quickly, help me save him!"

Frederick, Thomas, and Johnny ran forward and knelt beside John, trying to grab hold of Gryffyn's flailing arms.

"We must get him before he goes under the dock. Quick, Thomas, grab his arm!"

Both Thomas and Frederick were able to finally grab hold of an arm, but the wet, muddy skin caused it to slip from their grip.

They all watched in horror as Gryffyn disappeared under the dock.

"Hurry! To the other side! Surely, the current will have pulled him through. Mayhap we can save him."

John rose and ran across the dock and jumped into the river in search of Gryffyn Cane. He heard the three other men clomp across the dock and jump in behind him.

Thrashing through the brown, dirty waters of the River Thames, John flung his arms back and forth, attempting to find Gryffyn.

Nothing.

Where could he have gone?

John arose to peer along the edge of the dock in case Gryffyn's body had been caught on a piling. His heart sank when he saw Thomas dive under the dock and disappear.

No! Not Thomas!

Seconds ticked like minutes while John awaited the appearance of his eldest son from under the water. Frederick and Johnny had ceased their search and were also watching the dock where Thomas had gone under.

The beating of John's heart grew in intensity, his breath coming in rapid bursts.

Pushing forward through the water, John made his way to the piling where Thomas had disappeared. He flung his hands as far as they could reach under the dock, swishing them back and forth. Frederick and Johnny followed suit, and the three men worked their way along the edge of the wooden structure.

A cry from Johnny commanded John's attention. He glanced along the dock and realized Johnny held Thomas in his arms.

John slogged through the water toward Thomas and pulled him into an embrace.

"Thank you, Johnny. Thank you for finding him."

"Nay, Father," said Johnny. "He came up on his own."

"Oh, Thomas, my boy, I feared to have lost you."

"I am fine, Father, there is nothing to worry over. I know this river well."

John pulled back and watched the bright blue eyes shining through the mud on Thomas's face.

Mixed emotions tore at him. Thomas was safe, but where was Gryffyn? John drew in a troubled breath.

The cold, filthy river had swallowed Gryffyn Cane.

Elsabeth, Jane, Humphrey, and the younger children walked in their direction. He quickly waved them off and called over his shoulder to the other men.

"Let us not make mention of this incident to the others. We must keep the events surrounding Gryffyn Cane away from their tender souls."

John waved the children away and pointed toward the wherry. "Please turn back. We'll meet you down at the wherry in a moment."

He pulled himself from the water and sat upon the edge of the dock. Thomas, Johnny, and Frederick joined him. Spitting river water from his mouth, John brought his hand over his cropped hair and down his face and beard, flinging water back into the river.

Frederick turned to John and said, "Even though Gryffyn has brought you such pain and misery, I can tell it grieves your heart to realize he is gone. I understand you see him as a son of God and a soul worth saving."

"Aye, that I do. We cannot judge another by their actions. There is no way for us to truly understand what makes a person act the way they do. I know there has been much pain in the life of Gryffyn. Over time, it twisted his mind into what we saw today."

John continued, "We will never understand why someone acts the way they do. Only Jesus Christ can know what is truly in a person's heart."

Pushing against the dock, John winced at the pain from his burned palms. He slowly arose and said, "I guess the time has come to take care of the wherry. Frederick . . . I believe it prudent we accept your most kind and generous offer. We will continue our journey with you and join the others of our congregation at the harbor."

Frederick nodded and stood. "It fills my heart with joy to hear you say that."

John noted the wet, dripping faces of his two sons. "Come on, boys, let's go. We have a lot of work to do to get ready for travel."

He would not let the devastation of losing his supplies be the end of his quest for peace. With the help of his friends, he would rise above his current situation.

Though John had lost all of his worldly possessions, he sensed richness beyond mere money awaited him on the shores of a distant land.

For with him were his most treasured possessions.

His family and his friends.

Twenty-Two

LONDON HARBOR

The vast ocean played its tantalizing song as swells slid into waves and slithered across the water's surface until they were diffused by thick wharf pilings. John stared out over the water, bringing his hand up to block the sunlight sparkling across the water's surface like billions of stars glimmering in the night sky. Sea spray misted across his face, and the smell of salt filled his nostrils.

America lay across this great expanse of ocean. John wondered if the far-off land would provide the peace and safety he desired. They had suffered greatly in their pursuit of God's plan. But did not Christ Himself suffer even more?

John stepped to the edge of the wharf and gazed down into the gray water. Whirls of foam circled on the surface, making intricate patterns churn around each post until the next wave dragged them away.

Brisk footsteps pulled John from his reverie, and he saw Thomas heading in his direction. The smile his son wore bespoke of his excitement at beginning this new adventure.

"Father, it has been announced the winds and the tides are in our favor. I've been warned the shipmaster waits for no one. Jane is already below decks with the children."

"Now, at long last, the time has finally come," said John. "Let us make haste to the ship. I must ensure the flock has all gathered aboard."

Thomas turned and made his way back across the wooden structure toward the *Griffin*, the ship which would take them to Boston harbor.

Waving a hand in the air, Thomas said, "I will see you aboard soon, Father. I have been speaking with a sailor I met earlier. I have a few more questions for him in regards to working on a merchant ship."

"As you wish, Thomas. Do not dally too long."

Thomas laughed in response. "Perchance, do you feel I would miss the opportunity to board this ship?" He turned and quickly melded into the throngs of people scuttling about the harbor.

A few congregants stood near the landing stage while others stood upon the ship's deck, staring over the crowds. It filled his heart with love and thankfulness to realize so many were willing to follow him across the sea—off to a barely known place, where the number of Indians far outweighed the number of Englishmen.

He stopped short of the landing stage and read the name *Griffin* painted across the stern of the ship. This gave John pause as he recalled a man of the same name who had delivered such sorrow to his life—Gryffyn Cane.

John considered the legend of the mythical creature called a gryphon. The beast had the head and wings of an eagle with its front feet being eagle talons, and the remainder of the creature's body being that of a lion. Some said the gryphon was a trickster and took joy in hoodwinking man. Each gryphon hoarded a cache of gold somewhere deep within the mountains. If man discovered a gryphon's gold, its innate need to fool man overpowered the instinctive desire to protect its gold. A riddle would be asked of the man. If the correct answer was given, the man won the gold. If the answer was wrong, his life was forfeit.

The man Gryffyn had attempted to drag John down and destroy him. He prayed the ship *Griffin* would carry him onward to safety and peace.

The staging area of the ship bustled with activity as John made his way across the wharf to the ship. Tall ship masts rocked to and fro with the ocean's movement. Soon great sails would be run up the poles to catch the wind and carry them all across the ocean. He looked over the expanse of water they prepared to span, and the ship seemed small indeed.

A voice called out and pulled him from his thoughts. "Is this not a good day, Reverend Lothropp?"

John turned toward a gentleman from his congregation. "Aye, it is a good day. Is your family aboard and settled?"

"They are. I am the last of them on land. I trust you have heard the winds and the tides are good?"

"Aye." John pointed to the ship. "I am making my way to the *Griffin* as we speak. It seems incredible we are finally leaving for New England."

"That it does, Reverend. I will see you aboard." The man turned and made his way toward the landing stage of the ship.

Frederick waved at John from the main deck. "John Lothropp! Is your family aboard?"

Frederick, Elsabeth, and other members from the congregation had been kind enough to share their goods with him and his family. For this reason, John believed he must work even harder when he arrived at the new world so he might repay them for their sacrifice and their kindness to his family.

He stepped onto the gangplank, ascended the inclined wooden beam, and moved to the main deck of the ship. He worked through the crowd and over to where Frederick and Elsabeth leaned against the side rail.

A seaman called out, "All hands on deck!"

The main deck was crowded with the ship's crew preparing to put out to sea. Anxiety filled John's heart when he realized Thomas was nowhere to be seen. He perused the wharf and landing stage. He finally caught sight of him in the loading area.

Thomas was deep in conversation with a sailor who must be the man advising Thomas as to life aboard a merchant vessel. While they talked, John's eyes were drawn to a woman enshrouded by a hooded cloak weaving her way through the crowd and headed toward his son. She drew close to Thomas and stretched her hand out to him.

Thomas turned to face her, as though drawn to her like waves being pulled from the shore. His face fairly glowed with adoration, and he reached out to pull her into his arms.

They embraced, and the hood of the woman's cloak fell back. John realized the woman was Emma. Thomas pulled from her embrace, circled an arm about her waist, and led her away from the crowds to the edge of the wharf.

Activity on deck surrounding John and Frederick began to build to a new level of energy. Excitement filled the air like lightning streaking through a stormy sky.

The first mate called out from the quarter deck, "Avast! It be time t' weigh anchor th' harbor. All o' ye passengers make yer way below decks."

"Frederick, the time has finally come! Let us check the decks and landing stage to be sure the congregation is safely aboard. If you will circle forward, I will circle around the stern."

"Aye, that I will do. Afterward, we can meet below decks," said Frederick.

John stopped for a moment to peer over the crowds, attempting to catch sight of Thomas so he might call him onto the ship. The hordes of people melded into one great swarming mass, and he couldn't distinguish one person from the other.

He turned to Frederick. "Where do you suppose Thomas has taken himself to? I no longer see him on the wharf."

"I do not see him either. You go ahead and find your son. Elsa and I will scour the deck to make sure all are aboard and below decks."

"Thank you, my friend. I do grow anxious."

Making his way across the deck and down the gangplank, John's stomach began to churn. He'd failed to catch sight of Thomas.

All of the ship's crew, excepting one remaining sailor, were aboard and preparing the ship to set sail. Once the last crewman walked up the gangplank, he would pull it in and stow it away. Anyone left on the wharf would be unable to board the ship.

Anxiety filled every part of John's being. He stepped off the end of the gangplank and onto the wharf and pushed through the crowd in the direction he'd last seen Thomas. He grew more concerned as time passed and Thomas was nowhere. Looking into the face of anyone of Thomas's stature, he pressed on.

Nothing.

John knew he must return to the ship and pray Thomas had returned while he'd scoured the wharf. He made his way back through the crowd and onto the ship. Thomas was still nowhere to be seen.

The last sailor readied to pull the gangplank aboard. John waved his arms to get the man's attention.

"I beg of you, a few moments. My son must come aboard, and he has not yet returned."

"I give ye a moment, but that be all."

"I thank you, kind sir."

The tension in his neck and shoulders tightened. He skimmed over the bustle of activity on the wharf. Still, he caught no sight of Thomas. He leaned against the side rail and scanned across the entire wharf. A young couple drew his attention, and he watched them working their way through the crowd and toward the ship. It was Thomas and Emma.

Thank the Lord.

With two fingers in his mouth, John whistled loudly. Waving his arms in the air, he caught his son's attention. "Thomas! Hasten yourself aboard. As you said, the shipmaster waits for no one."

Thomas glanced up at John and nodded. He and Emma began to make their way to the gangplank and came up to where John stood on the main deck.

"My son, it does my heart good to have you aboard. The crew needs us out of the way so they can prepare the ship to set sail. We must all go below decks."

John looked from Thomas to Emma. "It is lovely to see you, Emma. I am happy you've come to say goodbye to Thomas. However, we are about to set sail. You two had best say your goodbyes quickly. After which, Thomas, will you please meet me below decks?"

"I beg of you a moment, Father." Thomas turned to face Emma, his smile as broad as the ocean. John could feel the energy emitting from the couple.

Thomas said, "Emma has come to join us on our migration to the New World."

John felt his heart leap with joy for his oldest son. He smiled and reached up to put a hand on each of their shoulders. "I knew you loved one another greatly, and I wondered how you were going to be apart for so long. Of course, she can join the congregation. She can stay with Jane and Barbara."

Thomas lowered his gaze to the ground. "Umm . . . Father, pray tell, will you will marry us once we have set sail?" Thomas put an arm around Emma and pulled her close to his side. Emma smiled up at John with a shy expression.

"Nothing would make me happier than to marry the two of you."

A loving gaze passed between the couple. It brought another surge of joy to John's spirit. At least one of his children had found love.

"What of your father, Emma? Does he not remain ill?" John said.

"He grows stronger each day. He insisted I join Thom on this migration, no matter how hard I fought against it. He is making plans to sell off our belongings and will make the journey as soon as possible."

"I am happy you have joined us and look forward to meeting your father some day in the future. Thom, why don't you take Emma below decks and get her situated with Jane now. Once you are married, we can make other arrangements."

"Aye, that I will, Father."

John worked his way amidships. He crawled through the hatch and down the ladder leading below decks. The overhead was low, and John bent down, proceeding aft, toward the makeshift quarters of the congregation.

Remembrances of the dark, dank conditions of Newgate, with its low ceilings and cramped quarters, poured into John's mind. He never thought to be in such a place again, yet here he was. The confined feelings of the ship brought back gruesome memories. How was he going to survive more than a month in these surroundings? He shook his head in a mock effort to shake off the past few years. He must look toward the future.

Turning aft, he saw Jane leaned back against the bulkhead with the younger children gathered around her. There was a hole in his family which Johnny had previously occupied. He would greatly miss his young son.

John kept his head low and worked his way to Jane's location, where he heard part of the tale she told the children about an exciting, new land.

John said, "Oh, my sweet children, I hate to interrupt such a pleasant story, but the shipmaster prepares to set sail. The time has finally come. We will be upon the great waters soon."

Benjamin jumped forward and grabbed John around the legs. "It scares me to be down inside the ship, Father."

John sat down and pulled little Benjamin onto his lap. "It scares me a bit, as well, Benny. Nevertheless, we will all be here together, and we will make it less frightful."

Frederick was hunched forward and coming his direction. "John, the congregants are gathering amidships. They long to hear their leader speak to them before we set sail."

"It would be my honor, Frederick." He glanced around at his children. They seemed torn between the excitement of the voyage and fear of the unknown. "Come, children, let us go see our friends."

Frederick turned and worked his way back the way he'd come. John arose as best he could. He grasped little Benjamin's hand and moved forward to join the congregation.

Jane said, "Father, let me take Benny for you." Little Benjamin took his oldest sister's hand. Jane shepherded the other children forward, and they all followed John as he made his way to the group.

John's heart swelled with gratitude and love for the people he saw gathered amidships, awaiting his word. Thomas and Emma had joined the group, and John's anxiety lessened. He worked his way toward the front of the congregation. Excitement radiated through the group. Though John was still hunched over, standing amidships allowed him to straighten up a bit.

"I bid you all welcome. It does my heart good to see you standing before me." He scrutinized the group and smiled. "As well as you *can* stand, I suppose, with the low overhead of this ship."

Several members of the group chuckled. His heart swelled with thankfulness for this group of people who would be the core of his congregation in New England.

"I express my gratitude to you who have freely and graciously joined me on this journey to a new land. I begin by thanking each of you for the generosity of spirit and substance you have shared with me and my family. We would not be here today if not for your charitable and loving support. I pray God will truly bless you for what you have done for us."

He continued, "By the grace of a most high God, who has granted us access to a new land, full of wonder and hope, I express a thankful heart for Him, that He may have more glory. I hope by grace, both by prayer and practice, that we shall endeavor to advance the throne of Christ. We have an obligation to maintain the straight and strong eye of the gospel in this new home we go forth to build.

"We stand steadfast in our resolution to remove ourselves from our beloved England and better prosper ourselves in New England. We would have our principle end be to glorify God, to make a better and more successful Zion, and to embrace our Lord and Savior, Jesus Christ.

"Let us be thankful and remember by whose grace we set upon the waters this day. Please join hands and bow your heads in silence and give thanks to Him who is the God of Gods. Let us pray that through His grace we will be guided on this journey and safely make land upon the New World."

John reached out and joined hands with those beside them. He waited until all the individuals of his group were connected by hands into one whole. After which, he bowed his head and felt the power and support of his family and friends. Love and appreciation for these people infused his heart with joy. The day had finally come!

The past few years had been filled with trial after trial. However, each time John felt like giving in, the hand of God comforted and guided him. This world could be filled with dread and dismay, but it could also be filled with excitement and wonder. The choice of misery or happiness was up to each individual. God gave free will to man, that he might choose his own way.

The ship began to shift, and John realized they were making their way out to sea. Raising his head, he opened his eyes and considered this small group of believers.

One by one, they lifted their heads and watched him. Each regarded him with appreciation and devotion on their faces. He was filled with the resolution to build a new future in a new land. By the grace and power of God, he would not lead them astray.

"Now, let us prepare. Soon we will be upon the depths of the sea. I say for now, and forevermore, I thank you for your friendship, your loyalty, and your generosity."

John's soul stirred at the courage he saw in the faces before him. His family and friends had stood by him through many years of persecution and now stood by him as they embarked upon a new life.

Though he had suffered in prison far longer than any other, many people standing in front of him had spent their own time in prison. Yet they had taken measures to shore up him and his family—during his time in Newgate, through the death of his wife, and by helping his children while he was away.

Frederick and Elsabeth stood to one side of the group. John saw in him a true friend who had never strayed, no matter the difficulty or the situation. John scanned the hopeful faces of those standing before him. He raised a fist to his shoulder.

"A new day has begun!"

AT SEA

Jane felt the salty air feather through her hair. She swept it back from her face, its blonde tendrils flickering out behind her. The starboard rail gave her some protection, and she leaned into the wind. A sprinkling of ocean mist blew across her arms bringing her a slight chill.

The loss of Edmund, who she had truly loved and believed to be the man she would have been with forever, scalded her heart like a burn. The gaping wound he'd created festered and gnawed at her soul. She knew not whether it was actually seasickness or heartsickness which continued to cause her so much pain and discomfort since setting sail a few days past.

The ship rose and fell over one or two larger swells, and she reached out for the rail, gripping it for added support. She closed her eyes and pulled the salty air into her lungs. It helped settle the sour feelings plaguing her since she'd stepped aboard the ship.

Though cutting ties with Edmund had been painful, Jane felt the excitement of a new life in the Americas. What would the new land be like? The mere thought caused a flutter in her already sick stomach.

She hugged her middle and leaned over the side rail, in case her stomach did truly rebel.

A gentle ocean breeze washed over her, and she slipped into the rhythm of the ship. She focused her attention on the white water curling out from the bow and, bit by bit, her stomach began to settle.

The immense ocean made her feel like a small duck bobbing upon the surface. It was a reminder of how small she truly was. Still, she knew God was aware of her.

She thought about Christ's teaching: *"Are not five sparrows sold for two farthings, and not one of them is forgotten before God? But even the very hairs of your head are all numbered. Fear not therefore: ye are of more value than many sparrows."* [v]

God *was* aware of her, and He would guide her in the New World. There were not many English colonists in the Americas, but they were growing in number as quickly as they could book passage on a ship and set sail.

Memories of Edmund still haunted her mind. Would she, perhaps, find a new love in that wild and untamed land? A man whom she might trust with her heart once again?

Jane tucked two fingers under her dress bodice and pulled a folded paper from the skirt's waistband. Turning her back to the wind, she unfolded the sheet and brought it up to her eyes.

Pain stabbed at her heart when she read the last lines of the sonnet Edmund had given her.

Rising up I heard the songbirds refrain
And waking whispered, "My beloved Jane."

Memories of Edmund filled her mind. Her teeth clenched in frustration, and she made quick work of the paper, easily tearing it into small pieces.

Turning back to the railing, she opened her hand to let go of the dreams she'd had with Edmund. She watched the breeze steal each little piece of paper from her hand as her feelings for him were carried away like these fragments upon the wind.

Every new minute of every new day brought with it the chance for her to change past memories into hopes for a brighter future. Forgiving would not erase hurt feelings, but instead, would open the way for new memories to take their place.

*****

Thomas leaned against the aft bulkhead, squinting in the dim light from a single candle. He'd fashioned a wooden crate into a table of sorts and dripped a puddle of wax onto the back corner to securely hold the candle upright.

Emma lay next to him, snuggled into his side. His arms held her close, and he never wanted to let her go. After the past few years of bitter trial and disappointment, he thanked God he'd been given a gift such as Emma.

Thomas stroked her hair and leaned down to kiss her on the cheek. Though he longed for the taste of her mouth, close quarters allowed for no privacy. He would have to steal a kiss when he could.

"Emma, you are the comfort of my soul and the joy of my heart. The height of all my hopes and happiness depends upon your love for me."

"Oh, Thomas, I feel the same way for you."

"Think what sad situation of mind I suffered the day I walked away from you. I was heartbroken that you would not join me on this voyage. You stood there watching me with such haunting eyes, and it almost killed me to withdraw. I longed for you to be by my side forevermore."

"How did I ever suppose I could let you sail away from me?"

Emma laid her head on Thomas's chest, her body warm alongside him. He leaned against the bulkhead once again. The sway of the ship lulled him, and his eyes grew heavy.

A loud bang jolted him alert. His eyes flew open to observe someone had dropped a wooden box, its contents spilling out over the lower deck. There were many people crowded into makeshift quarters surrounding the bulkhead. It was going to be an interesting trip across the great ocean.

Such a different life awaited him in New England, yet his former life still called out to him from old England. Having Emma by his side would help as they created a new life in a new land. He watched Emma, whose breathing had lengthened as she passed into slumber. He stroked her hair away from her face and noticed beads of sweat upon her brow. This had been a trying day for them all.

The call of the ocean urged him upward, and he longed to breathe in the cool salt air.

Barbara lay close by with little Benjamin tucked into her side.

"Barbara, will you please stay with the children whilst I go topside?"

"Aye, I will be here, Thom. You may go."

"Thanks be to you, Barbara."

Thomas leaned Emma against the bulkhead. Arising, he bent forward at the waist, and made his way amidships, up the ladder and through the hatch. Stepping onto the main deck, he noticed Jane resting against the starboard railing and made his way in her direction, adjusting for the movement of the ship as he walked. He stepped up behind her and put his arm around her in a brotherly hug.

Jane smiled up at him, and then turned back to gaze over the ocean. "It is quite a sight to see, is it not?" she said.

"I will never grow tired of watching the ocean. It has always brought me peace of mind."

"I usually find peace with the ocean as well. Yet now, it does me the injustice of reminding me I'm leaving behind my life in England and sailing into an unknown future."

"It is so, Jane, but what did England have to offer you any longer?"

Jane's shoulders lifted as she drew in a long breath. "What you say is true, Thom. England held no hope of a joyful future for me, and I have vowed to move on from that world. Yet still, I miss the life we had in Lambeth before Father was seized and hauled off to prison."

"I miss it as well. However, that life was taken from us and is no longer within our reach. The New World offers us the prospect of a hopeful, bright future—one we can make for ourselves, without the oppressive hand of an evil bishop who would take our father from us once again."

"Aye, that is the main advantage."

Thomas pulled Jane into his shoulder. He leaned down and kissed her forehead. "I believe Father is also topside somewhere. Let's try to find him and see how he fares."

He took Jane's hand and led her aft as he scanned the main deck for their father. Catching no sight of him, Thomas guided Jane forward, where he noted their father standing on the forecastle deck and leaning against the foremast.

"Look there, Jane, Father is up on the higher deck. Let's join him."

"I am a bit nervous about being up on the forecastle deck. It is high, and I have therefore avoided it thus far."

"Do not fear. I will be there to protect and support you. It is quite a thrill to see the ocean from such a vantage point."

Thomas took Jane's hand and helped her as they made their way forward toward the higher deck. "Would you like me to go first? Or should I stay in back, in case you slip?"

"Probably, behind me would help me feel the safest."

"As you wish, here we go." Thomas pulled Jane's hand forward. She took the first step upward, and he slipped behind her and held onto her waist.

"You do well, Jane, keep stepping up, I am right behind you."

As Jane trod up the steps and onto the forecastle deck, Thomas stepped up behind her and took her hand in his once again.

Because of his time spent on the river, Thomas had quickly grown accustomed to the swaying and rocking of the ship, and he was at one with the *Griffin*. Looking out over the ocean, his heart raced with excitement. He'd waited a long time to set out on his first great adventure.

Thoughts of Emma sleeping below decks filled his mind. Knowing she would soon be his wife brought joy to his soul.

Perhaps that would be the greatest adventure of all.

*****

John held onto the foremast with his left arm as he scanned the horizon. The ship had sailed but a few days across the waters toward the New World. A couple months of sailing were still in their future. Each time the *Griffin* rode a swell upward, John felt the agonies of Newgate lifting from his soul. A new world of hope, peace, and possibility lay before him.

Movement caught his eye, and he turned to see Thomas and Jane stepping onto the forecastle deck. Jane seemed a bit unsteady, but Thomas came up behind her and caught her hand in his, guiding her in the direction of the foremast. John reached out to take Jane's other hand, pulling her to him.

"What brings the two of you topside?"

"We came to check on you and see how you were faring," said Thomas.

"I do well, better still with each passing day. The sea air does me good, and I feel the weight of the past few years falling from my shoulders."

"I feel it as well, Father," said Jane.

He smiled at Jane and lifted his hand to cup her cheek. "Does Edmund still fill your thoughts each day?"

"Unfortunately, he often comes into my thoughts. I mostly feel the fool over him; however, I have faith I will be able to leave the memory of him far behind me."

"By the Grace of God, I pray you will be able to accomplish just that."

John lowered his hand and turned toward Thomas. "What of you, Thomas? How does it feel to have Emma aboard ship and joining you in the New World?"

"Nothing could have prepared me for seeing her on the dock that day. My heart had been fairly broken to leave her behind. I am a thankful man, indeed." Thomas smiled.

John chuckled and clapped his son on the shoulder. "I would have thought nothing less. I know you love her and look forward to your marriage. In fact, life seems to be fairly settled on the ship. I do believe it may be time for the marriage to take place. What say you, Thom? Are you ready to become a husband?"

"More than I ever thought possible, Father."

A broad smile spread across John's face. Happiness infused his soul, and he thanked God for his blessings.

He circled an arm around each child and turned them to face aft. "Jane, Thomas . . . look backward towards our precious England. Wave to her and wish her good eventide."

John lifted his hand in a wave, with Thomas and Jane following suit, as they each bid farewell to England.

Turning them forward to gaze past the bow of the ship, John said, "Now, look frontward towards New England and bid her good dawning."

Salty mist washed over John as he stood facing the Americas. His heart swelled with happiness as he thought of the bravery his children had shown over the past few years.

John continued, "Though, in the end, England brought us trouble and grief, she is the land of our nativity and will always hold a special place in our hearts. However, the time has come for a new place to fill our souls and become our new homeland.

"We must leave our dark trials behind us, yet hold onto our courage won. The courage of forgiveness when we felt betrayed. The courage of persistence when we felt despair. The courage of strength when we felt weak."

Never again would John sit in the dark, dank air of the devil's pit—for the light of a bright new day shone before him.

The *Griffin* dipped into the bottom of a swell and began to rise up the next, bringing more sea spray to mist over John and his two eldest children. He looked from one child to the next, and an added surge of love and respect filled his heart.

"We must now build a new life for ourselves. Whatever our challenges, whatever our trials, however we strive to overcome them, we must be who we are and nothing less."

More from the Author

Want to find out what happens next? Longing to see how John overcomes each ensuing hurdle on his way to the peace and serenity he so desires? Wondering if Thomas finds the adventure he desperately craves? Eager to learn what happens to Jane?

Follow the Lothropp family to the New World and experience the conflicts and trials that await them on a different shore.

Soul of **FAITH** - Book 2 in *The Soul Series*

Coming in 2018

Jeanette L. Ross grew up in Southern California basking in the sun and body surfing those wonderful white sand beaches. These days, you'll find her surfing the net for family history stories and doing other research. When she's not writing, working on genealogy, gardening, restoring old furniture, or building miniature houses you might catch her visiting yet another cemetery and taking photos of ancestor's headstones. She now lives in Meridian, Idaho with her husband and their little pooch Mandy.

You can visit her at:

www.JeanetteLRoss.com

www.Facebook.com/JeanetteLRossWrites

Interesting Information

Newgate or the Clink? Many question where John was actually incarcerated. It is recorded that John, along with others from his congregation, was sent ". . . in fetters to the old Clink Prison, in Newgate." I find that problematic because Newgate and the Clink were two different prisons in two different locations.

Newgate was a prison in London located at the corner of Newgate Street and Old Bailey. There is no way to determine just when the prison, which was originally a new Roman gatehouse (hence, Newgate), was originally built. It was to be the fifth gate into the city of London. The gatehouse was later enlarged into a prison, which went through several variations of restructuring and rebuilding, and remained in use for over seven hundred years. It closed in 1902, and was demolished for good in 1904.

The Clink prison was situated in Southwark and across the river from London. It was owned by the Bishop of Winchester. It opened in approximately 860 and was burned down by rioters in 1780. This prison is most likely the reason for the slang term "thrown into the clink," meaning being put into any prison.

There are no records for Newgate prison prior to 1770 due to the London fire. Records from the Star Chamber deteriorated and were ". . . in a very great heap, undigested, and without any covering from dust or security from rats and mice." Records from the Clink prison do not begin until 1690. So the precise location of John's incarceration has no proof through documentation.

John settled a town in Massachusetts called Barnstable (named after Barnstaple, a town in England). There is a plaque at the Lothrop Hill Cemetery located there which states that he was incarcerated in Newgate from 1632-1634.

American Ancestry: Giving the Name and Descent, in the Male Line, of Americans Whose Ancestors Settled in the United States Previous to the

Declaration of Independence, states on page 47 that John was ". . . imprisoned in Newgate on account of his nonconformity."

In an article written by Helene Holt, author of *Exiled*, she states: "Was Reverend John incarcerated in the Clink or in Newgate? One historical book on Newgate says the Queen was known to have petitioned the King for the release of prisoners in Newgate. It is not mentioned whether or not she ever petitioned for the release of prisoners from other prisons. It is known from the trial of John Lathrop that the husband of Abigail Delamar (she was one of the arrested conventiclers who was released on bond) served as part of the retinue of the Queen and that Abigail Delamar asked her husband to petition the Queen for their release. So the fact that one of Lathrop's conventiclers is recorded in history as having sought redress through the Queen and the fact that the Queen petitioned the King to release religious prisoners from Newgate was a bit of evidence for Newgate being the place of Lathrop's incarceration. Another historical record stated that Henry Dod, one of the conventiclers arrested with Reverend John, died during his imprisonment. That seemed far more typical of Newgate than the Clink (for reasons I elaborate upon in the Appendix). Plus, we know that Sam Eaton, Lathrop's close friend, died in Newgate. The more I researched the more I leaned toward Newgate as the place of his incarceration for numerous reasons, but especially since the plaque which had been erected at the Lothrop Hill Cemetery in 1939 specified Newgate as the prison in which Reverend John was incarcerated. Further reasons for my choice of Newgate are included in the Appendix."

Why did I choose to portray John as being housed at Newgate? After hours spent researching this topic, I felt there was more evidence to suggest that he was in Newgate, rather than in the Clink. Therefore in the end, for this fictional story, I chose the setting of Newgate as the location for John's imprisonment.

Archbishop William Laud was found "[. . .] guilty of endeavouring [sic] to subvert the laws; to overthrow the Protestant religion; and [. . .]

was an enemy to Parliament." He was imprisoned in the Tower of London on March 1, 1641, where he awaited trial for three years. He was brought to trial before the House of Lords on March 12, 1644, with the prosecution being led by William Prynne. The trial lasted for twenty days, and then, due to a lack of evidence, the Lords adjourned the trial without coming to a vote.

Laud was condemned to death by a bill which was passed by the House of Commons and the House of Lords. He was beheaded on Tower Hill in London January10, 1645.

King Charles I was "[. . .] guilty of all the treasons, murders, rapines, burning, spoils, desolations, damages, and mischiefs of the war." Charles was also considered a "[. . .] tyrant, traitor and murderer; and a public and implacable enemy to the Commonwealth of England. [. . .] out of a wicked design to erect and uphold in himself an unlimited and tyrannical power to rule according to his will, and to overthrow the rights and liberties of the people of England."

His trial started January 20, 1649 in Westminster Hall. The prosecution was led by the Solicitor General, John Cook. The King objected to the trial and asked, "I would know by what power I am called hither . . . I would know by what authority, I mean lawful; [. . .] Remember, I am your King, your lawful King, [. . .]" He claimed that his own authority to rule had been given to him by God and by England, and that the court had no jurisdiction over a monarch. Charles was charged with high treason, and then on January 27, 1649, he was sentenced to death. He was beheaded on January 30, 1649, at the Palace of Whitehall.

After Charles I, the monarchy was abolished and Parliament ruled for eleven years. Eventually his son, Charles II, was brought back to rule England. However, the monarchy would never again be afforded the same power.

Descendants of John Lothropp. It is estimated that John Lothropp has nearly two million lineal descendants living today. Some notable descendants include:

Aaron Wells Peirsol, Olympic medalist swimmer

Adlai Stevenson III, U.S. senator of Illinois

Alec Baldwin, TV and movie actor

Alexander S. Wadsworth, first lieutenant onboard the USS Constitution, War of 1812

Avery Robert Dulles, cardinal of the Catholic Church

Benedict Arnold, general in the American Revolutionary War

Charles Goodyear, discovered the vulcanization process for rubber

Clint Eastwood, movie actor

C. W. Post, founder of Post Cereals

Daniel Coit Gilman, founder of the Sheffield Scientific School at Yale College, president of the University of California

Dick Clark, TV personality, host of American Bandstand

Dickinson Woodruff Richards Jr., physician and co-recipient of the Nobel Prize

Eli Whitney, inventor of the Cotton Gin

Ephraim Peabody III, Unitarian clergyman

Ernest W. Longfellow, artist, art collector, benefactor of large art collection to the Boston Museum of Art

Franklin Delano Roosevelt, 32nd U.S. President

George H. W. Bush, 41st U.S. President

George Romney, U.S. governor of Michigan

George W. Bush, 43rd U.S. President

Henry A. Wallace, 33rd U.S. vice-president

Henry S. Morgan, banker and co-founder of Morgan Stanley

Henry Wadsworth Longfellow, American poet, writer, and Harvard professor

Jabez Huntington, major general of Connecticut Militia

Josiah Fay, captain in the 1st Continental Infantry Regiment

John Arthur Lithgow, TV and movie actor

John Foster Dulles, U.S. Secretary of State, Washington Dulles
    International Airport named for him
John Lathrop Jr., officer, French & Indian War
John Lathrop Sr., U.S. representative Connecticut legislature
Joseph Fielding Smith, tenth president of the LDS church
Joseph F. Smith, sixth president of the LDS church
Joseph Smith Jr., first president of the LDS church
Joseph Smith III, founder of the RLDS church
J. P. Morgan, banker
Julia Child, celebrity television chef
Kingman Brewster, president of Yale University
Marjorie Post, founder of General Foods
Mitt Romney, U.S. governor of Massachusetts
Oliver Cowdery, scribe of the Book of Mormon
Orson Pratt, one of the 12 original apostles of the LDS church
Parley P. Pratt, one of the 12 original apostles of the LDS church
Robert B. Borden, eighth prime minister of Canada
Samuel A. Eliot Jr., American novelist
Samuel H. Huntington, third governor of Ohio
Sarah Palin, ninth governor of Alaska
Tomáš Garrigue Masaryk, first President of Czechoslovakia
Ulysses S. Grant, civil war general and 18th U.S. President
Wilford Woodruff, fourth president of the LDS church
W.W. Phelps, composer

Acknowledgements

I first want to thank my wonderful husband, Robert Ross, whose patience in hearing me talk of old England, John Lothropp, and Newgate prison is greatly appreciated. His critique of my manuscript with reason and insight was extremely helpful in advancing the story forward in a logical way, and his awesome computer skills were of huge value to me. I thank him for understanding why I spent hours in front of my computer tapping away at the keys and why I couldn't seem to let my characters go to sleep at night.

Thoughts of thanksgiving cannot fully express the gratitude I feel toward my dear friend, Kathleen Brebes. Her never-ending support, critiques, and guidance in creating this manuscript were vital in helping the work come to fruition. I can say in all honesty that this manuscript would never have come to be, if not for her counsel, support, and understanding. She helped my characters stay honest and real, and my story move forward. I am deeply grateful for her years of patient friendship and love in things both literary and personal. She's a wonderful person and a priceless friend.

The help and support of a friend from my youth, Rick Oyler, was a surprise and a blessing. I'm grateful he shared with me his own gift of writing in the poem *Courageous Souls*, also Edmund's sonnet *For Jane*—both of which added a nice touch to this work. His knowledge and experience of rowing, kayaking, and sculling were invaluable in helping me write of Thomas's experiences on the river. I thank him for his honest reading of my manuscript and wonderful story advice, and for being a great friend.

My daughter, Bethany Tolman, and I spent hours talking over plot, characters, and scene ideas. I'm thankful for her thoughts, insights, and patience. She never stopped encouraging me and helping me feel that I could actually accomplish the huge task of writing this story. I am truly grateful for her guidance and support not only with the story, but in helping me build my business as well.

My son, Christopher Ross, was kind and patient as he shared his computer and Photoshop skills with me. His tutelage helped me develop many of the computer skills I needed to create my book covers, website, and other marketing materials. In fact, I thank him for many years of perseverance and support in my computer training.

I voice my appreciation to my son, Joshua Keuning, for being my book cover model. He was kind and patient as I dressed him in period clothing and took him down to the old penitentiary for a photo shoot with the photographer. I thank him for taking time out of his busy schedule and becoming John Lothropp for the afternoon.

And, Rick Tolman, thank you for digging up those bushes for me. ☺

Lastly, I would be truly ungrateful if I didn't mention all of those who have previously spent hours researching John Lothropp and his family. I enjoyed reading many books and articles on his life, which are listed in the bibliography. If not for them, I would never have learned of John and the many trials he endured during his life. I'm grateful that I came to know the Lothropp family through previous research and the many hours that were spent documenting and protecting his life story.

I feel as though I've really come to know John, Hannah, Thomas, Jane, and all the children. My testimony of God has been strengthened through my study of their trials, which they so beautifully overcame, and of their sacrifices made in service to God. They have forever touched me and changed my life in positive and uplifting ways.

I hope and pray that reading this story has blessed your life and helped you come to appreciate the sacrifice of those who fought the battles that enable us to be where we are today.

References

Finch, Peter. *Access to the River Thames Steps, Stairs, and Landing Places on the Tidal Thames*, London: The River Thames Society, 2010

Fuller, Gerald R., complied by. *Ancestors and Descendants of Andrew Lee and Clarinda Knapp Allen* Arizona: The Andrew Lee Allen Family Organization, 1952

Holt, Helene. *Exiled: The Story of John Lathrop* New York: Paramount Books, 1987

Hughes Thomas P., *American Ancestry: Giving the Name and Descent, in the Male Line, of Americans Whose Ancestors Settled in the United States Previous to the Declaration of Independence, A.D. 1776, Volume 1* New York: Joel Munsell's Sons, 1887

Huntington, Julia M. *A Genealogical Memoir of the Lo-Lathrop Family in This Country* Connecticut: The Case, Lockwood & Brainard Company, 1884

Loomis, Lucy, complied by. *John Lothrop in Barnstable* Massachusetts: Sturgis Library, 2011

Martyn, W. Carlos. *The Pilgrim Fathers of New England a History* New York: American Tract Society, 1867

O'Riordan, Christopher. *The Thames Watermen in the Century of Revolution*, 1992, 2000

Otis, Amos, revised and complied by Swift, C. F. *Genealogical Notes of Barnstable Families, Volume I & II* Massachusetts: F.

B. & F. P. Goss, [The Patriot Press], 1888, 1890 originally published in the *Barnstable Patriot*

Price, Richard W. *John Lothropp: A Puritan Biography & Genealogy* Utah: Richard W. Price and Associates, 1989

Sprague, William B. *An Address Delivered at West Springfield August 25, 1856 on Occasion of the One Hundredth Anniversary of the Ordination of the Reverend Joseph Lathrop* Massachusetts: Samuel Bowles and Company, 1856

Taber, Helen Lathrop. *A New Home in Mattakeese* Massachusetts: Rock Village Publishing, 2013

The Court of Star Chamber Records United Kingdom: The National Archives, 1485-1642

John Lathrop Arrival in America and Family Tree Utah: Apocalypse Books, 1988

John Lathrop Reformer, Sufferer, Pilgrim Man of God Utah: Institute of Family Research, Inc., 1978

The Seven Villages of Barnstable Massachusetts: Town of Barnstable, 1976

Notes

---

i   KJV Psalms 41: 9
ii KJV Psalms 23: 4
iii KJV Nehemiah 4:14
iv KJV Ephesians 6: 11-12
v   KJV Luke 12:6-7

CPSIA information can be obtained
at www.ICGtesting.com
Printed in the USA
FFHW021253251119
56472076-62266FF